Other Books by Gilbert Sorrentino

POETRY

The Darkness Surrounds Us
Black and White
The Perfect Fiction
Corrosive Sublimate
A Dozen Oranges
Sulpiciae Elegidia: Elegiacs of Sulpicia
White Sail
The Orangery
Selected Poems 1958-1980

FICTION

The Sky Changes
Steelwork
Imaginative Qualities of Actual Things
Flawless Play Restored: The Masque of Fungo
Splendide-Hôtel
Mulligan Stew
Aberration of Starlight
Crystal Vision
Blue Pastoral
Odd Number
A Beehive Arranged on Humane Principles
Rose Theatre
Misterioso
Under the Shadow
Red the Fiend
Pack of Lies
Gold Fools
Little Casino

ESSAYS

Something Said

BIBLIOGRAPHY

Gilbert Sorrentino: A Descriptive Bibliography by William McPheron

The Moon in Its Flight

STORIES BY

Gilbert Sorrentino

COFFEE HOUSE PRESS
MINNEAPOLIS

2004

Coffee House Press books are available to the trade through our primary distributor, Consortium Book Sales & Distribution, 1045 Westgate Drive, Saint Paul, MN 55114. For personal orders, catalogs, or other information, write to: Coffee House Press, 27 North Fourth Street, Suite 400, Minneapolis, MN 55401.

Coffee House Press is a nonprofit literary publishing house. Support from private foundations, corporate giving programs, government programs, and generous individuals help make the publication of our books possible. We gratefully acknowledge their support in detail in the back of this book. To you and our many readers across the country, we send our thanks for your continuing support.

LIBRARY OF CONGRESS CIP DATA
Sorrentino, Gilbert.
The moon in its flight : stories / by Gilbert Sorrentino.
p. cm.
ISBN 1-56689-152-3 (alk. paper)
1. United States—Social life and customs—Fiction. I. Title.
PS3569.07M66 2004
813'.54—DC22 2004000665
PRINTED IN CANADA

Grateful acknowledgment is made to the editors of the following magazines in which many of these stories first appeared: The Moon in Its Flight *(New American Review,* 1971), Decades *(Esquire,* 1977; *The Best American Short Stories 1978),* Land of Cotton *(Harper's,* 1977), A Beehive Arranged on Humane Principles *(Conjunctions,* 1985), The Sea, Caught in Roses *(Zyzzyva,* 1990), Times Without Number *(Private Arts,* 1992), Pastilles *(Trafika* [Prague], 1994), In Loveland *(Common Knowledge,* 1996), Things That Have Stopped Moving *(Conjunctions,* 1997), Sample Writing Sample *(Arshile,* 1997), Allegory of Innocence *(Matrix* [Montreal], 1998), Facts and Their Manifestations *(The Southern California Anthology,* 1999), Gorgias *(Conjunctions,* 2001), Life and Letters *(Conjunctions,* 2001), It's Time to Call It a Day *(Bluesky Review,* 2003), *Perdido (BOMB,* 2004), Lost in the Stars *(Fence,* 2004).

"A Beehive Arranged on Humane Principles" was also published in a signed, limited edition, with woodcuts by David Storey, by the Grenfell Press (New York, 1986).

CONTENTS

7 THE MOON IN ITS FLIGHT

21 DECADES

39 LAND OF COTTON

49 THE DIGNITY OF LABOR

69 THE SEA, CAUGHT IN ROSES

75 A BEEHIVE ARRANGED ON HUMANE PRINCIPLES

87 PASTILLES

97 ALLEGORY OF INNOCENCE

106 SAMPLE WRITING SAMPLE

121 TIMES WITHOUT NUMBER

131 SUBWAY

134 FACTS AND THEIR MANIFESTATIONS

140 IT'S TIME TO CALL IT A DAY

146 LIFE AND LETTERS

155 PERDIDO

168 LOST IN THE STARS

174 PSYCHOPATHOLOGY OF EVERYDAY LIFE

191 GORGIAS

204 IN LOVELAND

227 THINGS THAT HAVE STOPPED MOVING

THE MOON IN ITS FLIGHT

This was in 1948. A group of young people sitting on the darkened porch of a New Jersey summer cottage in a lake resort community. The host some Bernie wearing an Upsala College sweatshirt. The late June night so soft one can, in retrospect, forgive America for everything. There were perhaps eight or nine people there, two of them the people that this story sketches.

Bernie was talking about Sonny Stitt's alto on "That's Earl, Brother." As good as Bird, he said. Arnie said, bullshit: he was a very hip young man from Washington Heights, wore mirrored sunglasses. A bop drummer in his senior year at the High School of Performing Arts. Our young man, nineteen at this time, listened only to Rebecca, a girl of fifteen, remarkable in her New Look clothes. A long full skirt, black, snug tailored shirt of blue and white stripes with a high white collar and black velvet string tie, black kid Capezios. It is no wonder that lesbians like women.

At some point during the evening he walked Rebecca home. She lived on Lake Shore Drive, a wide road that skirted the beach and ran parallel to the small river that flowed into Lake

Minnehaha. Lake Ramapo? Lake Tomahawk. Lake O-shi-wa-noh? Lake Sunburst. Leaning against her father's powder-blue Buick convertible, lost, in the indigo night, the creamy stars, sound of crickets, they kissed. They fell in love.

One of the songs that summer was "For Heaven's Sake." Another, "It's Magic." Who remembers the clarity of Claude Thornhill and Sarah Vaughan, their exquisite irrelevance? They are gone where the useless chrome doughnuts on the Buick's hood have gone. That Valhalla of Amos 'n' Andy and guinea fruit peddlers with golden earrings. "Pleasa No Squeeza Da Banana." In 1948, the whole world seemed beautiful to young people of a certain milieu, or let me say, possible. Yes, it seemed a possible world. This idea persisted until 1950, at which time it died, along with many of the young people who had held it. In Korea, the Chinese played "Scrapple from the Apple" over loudspeakers pointed at the American lines. That savage and virile alto blue-clear on the sub-zero night. This is, of course, old news.

Rebecca was fair. She was fair. Lovely Jewish girl from the remote and exotic Bronx. To him that vast borough seemed a Cythera—that it could house such fantastic creatures as she! He wanted to be Jewish. He was, instead, a Roman Catholic, awash in sin and redemption. What loathing he had for the Irish girls who went to eleven o'clock Mass, legions of blushing pink and lavender spring coats, flat white straw hats, the crinkly veils over their open faces. Church clothes, under which their inviolate crotches sweetly nestled in soft hair.

She had white and perfect teeth. Wide mouth. Creamy stars, pale nights. Dusty black roads out past the beach. The sunlight on the raft, moonlight on the lake. Sprinkle of freckles on her shoulders. Aromatic breeze.

Of course this was a summer romance, but bear with me and see with what banal literary irony it all turns out—or does not turn out at all. The country bowled and spoke of Truman's grit and spunk. How softly we had slid off the edge of civilization.

The liquid moonlight filling the small parking area outside the gates to the beach. Bass flopping softly in dark waters. What was the scent of the perfume she wore? The sound of a car radio in the cool nights, collective American memory. Her browned body, delicate hair bleached golden on her thighs. In the beach pavilion they danced and drank Cokes. Mel Tormé and the Mel-Tones. Dizzy Gillespie. "Too Soon to Know." In the mornings, the sun so crystal and lucent it seemed the very exhalation of the sky, he would swim alone to the raft and lie there, the beach empty, music from the pavilion attendant's radio coming to him in splinters. At such times he would thrill himself by pretending that he had not yet met Rebecca and that he would see her that afternoon for the first time.

The first time he touched her breasts he cried in his shame and delight. Can all this really have taken place in America? The trees rustled for him, as the rain did rain. One day, in New York, he bought her a silver friendship ring, tiny perfect hearts in bas-relief running around it so that the point of one heart nestled in the cleft of another. Innocent symbol that tortured his blood. She stood before him in the pale light in white bra and panties, her shorts and blouse hung on the hurricane fence of the abandoned and weed-grown tennis court and he held her, stroking her flanks and buttocks and kissing her shoulders. The smell of her flesh, vague sweat and perfume. Of course he was insane. She caressed him so far as she understood how through his faded denim shorts. Thus did they flay themselves, burning. What were they to do? Where were they to go? The very thought of the condom in his pocket made his heart careen in despair. Nothing was like anything said it was after all. He adored her.

She was entering her second year at Evander Childs that coming fall. He hated this school he had never seen, and hated all her fellow students. He longed to be Jewish, dark and mysterious and devoid of sin. He stroked her hair and fingered her nipples, masturbated fiercely on the dark roads after he had seen her home. Why didn't he at least *live* in the Bronx?

Any fool can see that with the slightest twist one way or another all of this is fit material for a sophisticated comic's routine. David Steinberg, say. One can hear his precise voice recording these picayune disasters as jokes. Yet all that moonlight was real. He kissed her luminous fingernails and died over and over again. The maimings of love are endlessly funny, as are the tiny figures of talking animals being blown to pieces in cartoons.

It was this same youth who, three years later, ravished the whores of Mexican border towns in a kind of drunken hilarity, falling down in the dusty streets of Nuevo Laredo, Villa Acuña, and Piedras Negras, the pungency of the overpowering perfume wedded to his rumpled khakis, his flowered shirt, his scuffed and beer-spattered low quarters scraping across the thresholds of the Blue Room,

Ofelia's, the 1-2-3 Club, Felicia's, the Cadillac, Tres Hermanas. It would be a great pleasure for me to allow him to meet her there, in a yellow chiffon cocktail dress and spike heels, lost in prostitution.

One night, a huge smiling Indian whore bathed his member in gin as a testament to the strict hygiene she claimed to practice and he absurdly thought of Rebecca, that he had never seen her naked, nor she him, as he was now in the Hollywood pink light of the whore's room, Jesus hanging in his perpetual torture from the wall above the little bed. The woman was gentle, the light glinting off her gold incisor and the tiny cross at her throat. You good fuck, Jack, she smiled in her lying whore way. He felt her flesh again warm in that long-dead New Jersey sunlight. Turn that into a joke.

They were at the amusement park at Lake Hopatcong with two other couples. A hot and breathless night toward the end of August, the patriotic smell of hot dogs and French fries and cranky music from the carousel easing through the sparsely planted trees down toward the shore. She was pale and sweating, sick, and he took her back to the car and they smoked. They walked to the edge of the black lake stretching out before them, the red and blue neon on the far shore clear in the hot dark.

He wiped her forehead and stroked her shoulders, worshiping her pain. He went to get a Coke and brought it back to her, but she only sipped at it, then said O God! and bent over to throw up. He held her hips while she vomited, loving the waste and odor of her. She lay down on the ground and he lay next to her, stroking her breasts until the nipples were erect under her cotton blouse. My period, she said. God, it just ruins me at the beginning. You bleeding, vomiting, incredible thing, he thought. You should have stayed in, he said. The moonlight of her teeth. I didn't want to miss a night with you, she said. It's August. Stars, my friend, great flashing stars fell on Alabama.

They stood in the dark in the driving rain underneath her umbrella. Where could it have been? Nokomis Road? Bliss Lane? Kissing with that trapped yet wholly innocent frenzy peculiar to American youth of that era. Her family was going back to the city early the next morning and his family would be leaving toward the end of the week. They kissed, they kissed. The angels sang. Where could they go, out of this driving rain?

Isn't there anyone, any magazine writer or avant-garde filmmaker, any lover of life or dedicated optimist out there who will move them toward a cottage, already closed for the season, in whose split log exterior they will find an unlocked door? Inside there will be a bed, whiskey, an electric heater. Or better, a fireplace. White lamps, soft lights. Sweet music. A radio on which they will get Cooky's Caravan or Symphony Sid. Billy Eckstine will sing "My Deep Blue Dream." Who can bring them to each other and allow him to enter her? Tears of gratitude and release, the sublime and elegantly shadowed configuration their tanned legs will make lying together. This was in America, in 1948. Not even fake art or the wearisome tricks of movies can assist them.

She tottered, holding the umbrella crookedly while he went to his knees and clasped her, the rain soaking him through, put his head under her skirt and kissed her belly, licked at her crazily through her underclothes.

All you modern lovers, freed by Mick Jagger and the orgasm, give them, for Christ's sake, for an hour, the use of your really terrific little apartment. They won't smoke your marijuana nor disturb your Indiana graphics. They won't borrow your Fanon or Cleaver or Barthelme or Vonnegut. They'll make the bed before they leave. They whisper good night and dance in the dark.

She was crying and stroking his hair. Ah God, the leaves of brown came tumbling down, remember? He watched her go into the house and saw the door close. Some of his life washed away in the rain dripping from his chin.

A girl named Sheila whose father owned a fleet of taxis gave a reunion party in her parents' apartment in Forest Hills. Where else would it be? I will insist on purchased elegance or nothing. None of your warm and cluttered apartments in this story, cats on the stacks of books, and so on. It was the first time he had ever seen a sunken living room and it fixed his idea of the good life forever after. Rebecca was talking to Marv and Robin, who were to be married in a month. They were Jewish, incredibly and wondrously Jewish, their parents smiled upon them and loaned them money and cars. He skulked in his loud Brooklyn clothes.

I'll put her virgin flesh into a black linen suit, a single strand of pearls around her throat. Did I say that she had honey-colored hair? Believe me when I say he wanted to kiss her shoes.

Everybody was drinking Cutty Sark. This gives you an idea, not of who they were, but of what they thought they were. They worked desperately at it being August, but under the sharkskin and nylons those sunny limbs were hidden. Sheila put on "In the Still of the Night" and all six couples got up to dance. When he held her he thought he would weep.

He didn't want to hear about Evander Childs or Gun Hill Road or the 92nd Street Y. He didn't want to know what the pre-med student she was dating said. Whose hand had touched her secret thighs. It was most unbearable since this phantom knew them in a specifically erotic way that he did not. He had touched them decorated with garters and stockings. Different thighs. She had been to the Copa, to the Royal Roost, to Lewisohn Stadium to hear the Gershwin concert. She talked about *The New Yorker* and *Vogue,* e.e. cummings. She flew before him, floating in her black patent I. Miller heels.

Sitting together on the bed in Sheila's parents' room, she told him that she still loved him, she would always love him, but it was so hard not to go out with a lot of other boys, she had to keep her parents happy. They were concerned about him. They didn't really know him. He wasn't Jewish. All right. All right. But did she have to let Shelley? Did she have to go to the Museum of Modern Art? The Met? Where were these places? What is the University of Miami? Who is Brooklyn Law? What sort of god borrows a Chrysler and goes to the Latin Quarter? What is a supper club? What does Benedictine cost? Her epic acts, his Flagg Brothers shoes.

There was one boy who had almost made her. She had allowed him to take off her blouse and skirt, nothing else! at a CCNY sophomore party. She was a little high and he—messed—all over her slip. It was wicked and she was ashamed. Battering his heart in her candor. Well, I almost slipped too, he lied, and was terrified that she seemed relieved. He got up and closed the door, then lay down on the bed with her and took off her jacket and brassiere. She zipped open his trousers. Long enough! Sheila said, knocking on the door, then opening it to see him with his head on her breasts. Oh, oh, she said, and closed the door. Of course, it was all ruined. We got rid of a lot of these repressed people in the next decade, and now we are all happy and free.

At three o'clock, he kissed her good night on Yellowstone Boulevard in a thin drizzle. Call me, he said, and I'll call you. She went into her glossy Jewish life, toward mambos and the Blue Angel.

Let me come and sleep with you. Let me lie in your bed and look at you in your beautiful pajamas. I'll do anything you say. I'll honor thy beautiful father and mother. I'll hide in the closet and be no trouble. I'll work as a stock boy in your father's beautiful sweater factory. It's not my fault I'm not Marvin or Shelley. I don't even know where CCNY is! Who is Conrad Aiken? What is Bronx Science? Who is Berlioz? What is a Stravinsky? How do you play Mah-Jongg? What is schmooz, schlepp, Purim, Moo Goo Gai Pan? Help me.

When he got off the train in Brooklyn an hour later, he saw his friends through the window of the all-night diner, pouring coffee into the great pit of their beer drunks. He despised them as he despised himself and the neighborhood. He fought against the thought of her so that he would not have to place her subtle finesse in these streets of vulgar hells, benedictions, and incense.

On Christmas Eve, he left the office party at two, even though one of the file girls, her Catholicism temporarily displaced by Four Roses and ginger, stuck her tongue into his mouth in the stock room.

Rebecca was outside, waiting on the corner of 46th and Broadway, and they clasped hands, oh briefly, briefly. They walked aimlessly around in the gray bitter cold, standing for a while at the Rockefeller Center rink, watching the people who owned Manhattan. When it got too cold, they walked some more, ending up at the Automat across the street from Bryant Park. When she slipped her coat off her breasts moved under the crocheted sweater she wore. They had coffee and doughnuts, surrounded by office party drunks sobering up for the trip home.

Then it went this way: We can go to Maryland and get married, she said. You know I was sixteen a month ago. I want to marry you, I can't stand it. He was excited and frightened, and got an erection. How could he bear this image? Her breasts, her familiar perfume, enormous figures of movie queens resplendent in silk and lace in the snug bedrooms of Vermont inns—shutters banging, the rain pouring down, all entangled, married! How do we get to *Maryland?* he said.

Against the tabletop her hand, its long and delicate fingers, the perfect moons, Carolina moons of her nails. I'll give her every marvel: push gently the scent of magnolia and jasmine between her legs and permit her to piss champagne.

Against the tabletop her hand, glowing crescent moons over lakes of Prussian blue in evergreen twilights. Her eyes gray, flecked with bronze. In her fingers a golden chain and on the chain a car key. My father's car, she said. We can take it and be there tonight. We can be married Christmas then, he said, but you're Jewish. He saw a drunk going out onto Sixth Avenue carrying their lives along in a paper bag. I mean it, she said. I can't stand it, I love you. I love *you*, he said, but I can't drive. He smiled. I *mean* it, she said. She put the key in his hand. The car is in midtown here, over by Ninth Avenue. I really *can't* drive, he said. He could shoot pool and drink boilermakers, keep score at baseball games and handicap horses, but he couldn't drive.

The key in his hand, fascinating wrinkle of sweater at her waist. Of course, life is a conspiracy of defeat, a sophisticated joke, endless. I'll get some money and we'll go the holiday week, he said, we'll take a train, O.K.? O.K., she said. She smiled and asked for another coffee, taking the key and dropping it into her bag. It was a joke after all. They walked to the subway and he said I'll give you a call right after Christmas. Gray bitter sky. What he remembered was her gray cashmere coat swirling around her calves as she turned at the foot of the stairs to smile at him, making the gesture of dialing a phone and pointing at him and then at herself.

Give these children a Silver Phantom and a chauffeur. A black chauffeur, to complete the America that owned them.

Now I come to the literary part of this story, and the reader may prefer to let it go and watch her profile against the slick tiles of the IRT stairwell, since she has gone out of the reality of narrative, however splintered. This postscript offers something different, something finely artificial and discrete, one of the designer sweaters her father makes now, white and stylish as a sailor's summer bells. I grant you it will be unbelievable.

I put the young man in 1958. He has served in the Army, and once told the Automat story to a group of friends as proof of his sexual prowess. They believed him: what else was there for them to believe? This shabby use of a fragile occurrence was occasioned by the smell of honeysuckle and magnolia in the tobacco country outside Winston-Salem. It brought her to him so that he was possessed. He felt the magic key in his hand again. To master this overpowering wave of nostalgia he cheapened it. Certainly the reader will recall such shoddy incidents in his own life.

After his discharge he married some girl and had three children by her. He allowed her her divers interests and she tolerated his few stupid infidelities. He had a good job in advertising and they lived in Kew Gardens in a brick semi-detached house. Let me give them a sunken living room to give this the appearance of realism. His mother died in 1958 and left the lake house to him. Since he had not been there for ten years he decided to sell it, against his wife's wishes. The community was growing and the property was worth twice the original price.

This is a ruse to get him up there one soft spring day in May. He drives up in a year-old Pontiac. The realtor's office, the papers, etc. Certainly, a shimmer of nostalgia about it all, although he felt a total stranger. He left the car on the main road, deciding to walk down to the lake, partly visible through the new-leaved trees. All right, now here we go. A Cadillac station wagon passed and then stopped about fifteen yards ahead of him and she got out. She was wearing white shorts and sneakers and a blue sweatshirt. Her hair was the same, shorter perhaps, tied with a ribbon of navy velour.

It's too impossible to invent conversation for them. He got in her car. Her perfume was not the same. They drove to her parents' house for a cup of coffee—for old times' sake. How else would they get themselves together and alone? She had come up to open the house for the season. Her husband was a college traveler for a publishing house and was on the road, her son and daughter were staying at their grandparents' for the day. Popular songs, the lyrics half-remembered. You will do well if you think of the ambience of the whole scene as akin to the one in detective novels where the private investigator goes to the murdered man's summer house. This is always in off-season because it is magical then, one sees oneself as a being somehow existing outside time, the year-round residents are drawings in flat space.

When they walked into the chilly house she reached past him to latch the door and he touched her hand on the lock, then her forearm, her shoulder. Take your clothes off, he said, gently. Oh gently. Please. Take your clothes off? He opened the button of her shorts. You see that they now have the retreat I begged for them a decade ago. If one has faith all things will come. Her flesh was cool.

In the bedroom, she turned down the spread and fluffed the pillows, then sat and undressed. As she unlaced her sneakers, he put the last of his clothes on a chair. She got up, her breasts quivering slightly, and he saw faint stretch marks running into the shadowy symmetry of her pubic hair. She plugged in a small electric heater, bending before him, and he put his hands under her buttocks and held her there. She sighed and trembled and straightened up, turning toward him. Let me have a mist of tears in her eyes, of acrid joy and shame, of despair. She lay on the bed and opened her thighs and they made love without elaboration.

In the evening, he followed her car back into the city. They had promised to meet again the following week. Of course it wouldn't be sordid. What, then, would it be? He had perhaps wept bitterly that afternoon as she kissed his knees. She would call him, he would call her. They could find a place to go. Was she happy? Really happy? God knows, he wasn't *happy!* In the city they stopped for a drink in a Village bar and sat facing each other in the booth, their knees touching, holding hands. They carefully avoided speaking of the past, they made no jokes. He felt his heart rattling around in his chest in large jagged pieces. It was rotten for everybody, it was rotten but they would see each other, they were somehow owed it. They would find a place with clean sheets, a radio, whiskey, they would just—continue. Why not?

These destructive and bittersweet accidents do not happen every day. He put her number in his address book, but he wouldn't call her. Perhaps she would call him, and if she did, well, they'd see, they'd see. But he would *not* call her. He wasn't that crazy. On the way out to Queens he felt himself in her again and the car swerved erratically. When he got home he was exhausted.

You are perfectly justified in scoffing at the outrageous transparency of it if I tell you that his wife said that he was so pale that he looked as if he had seen a ghost, but that is, indeed, what she said. Art cannot rescue anybody from anything.

DECADES

Ben and Clara Stein were made for each other. I won't go so far as to say that they were meant for each other, but it all comes out the same way. It is impossible for me, even now, after these fifteen or so years since I first met them, to think of them as anything but "the Steins."

I have no idea how and where they met, but it might have been at a party during the Christmas vacation—this would have been back in 1955 or thereabouts. Clara was a Bard student at the time, having gone there from Bennington, to which she had gone from Antioch, to which she had gone from Brooklyn College. All this moving about had something to do with art, i.e., she went where art was "possible." All right, I don't know what it means, either. She published some poems in various student magazines, and in one of them an essay on Salinger's *Nine Stories,* which won her a prize of twenty-five dollars' worth of books. She was a dark, slender, hyper-nervous girl, whose father thought that she was going to be a teacher. He comforted himself with this, although I assure you that he would have sent her to school no matter what he thought she wanted to be, for, to her father, school was good, it was sunshine and bananas with cream. He had plenty of money from his business, which had something to do with electronic hospital equipment, and Clara was denied nothing.

Ben was an English major at Brooklyn College when he met Clara at this party. I will put their meeting at this party since all college parties are essentially the same and I am saved the trouble of describing it. But they met, conversation in the corner, coffee at Riker's, and so on. Ben wore blue work shirts, tweed jackets with leather elbow patches, long scarves wound around his neck and thrown over the shoulder. His father did something. Whatever your father does, that's what he did: the years shuffling by, marked by decaying Chevys and fevered vacations, the World Series and Gelusil. Ben's minor was French, and he read Apollinaire and Cocteau. His reading of French anglicized him in a Ronald Firbank kind of way, and he affected a weariness and sensitivity that, on Flatbush and Nostrand, was something to see. He had a darting, arcane mind, of a kind that made Clara forever obscure the fact that she had once admired Salinger. Somewhere they found a place to be alone, and in two months Clara was pregnant. Ben married her, after a long, serious talk with her father and mother, during which Ben shook his foot nervously, flashed his compulsive smile at them, and made bewildering jokes about W. H. Auden. Clara's father shook Ben's hand and they both stood there, in wordless misery, laughing cordially. The father couldn't understand how Clara had allowed this silly boy into her slim, straight body.

I first met Ben in a class in classical civilization at Brooklyn College. At the time, I was attending school on the Korean War GI Bill, and my school friends were other ex-soldiers like myself, a penurious and shabby bunch indeed. Ben was the first non-veteran I had come across who seemed to have something to do with what I then thought of as reality. We sat in the back of the room, composing obscene sonnets, to which we wrote alternate lines, while the rest of the class relentlessly took notes. Why I was going to school I really can't tell you in any clear way: let's say that I wanted to learn Latin. All right.

Ben and I failed that course, but Ben, who was being supported by Clara's father, panicked. He was afraid that their monthly stipend would be cut off and that he might have to drop out of school or go to work. The reader must know that in the fifties, Ben was a member of a large minority of young people that thought that life was somehow nonexistent outside of the academy, that is, life within the university was real life—outside were those strange folk who spoke ungrammatical English and worshiped the hydrogen bomb. God knows what has happened to those scholars; I know only what has happened to Ben and Clara. In any event, I myself didn't care about my F, but it was interesting to see Ben's reaction to the failing grade: he begged, he pleaded, he took a makeup exam and wound up with a C for the course. When I say it was interesting, I mean that I saw that Ben was not that romantic Byronesque figure I had taken him to be. He somehow had a goal, a—what shall I call it?—"stake in life." On the other hand, I am more or less still searching for myself, if you can stomach that phrase. Well, let that be; this is the Steins' story.

I suppose it was at about this time that I met Clara, Ben's other half—the banality of that expression is, in this case, perfection itself. The scene: a hot day in June. Ben had received permission to take his makeup exam. I was invited to their apartment to have a drink and some supper and "see the baby," Caleb. At the time, I was going with a girl who regularly contributed to the Brooklyn College literary magazine, and whose father was a shop steward in what used to be a Communist local. She read *The Worker,* and pressed on me the novels of Howard Fast. If she has followed the pattern of her generation, she has married a pharmacist and lives in Kips Bay—but in those days she was my mistress: or, let me write it, My Mistress. How flagrantly serious we were! Lona carried her diaphragm in her bag and we discovered that John Ford was a great artist. We went together to see the Steins in their apartment in Marine Park.

The most exquisite tumblers, tall and paper-thin, filled with icy Medaglia d'Oro topped with whipped cream. Hennessy Five Star. Sliced avocados with lime wedges. Crisp, salty rye and Brie. In my faded khaki shirt, the shoulder ripped where I had fumbled in removing the patch that had once identified me, I ate and drank and understood why Ben had been concerned with his grade. Clara made it clear that the Hennessy was a gift from her father, who apparently was good for little else. "In his freaking air-conditioned Cadillac!" she said. "What else?" Ben said. "De gustibus." Lona was into her harangue on the symmetrical beauties of *Barbary Shore,* Ben was depleting the Cognac, the baby was crying. We spoke of Charles Olson, of whom I was then scarcely aware. Clara thought he was "pure shit," a fake Ezra Pound: she knew him from Bard or Bennington or someplace. Norman Mailer was also "shit," as was the Communist party, Adlai Stevenson, peace, war, and Ben. Ben would twitch slightly and say Cla-ra, Claa-ra, Claa-rr-aa? Lona and I soon left. At the door, Ben showed me a split in the sole of his shoe, to demonstrate his penury. I soon came to realize that Ben was always broke—I mean that was his mask. His life, financially speaking, was remarkably stable—but he was always broke. The attainment of this attitude was a talent of Ben's class, which attitude has persisted, and even refined itself. At the time, I was naïve enough to think that one had to be without money to be broke.

Lona and I separated soon after. I remember taking a ferry ride that afternoon and, later in the day, going to Luigi's, a bar near the college, where I got drunk on 2-for-35 Kinsey and beer chasers. Sad, sad, I wanted to be sad. It was delicious.

Some time passed and I lost track of the Steins. Ben had graduated and he and Clara and the baby had left town, Ben gone to some assistantship in the Midwest. I had left school and was working in a factory on Pearl Street, operating a punch press that stamped out Teflon gaskets and couplings. The work exhausted me, but I took comfort in the fact that it left my mind free to write. Of course, if one's mind is too free while working a punch press, one can part with a finger or two. But I was caught in the mythology of the struggling writer in America; in retrospect, I see that I contributed some small part to the myth myself. It is not a comfort— but then, what is? At night, I was slogging through a gigantic and unwieldy novel, *From Partial Fires*, which had long before got completely out of control, but which I persisted in thinking would make my name. I don't know what else I did. I did have an affair with a girl who worked in the factory office, who regarded my manuscript with awe; we saw a lot of movies together and afterward would go to my apartment on Coney Island Avenue and make love. She would leave at midnight; I would walk her to the subway, then return to stare at the thick prose I had last composed. I don't think I have ever been closer to despair.

Suddenly the Steins were back, just for the summer. Ben was going to work in some parks program to bring culture to somebody in the guise of demotic renderings of Restoration comedy. Almost every Saturday we all went to the beach in Ben's car. June, my lover, could not understand the Steins, and they thought of her as an amusing yahoo. Clara delighted in asking June questions like which of "the Quartets" she preferred most. Ben drank vast quantities of vodka and orange juice, as did I. One day I was fired for having taken off three Mondays in a row, and was lucky enough to get on unemployment. June hit me with her beach bag the next Saturday when I called her my "little Polack rose," and she walked off to the bus, crying. Clara seemed delighted and cheerful the rest of the day, and toward twilight we swam together far out into the ocean. Ben seemed to me then the luckiest of men.

Toward Labor Day, Ben became entangled in an affair with a girl named Rosalind, a flautist who attended Juilliard. He would spend the afternoons with her in her loft on East Houston Street. Clara said nothing, but began to take Dexedrine in large amounts, and to comment on my sexual attractiveness whenever Ben was paying attention. Ben would grimace, and say Claa-r-aa, Claa-rr-aaa? One day, when Rosalind had come to the beach with us, and she and Ben had gone walking along the water's edge, hand in hand—innocent love!—collecting shells, I leaned over and kissed Clara and she slapped me, then scratched my face. She was trembling, and flushed. "You rotten son of a bitch! You rotten bastard son of a bitch!" But she said nothing to Ben—as if he would have heard her.

When the Steins left in September for their Midwestern life, Rosalind went with them. I heard that Ben had jumped the island on some eight-lane highway in Indiana and almost killed them all. I can't imagine that it was anything other than an accident; he had Rosalind, he had Clara, he had money. I think I got another job at just about that time, dispatching trucks for a soap company located on the North River. The foreman kept telling me stories about how he used to screw his wife every night so that she wept in hysterical joy. It would be nice if I could say that I thought the foreman was telling the truth, but he was not. He lied desperately, almost gallantly, watching the sun go down over the ugliness of north Jersey each evening as we waited for the trucks to return.

Occasionally, one of these old coffeepots would break down outside of Paterson or Hackensack, and we would have to wait some hours into the evening for it to come in before we could leave. At these times, the foreman would send out for sandwiches and coffee, and tell me about some terrific broad's legs and ass and "everything else" that he had seen somewhere, anywhere. His eyes would widen in his remarkably precise nostalgia for something that had never happened. Once I invented and told him about a wild bedroom scene I had had with a "crazy hot broad" who was the wife of a good friend of mine. As I spun out the details of this lie, I realized that I was envisioning Clara Stein. So you will see the pass to which I had come.

My novel was completed, and I began the process of retyping the ragged manuscript to which I liked to think I had given my best. I began to frequent the bars I had gone to before beginning work on the book, and in them heard various reports of the Steins. Ben, Clara, and Rosalind had tried to keep their ménage going, but it was hopeless, and Ben left with Rosalind for Taos, where she left him for an Oklahoma supermarket-chain owner who had controlling interest in two of the Taos galleries. "Mountains, mountains, bring me more mountains!" the gallery directors would indubitably command their stables of rustic hacks. Then the Steins were back together again and Ben got Clara pregnant, to prove his love or his manhood or his contempt. At just about the time I heard this story, the Steins came back into New York for Clara's abortion. Her father didn't like the idea, but abortion, in its place . . . it was something like school and the sun, it was good. Their visit was a flying one, and I didn't get to see them, but I did speak briefly with Ben on the phone. He despised the doomed fetus almost as much as he despised Clara and himself. At least that was my impression. But perhaps I was wrong, perhaps Ben was just nervous.

I had finished my novel and sent it to an editor at one of the big houses, a man whom I had met some years before at one of my English professors' "teas." The editor was heavy and shambling, and vodka martinis had kept him from a brilliant career. We had lunch at one of those boozy little French restaurants in the East Fifties, which I remember quite clearly because two women and a man at the table next to ours drunkenly, but seriously, talked over their sexual adventures of the previous weekend. In any event, *From Partial*

Fires was too long, too cluttered plot-wise, it was really two novels, the characters were undeveloped and not really convincing except for the woman who was married to Jerry, what was her name? Perhaps if I rewrote? I went home, fuzzily drunk, and tore the manuscript up. My sense of relief was almost as great as it had been on the day that my Polack rose had walked out of my life. I felt free now to—do things. To do things.

One of the first things I did was to meet, at a party for somebody's reading at the Y, a really lovely girl who studied yoga and wrote poems that were a marvel of abstract nouns, all counted off in the most meticulous measure this side of John Betjeman. She lived on St. Marks Place in a beautifully appointed apartment, into which I moved with her soon after our first lust had passed. Just before I quit my job at the soap company, I asked her to pick me up there one day after work, so that I could show her off to the foreman. Such small cruelties often return to plague me now. I like to think of them as aberrations, or deviations from a true path.

So Lynn supported me. While she worked at her job—let's say it was in a publishing house where her intelligence would soon be revealed—I walked around a lot, drank coffee, and went to the movies. Occasionally, I wrote poems on her Olivetti, a machine that has the knack of making all poems look amateurish, or I took Lynn's poems and tried to rework them in different rhymes. She was a demon for rhyming.

In my restless peace, after I had done my walking or my typing for the day, and while I was waiting for Lynn to come home, I often thought of the Steins, and wondered how Clara would like Lynn, or, I should say, I wondered how much Clara would dislike her. Lynn would come in around five-thirty or six, with something to make the place "cheery," as if such things could fend off New York, lying in wait outside the windows. She would bring in some flowers, or a tiny Japanese vase; perhaps a cake from Sutter's; a paper lantern to illuminate the late supper of linguini and clam sauce, the Chablis and Anjou pears. We would talk about art and movies and her poems. She had almost put together a first collection and was thinking of publishing it privately in a small offset edition. One of the men in the art department (that is a remarkable phrase) at the office would do a cover drawing for her—he was really good. What else would he be? Does anyone know a bad artist?

One afternoon I got very drunk at Fox's Corner, a bar—now gone—on Second Avenue frequented by gamblers and horse-players. The reason I remember it is because that was the day Kennedy was shot in Dallas. When I got home, Lynn was waiting for me, the TV and radio both on, her face serious and white, and the ashtray filled with her half-smoked Pall Malls. She looked at me, stricken, as if someone who had loved her had died. For some reason, I was sexually aroused and knelt in front of her, then began to work her skirt up over her thighs, opening them with delicate care. She slapped at my hands, and stood up. "My God! You're *drunk!* You're drunk and can't you see? Don't you know what's happened? They shot Kennedy! Kennedy is dead!" She was in a rage, and she annoyed me more than I can say—she annoyed me past reason. Smiling in a vague imitation of Ben's compulsive rictus, I chose to be light—ah, light, gay, and facetious. "Ah, well, but what has Kennedy ever done for the novel?"

I suppose that Lynn was right to strike me—even fools can rise to what I suppose they consider to be dignity. So that was the end of that affair. It is only our own deaths that we are allowed to ridicule. I left the next day, while Lynn was at work, placing my key in the mailbox, wrapped in a piece of paper on which I had written: *Ars gratia artis.*

I got another job as a clerk/typist in a small printing house, and settled into a new place on Avenue B, near the Charles movie theater. At a party one night, a drunk told me that Ben and Clara and some art student had set up housekeeping together. Ben was working toward his doctorate, a study of the relation between the songs in Shakespeare's plays and the choruses of Greek drama, and they were in Cambridge. Their son, Caleb, was at boarding school—too late to matter, of course—Ben studied and wrote and drank, the art student painted and drank, and Clara—I couldn't imagine anything that Clara did. My only picture of it all was of Clara and the art student, arms around each other's waists, stumbling into the bedroom while Ben groaned Claa-ra, Claa-rr-aaa? his nose in the sauce.

Soon after, I met a girl who had known Clara from high school, and she said that Clara often spoke of me in her letters; I was touched. We went, later that week, to the New Yorker, and saw *La Grande Illusion* for the seventh time, then took a cab to my place. The following Friday, she called and asked me if I'd like her to come over for the weekend, and I said it was fine with me. When she came in, she had a Jon Vie cake and a teal-blue candle that had been "handcrafted." I kept still. Making love that night, she began to cry, and I thought of the foreman and his fantastic wife. Perhaps he had been telling the truth, after all.

The next few years are a blur of the most disparate things, all of them, however, very much the same in essence. My Jon Vie girl left me one night in a bar when I began to insult her because she had been talking incessantly about Saul Bellow. "Fuck you and your mockie writers," I said, or words to that effect. "Them Jew writers don't speak for us proletariats and blue-collar woikers." I don't know why I said this: I have nothing against Saul Bellow; I've never even read him.

At about the time of this unpleasantness, I began to write again, but found it unsatisfying, both as act and product. I thought that I might write a detective story and get enough money to leave my job and go somewhere, but I couldn't get past the first chapter. What made me quit the whole thing was coming across a magazine one day in the 8th St. Bookshop; in it, there was a poem by Benjamin Stein. I can't remember all of the poem, but it was cast in a curious and affected language, a kind of modernist cant then abounding. The first few lines ran:

> *I touch ya, ya touch*
> *me, yer bellie an mine.*
> *ole catullus wuz rite*
> *1,000,000 kisses . . .*

On the contributors' page, it said that Mr. Stein was an "ex-professor of English now living in the Bay Area with his wife and son." I can't express the feeling of defeat that this little poem carried into my very spirit. I did understand, however, that my own aborted "return to writing" had the closest affinities to this ridiculous trash of Ben's.

I didn't go back to work the next day, nor the next, and then I went in to collect my pay and tell the boss that I had to leave for Chicago because of a family emergency. I lived frugally on some money I had saved, supplemented by occasional freelance proof-reading jobs, looked out the window, and mentally composed hundreds of letters to Ben and Clara. But they were impossible to write, filled, as they would have to be, with no facts at all. I suppose I was vaguely ashamed of myself.

About six weeks before the last of my savings ran out, I got into a silly conversation with some idiot I had known for years. He was buying the drinks and I, in a sponger's honesty, kept telling him, as we got drunk, that I could not buy back. Somehow, we made plans to collaborate on a play that would exploit the ludicrous side of the flower children. "A winner, man, a winner! Maybe we could get a goddamn grant and do it in the parks even!" So we became collaborators, and I moved in with him after explaining my wretched financial status. Oh, well, not to go into it, but I began to carry on with his girl, who was always conveniently at home when he was not. She was a true Miss Post Toasties, white teeth, blue eyes, sunny California hair—ah, dear God. She, of course, told him of our indiscretions after we had had a bitter argument one night over the ultimate artistic value of the Beatles. The Beatles! You can see that I had gone beyond foolishness.

He threw me out, and I took a room by the week in the Hotel Albert until I could get up the nerve to write Ben and ask him for enough money to put down as security and the first month's rent on a shotgun flat on Avenue c. It struck me as I wrote him that I had no one else to write to. I didn't expect him to send me the money, but two weeks later he did, a money order for a hundred and fifty dollars, and a note: *Peace*. The letter was postmarked from Venice, California, another outpost of the lost battalion. I moved into the new place, started working temporary office jobs, and recovered some of my solvency. I even managed to send Ben ten or fifteen dollars a week to pay off the debt. Some months passed, during which time I heard no more from Ben, nor from Clara, either. My experience had got me another truck-dispatching job with a direct-mail company on Fourth Avenue, a few blocks north of Klein's. I handled the trucks that made the daily post-office runs, and acted as a kind of foreman over the constantly changing personnel. Since I despised the management as much as the laborers despised me, the job was a nightmare, and I began to drink my lunches in a Fourteenth Street bar. My afternoons were passed in a boozy haze of sweat, curses, and shouts. For this, I got eighty-five dollars a week.

One afternoon, Clara called me on the job. She wanted to know if I'd like to have a drink with her after work—someone had told her where I was working and she thought . . . Her voice was gentle, almost gentle, and, I thought, resigned. Ben was doing what he wanted to do, write. He was happy. Did it matter to him or to Clara that he wrote badly? Did it matter to anyone? We made a date to meet in a little bar on University Place at five-thirty.

When I got there, Clara was already at the bar, working on what seemed to be, from her manner, her third Gibson. She was cool and brown in a yellow dress and yellow sandals, her hair drawn back from her face. I ordered a bourbon and soda and sat on the barstool next to her, giving her wrist what I hoped she would take to be a friendly squeeze. How I despised myself. What could I possibly have said? It is amazing that I am utterly unable to recall our conversation. Well, you must remember that I was half-drunk when I got there, and the bourbons that I subsequently drank did nothing to make me less drunk. It is odd that this should be, that I can't remember anything of what was said, since this was surely one of the most important conversations of my life—that is, if you are willing to accept that my life is of any importance at all. On the way to the bar, I had determined to ask Clara if she would consider "being" with me during her stay in the city. Then we would see—we would see what would happen. God knows, I was no worse than Ben; in some ways, I was better. I had stayed in the city, I had stuck it out, I hadn't fooled myself that I was a writer. I had, in short, faced the music. I don't think that I thought of myself as a failure; not that I do now, of course. But I have come to realize that there are certain options, let us say, that are closed to me. The fashionably grubby artistic circles in New York are filled with people like me, people who are kind enough to lie about one's chances in the unmentioned certitude that one will lie to them about theirs. Indeed, if everyone told the truth, for just one day, in all these bars and lofts, at all these parties and openings, almost all of downtown Manhattan would disappear in a terrifying flash of hatred, revulsion, and self-loathing.

Well, we spoke of Ben, that's for certain. Ah, how marvelously drunk we were getting, gazing at each other through those rose-colored glasses all drinkers wear. Ben had left Clara again and gone to a commune in Colorado with some young girl he had met at a rock concert in Los Angeles. I must have subtly inquired as to Clara's feelings on the matter; I mean, I wanted to know if she cared, I wanted to know if she wanted him back. I clearly remember her facing me, her legs crossed, one of them brushing my calf as she swung it back and forth, the fragile glass to her mouth. Oh, I don't know. I don't know how I said it, said anything. Probably something like, "Why don't we just give it a try for a while? For a few days?" What I wanted to say was: "Your yellow dress. Your yellow sandals. Your dark and sweet skin. Your legs. I don't care about Ben or anything else but you." But I do remember her saying, "Let's go to my hotel. That's what you want, isn't it? Isn't that what you want?" And I said something like—oh, I was determined to force her to spoil our chances, if chances they were—"Is it all right? I mean, with Ben?"

I bought a bottle of Gordon's on the way to the Fifth Avenue Hotel, and we started to drink as soon as we got to her room—no ice, no soda, just the harsh, warm gin out of the bottle. I held the bottle to her mouth as she let her dress and half-slip fall around her feet.

We made love under the shower, weaving and thrusting and shuddering in the drenching spray of hot water that seemed to make me drunker. Clara was leaning against the porcelain tiles of the stall, bent over, and I behind her, my eyes blinded by the streams of water, my mouth open to its metallic heat. "Ben!" she laughed. "Oh, Ben! You rotten son of a bitch! Split me apart, you rotten bastard! Rotten son of a bitch!" I didn't care. I didn't care.

After I dried myself and her, she lay on the bed, smiling at me. "I'm here for two days," she said. "You're not mad at me? Am I all right?" "Why should I be mad at you?" "Come and sleep," she said, "and when we wake up I'll show you some funny things I can do." "Sure," I said, and then she closed her eyes and was asleep in a minute. I dressed and left, and walked aimlessly for an hour, wanting to go back to the hotel. She could call me Ben again. She could show me the funny things she knew how to do. I finished my drunk in a bar on Sixth Avenue, just off Fourteenth Street, and lost my wallet in the cab that took me home.

The next day I called Mrs. Stein at the hotel, and the desk clerk told me that she had checked out very early. It strikes me now that I never even knew why she had come in, that she might have come in for no other reason than to see me. But if I know Clara, she came in to see her mother and father, or to have her teeth checked, or to buy some clothes. She wouldn't come all the way from California just for old times' sake. I know Clara.

I'm living now in a very decent apartment in an old, rather well-kept building on Avenue B and Tenth Street, with the estranged wife of a studio musician. She makes a very good salary as a buyer for Saks, so I have quit my job. Outside, Tompkins Square Park and the streets reel under the assaults of the hordes of mindless consumers of drugs. But in here we are safe behind our triple locks and window gates. About once a month my girl, who is really quite brilliant—she graduated magna cum laude in political science from Smith—and I invite a young filmmaker and his wife over, and we watch blue movies that they shot in a commune in Berkeley. We drink wine and smoke a great deal of marijuana and what happens happens. Each time they come over, we all pretend horror that "something" may happen, what with the wine and the grass and the movies. We laugh and make delicately suggestive remarks to each other. It seems clear that the young filmmaker's wife likes me a great deal. Each time they come is a new time, and no one speaks of the last time.

I've begun to write poems again, or let me be honest and say that they are attempts at poems. But they seem sincere to me. They have a nice, controlled flow. My girl likes them.

This morning I got a letter from Ben. It had taken three weeks to reach me because it had been sent to the Avenue c address. I don't really know what I'm going to do about it.

I'm reading it again now. Somewhere in the building a young man is singing a song, accompanying himself on the guitar. I can't make out the words, but I know that they are about freedom and love and peace—perfect peace, in this dark world of sin.

dere old pal—

you wuz alwaze crazee not to be into life. out here in colorado—the country will *bring us peace—we are together, all together, suzanne, a sweet luvlee thing an clara too. come out an see us. good bread an good head aboundin. a commune for all us lost -ists. dig on it!*

ah jeezus! we all wuz sikk or wounded but now we're gunna get healed. come on! you aint so g/d old.

luv,

ben

LAND OF COTTON

Joe Doyle was born a bastard whose natural father's name had been Lionni, or Leone. I have no idea what man owned the name Doyle. Let's imagine his true sire to be a loudmouth who spent his days in a candy store in the Bronx, reading *The Green Sheet* and betting hopeless long shots. When one speaks of the People, one must remember that Joe's father is always to be included among them. Whole novels, inexplicably, have been written exploring such characters. Perhaps these novels allow them to persist.

Along about the time that Joe decided that he would be a "writer," his father's name shifted in his head so that he came to think of it as Lee. In any event, he led everyone he knew to believe that *he* believed that the name was Lee. Ah, mystery. Why his father would have changed his name from Lee to Lionni was unexplained, but such a puzzle only served to make everything more hazily romantic. Once an aberration is seized upon, its possible variations are virtually limitless: consider advertising. Soon after this, Joe came to consider himself, I swear it, a descendant of Robert E. Lee, and the dear old shattered South, the grand old decayed plantations, the beautiful old smoldering mansions became part of his heritage. It might have been true if things had been a little this way, or a little that way, right? So Joe perhaps thought of it.

This spangled rubbish was useful to Joe's life; with it, he could wrench his father out of roachy shotgun flats and busboy jobs in Horn and Hardart's and fold him into pink clouds that glowed with the light of romance. He was no longer the man his mother had often bitterly and mockingly described to him, an unemployed lover in a Crawford suit-with-two-pairs-pants and Woolworth's rose-oil pomade, shining his hair to oilcloth, but a quixotic, footloose hero whose rebel blood drove him to disappear from the verminous kitchens in which Joe had grown up. Joe, of course, had this same imaginary blood.

He kept all this glittering lost glory subtly in the background, exposing it discreetly when it could get him something, and functioned off its energy. It was indeed an engine of sorts, and did not at all interfere with his job, his social life, or his "writing." Joe *became* what he called an artist—and how he loved that word; I can hear him now: "Well, as far as Flaherty being an *artist* . . ."—because to be an artist was to be the stubborn Reb in retreat. He began to write poems, actual words, count 'em, words, on actual paper. It was "interesting," and admitted him to a world that seemed to offer more than the world of, say, numismatics. That the poems were indeed accepted as art has little bearing on this story—although I suspect that it is not so much a story as a minor change upon a common fable. The world is filled with talented and intelligent people who produce arty bits and pieces by which other talented and intelligent people are somehow nourished; they get what they need for their ailments.

Sometimes I think it is all nothing but Joes with their variants of sham honeysuckle and Alabama nights on the one hand, and on the other those who come within range of that nailed-together glamour. It is all exciting and everyone is very pleased.

Joe first met Helen Ingersoll in 1965, some five years after he manufactured his paper-magnolia legend. He and a friend, Ed Manx, had gone to a poetry reading at a grim, creaking little theater downtown, just off Second Avenue. I believe the theater is now a macrobiotic restaurant or a "head shop"—it is not my fault that the generation's nomenclature is spectacularly ugly. The poet was a smudgy friend from the fifties who had been living in the Southwest for years and had returned for a month or so to attend to some family matter. His current poems were about freedom and adobe and white sand, mesas and mountains, in the way that Robert Frost's poems are about America—that is, these concepts were laid on like high-gloss enamel. One can imagine the scarred little table behind which the bard sat, his can of beer and black spring binders at his elbow, reading, oddly enough, from a book of verse he had published almost ten years earlier, at a time when he had entertained a powerfully unreal conception of his gifts. He read these old poems as if they were examples of youthful aberration. Which is to say that he laughed at what he now considered to be their "boudoir sentiments"—his term. When Joe asked him about New Mexico or Colorado or some other chic wasteland, he said, "I never knew what a long line could be, baby, till I saw those mountains." You get the idea. Joe and Ed drank from a pint of Dant that Ed had in his raincoat, their faces fixed in a blank, intense look behind which boredom crawled and scuffled. At the intermission, they went across the street to a bar and never got back to the reading.

Joe began talking to Ed about Hope, his wife, how terrific she was, how lovely, how understanding and intelligent, what a son of a bitch he had been to her, and yet, and yet, what good friends they were now that they were separated. I'm certain that he even did a few time steps to the old tune that goes, "We see more of each other than when we were together." He could be a master of nausea without half trying. She was doing well, working as a secretary-receptionist-girl Friday in an uptown gallery devoted to the What's Selling School. She really had great taste, Joe said; she felt useful now, truly involved with the art world she had always just touched the edges of. I can almost see Hope's lacquered face placid among the wares on display; I can almost hear her telling some broke painter, desperate in his wrinkled tie, to bring in a selection of color slides. They drank some more, silent in the contemplation of Hope's splendor. Then, just for the ride, and because he was a little drunk, Joe went uptown with Ed to see Helen.

She had asked Ed up to advise her on the right mat and frame for a small ink drawing that she had been given as a gift, and while Ed and she talked things over, Joe walked around the apartment, looking at her small and somewhat precious collection of pictures and books. He was, one might say, zeroing in on his intentions regarding this attractive woman. She was mature—another word that Joe liked; she was the Sarah Lawrence or Barnard alumna who had been around. Life had *used* her, as she had *used* life, and so on. Joe felt as if he were strolling into a relevant movie, all pained faces and swallowed dialogue and blurred focus. He helped himself to another vodka and caught Helen's eye. She seemed delicately faded to him; there was something irrevocably broken about her. He slouched against the wall, gallant and aristocratic; against the tattered and streaming gray sky of his mind the Stars and Bars cracked in the wind.

On the way downtown, Ed told him that she was forty-two and undergoing chemotherapy treatments for leukemia. To Joe, this was an unexpected perfection—how could she resist, her tragedy upon her, the gift of himself that he would offer? Joe's opinion of himself was based solidly on his being a product of that solipsistic aristocracy that clumps itself about the nucleus of art—which latter gives it breath and rationale. He was, in his sham individuality, a dime a dozen. So was Helen.

Joe didn't know this about Helen—nor did he know it about himself, certainly. Helen, in fact, qualified for him as representative of that breeding and careless grace with which his fabulous past was suffused, and she took her place in that misty locale where Joe's father sipped juleps and played croquet on emerald lawns, the sun dazzling off his white flannels and linen cap. There was a patina he felt he could scrape and strip off her very person and place on his own in mellow and lustrous layers. For Helen, Joe was young enough to be interesting, but not so young as to be gauche and trite in his desire. So they became lovers. I don't know how to say this without seeming either cold or vulgar, but Helen thought of Joe as a last fling. Joe's feelings concerning Helen were, as you will have guessed, cold and vulgar.

Concerning Helen's past, there isn't much to say. She had hacked and hewn out a lopsided icon that passed for taste, had achieved an arresting face, and had been twice married to vaguely creative men who were moderately successful in vaguely creative jobs—the sort of men who wore ascots and smoked little Dutch cigars. In her thirties she had painted a little and clumped through a few parts in off-off-off-Broadway theater; a modern-dance class and a poetry workshop were also buried in the sludge. You will understand that she was a female counterpart to Joe. The one element that totally differentiated her from him was the fact of her critical illness: death and disease are impenetrable masks behind which the pettiness and shabbiness of personality are absolutely obscured. That we tend to forgive or overlook the flaws of the doomed probably saves us all from total monstrosity. But it must be borne in mind, however ungenerously, that Helen was a shambles of half-baked ideas, insistent on her thin skin yet an opportunistic traitor to her husbands and children, the latter now grown into drugs and therapy, sickened by the mother who embraced the "idea" of, for instance, Mick Jagger as Prophet with a moronic fervor. Young, young, she was forever young as she slid toward her death, brandishing a copy of the *Village Voice*.

It is important to know that Joe thought, in the first weeks of their relationship, that it was his "art" that had seduced her; it had always been his "art" that had brought him his platoons of rutting young women—it was a subtle hook that he used to snare them and then lift their skirts. And if "art" failed, Dixie would materialize out of thin—very thin, indeed—air. When Joe discovered that this was not the case with Helen he was nonplussed, then hurt, then angered. She simply took Joe to be another charming and aesthetically intense young man—much like her husbands and previous lovers. She was right, but no one had ever before so squarely confronted Joe with the fakery of his life and its picayune products. He moved in a world of fakes like himself, so that their mutual interest lay in interdependent lying. Joe thought of himself as a "coterie" poet of carefully controlled output—and so did his friends. Now, suddenly, here was Helen, who with unfeigned equanimity treated him as the amateur dilettante—in Joe's case the phrase is not tautological—he was and always would be. It never occurred to her that Joe thought of his fabrications as poems. One night she said a poem of his reminded her somehow of saltwater taffy. That's not bad at all. Joe wasn't used to this sort of comment on his work; he had never got anything like it from Hope, who thought of him as a serious and neglected artist, although she would not have recognized art if it fractured her skull.

Joe and Hope had dinner together once a week—they were civilized and understanding and good friends and so on. How they rang and rang again each boring modern change. Hope was aware that Joe and Helen were having an affair; Ed Manx had told her about Helen, and Joe had corroborated the tale—and how. In her mind it was a "friendly" affair, and somehow good for Joe: a good, mature woman to discuss art with her husband—oh, once in a while they discovered themselves in bed together, but that was almost an accident, or the price one pays for the nurture of beauty. Over her shrimp cocktail she was reliably bright and engaging. Peck and Peck all the way, with plenty of small talk about some up-to-the-minute painter "into some wild things." Her eyes were blank with that flat stare peculiar to natives of Southern

California, the ocular equivalent, one might say, of a slack mouth. She had practiced for years to achieve it, God knows why: I suspect she confused it with *sang-froid*. Ah, she still had something for Joe; he looked at her with false warmth and affection and she looked back, laboring to emulate his falsity. What moments divine, what rapture serene.

"It's nice and transparent," Helen said one night of a new poem that Joe modestly represented as a "breakthrough." Joe had been writing for five or six years and each year had one of these breakthroughs. His poems neither changed nor improved, but there was, in his insistence on aesthetic discovery, an illusion for him of amelioration in his jottings. Joe was one of those "writers" of whom one constantly thinks as a tyro; then one day the realization that the person has been pottering around for ten years or so crystallizes. It is enough to make one a yahoo. "I mean it's very—clear, yes, right. Transparent." Joe, in a rage, but silent, reclining on the couch under the ink drawing whose mat and frame had brought out its weakness, allowed her to unbuckle his belt and open his trousers. It was *she* who was controlling *him!* What a bitch he thought her. He watched her face disappear in the lace of her slip, her arms above her head graceful and quick. A horny old bitch. He might as well have been a truck driver or a plumber or a goddamned teacher the way she so casually used him. A journalist or editorial assistant who wanted to write a novel! God! At that moment, he began to hate her, his spurious heritage stirring him to combat, gallant. She gently pushed him back on the couch and reached behind to unhook her brassiere. Old raunchy dumb bitch.

So Joe began to speak of her, vulgarly and openly, at the bar in which he was something of a figure. It was a mean and poisonous place of third-rate painters, hangers-on, dedicated filmgoers, and arty idiots, pots and looms in every pocket, who were just passing through. The controlled and amused voice came forth from his expertly hirsute face, his Italian leather jacket was creased—so—in soft, elegant folds. He joked of her tremendous passion for him, her raging and almost "embarrassing" sexual hungers, the luscious nightgowns and intriguing underwear she bought to excite him. It was pathetic. He felt it almost his duty. Her tears. Her moans of gratitude. Where did they think he got this leather jacket? Nothing like an old broad! He and his auditors shuffled and chuckled, a bunch of regular guys that *la vie d'art* would never change. His words punctuated the long tale of malice and vindictiveness and failure that the bar spun out endlessly.

As Helen got sicker, she made herself progressively more ridiculous by trying to be vivacious and girlish for Joe—who rarely went out with her anymore. She played right into the hands of his shabby stories about her, so that when they did meet someone that Joe knew, her behavior was such that Joe all but snickered and winked. He was contemptuous toward her, rude and arrogant—he assaulted her, getting even and getting even again for that "saltwater taffy," that "transparent," her sexual aggressiveness, the Italian leather jacket. Those ragged cavalrymen of his fantasy rode their broken nags out of the morning mists, bent on slaughter.

As it would happen, Helen, with the predictability of melodrama, fell in love with Joe. He was so delicate, so vulnerable, yet so proud. At the moment that Joe realized that, he lied that he and Hope were thinking of "trying it again together." He was precisely if not subtly cruel.

He visited her almost daily at the hospital during her final confinement, bringing her flowers, magazines, books—once, quite unbelievably, he brought her a copy of *As I Lay Dying:* he had turned almost recklessly mean. What was there to lose? He occasionally held her hand and felt generous and forgiving. I like to think that Joe considered these small attentions instances of a refined sense of *noblesse oblige*.

He of course went to the funeral in a new midnight-blue suit: nothing could have kept him out of the first rank of mourners. What is surprising is that Hope went with him. Joe stood there in the calm morning, his face a marvel of abstraction, Hope beside him, her flat stare finding useful employment, in a strikingly severe black-and-silver dress that she had bought a month earlier for an important opening. They were so anxious for each other that they kissed and clutched and fumbled in the taxi home from Queens. Perhaps it was the first step to trying it again together.

THE DIGNITY OF LABOR

≈ The White Shirt

Some young man, Bill will do for a name, out of the Army for three months and tinged, if you will, all right, tinged with a gloom well short of despair, got a job. This was Bill's first job, save for six months spent as a dishwasher and three years as an infantryman, neither of which are now considered actually to be *jobs,* but are thought of as burdens, or perhaps misfortunes. How wise and wonderful the world has become, filled to bursting with careers!

There he was, in the basement stockroom of Art Adventures, an art-supply store in midtown Manhattan. One of the somewhat shabby and unenthusiastic of Bill's chores was to fill exceedingly small glass jars with glaringly bright poster paints "in all popular colors," these paints having been mixed in hundred-gallon vats in Art Adventures' laboratory, you'll pardon the word, affix identifying labels to these filled jars, and stack them, in neatest rows, on the steel shelves reserved for them and other sundries of the art business.

Bill's immediate boss was an adenoidal schlepper from Ozone Park whose name was Stewie, a self-proclaimed hipster, drenched in mambo lore, who sang, hummed, and whistled, day in and day out—to employ a poster-paint phrase—"Rock Around the Clock." Had Stewie's name not been Stewie, it would have been Carl, Ernie, Cliffie, or Sheldon. Now you know who he is! Of course, Stewie took stern delight in telling Bill and his colleague, a Puerto Rican headbreaker, Felix, what to do and how to do it. Felix had been "given a break" and hired, freshly paroled, God only knows why, out of Coxsackie; he often quietly mused, when he and Bill took a smoke break, on the possibility of accidentally maybe stabbing Stewie to death. So the days of that sunny, crisp fall passed, a ragged dream of honest work's rewards and the second chance.

One morning, Stewie told Bill and Felix that he wanted the jars of poster paint shelved so that the virtually unnecessary labels—which comically and redundantly described the startling red or sickly green paints within their jars as RED or GREEN—faced forward, so that, Stewie wisely reasoned, you fuckin well know what you're fuckin pickin when you fill a fuckin order. He was a logical sort, take him all in all. Bill suggested, gently, gently, that this seemed wasteful of time and effort, for a half-blind drunken idiot could tell the difference between colors, and in the dark, for Christ sake. But Stewie, with the sort of ravaged and tottering intelligence that might well have sent him to law school had he not been so ambitious, was not having any of *this*. Yizzel fuckin do what I say, he noted; or, perhaps, yizzel fuckin do it right; or yizzel fuckin well do it. Bill rejoined, weakly, that, hell, come on, there's nobody who could mistake RED for YELLOW, etcetera. But this argument cut no ice with Stewie. Felix, attentive to this dialogue, fingered the switch-blade knife in his pocket, his eye on Stewie's pallid neck, till the latter ended the conversation by arguing that Bill just thought he was a wise guy because he'd been in the fuckin Army. Bill fell silent, searching for the arcane meaning hidden in this observation, but gave up. What the hell. Felix, in a quiet aside, suggested to Bill that they might seriously injure Stewie's sconce with a carelessly wielded gallon jug of India ink, the faggot punk jive motherfucker.

I have not yet mentioned Mr. Pearl, the stockroom supervisor, shipping (he preferred to call it "traffic") coordinator, keeper of the inventory, and he who answered to Art Adventures' purchasing agent. Mr. Pearl had a sad little desk, about as big as a minute, as simple people were wont to say in "a more innocent time" (see: Second World War, the Holocaust, Korean "police action," etc.). On this lugubrious surface, he marshaled his inventory records, daily-order forms, back-order memoranda, pens, pencils (red, green, blue), erasers, and scarred wooden ruler. And off it he ate his lunch, a homely, unassuming, and pedestrian sandwich, a nice piece of fresh fruit, and a pint of milk, the last wrapped in wax paper in the superstitious belief—daily disproved—that this helped keep the milk cool. He was, one might say, a sap. And from the vantage of this handkerchief-sized desk, he looked kindly upon young Stewie, and why? As if you didn't know! *Because he had once been just like young Stewie.* Yea, even unto his sweaty face and dingy cardigan.

Bill, poor Bill, then made the classic yet banal mistake, common enough among all lowly and callow employees, of appealing the irrational decisions of the corporal-mind to a higher, and supposedly saner authority. (May I digress for a moment? Ho! Ho! Ho!)

Or, as Felix put it when Bill told him of his intentions, You must have shit for brains, coño. Cruel yet clear-eyed Felix. Mr. Pearl, seated at his toy desk, a partially destroyed baloney-and-American-cheese sandwich before him on a white handkerchief somewhat drearily adorned with a frayed, faded, embroidered "P" in an infirm pale green, his hands, shiny and grimy with charcoal dust from the drawing pencils he had personally unpacked that morning, resting on the *Mirror,* looked at Bill. Then he spoke:

Stewie is your boss just like I am, your boss, and when Stewie talks I, talk, it's like I talk you unnastan, but, different but, like a, second boss so do as you're told and you'll you'll, get along cause one hand washes, the other am I correct or, am I correct, you ain't like the, other gazabo, the Spanish, Spanish boy from the reform, school you don't want to be like, him, from Harlem, is he, Spanish, you're not, Spanish are you, no offense, I get along, with all kinds of, all people, ask Stewie, Porto Rickans, the colored, ask Stewie, but you, you want to be, a real man, a mensch like they say in Jewish, like Stewie like, me, a man with a wife some day you can look up at a clean fine, American sort of a young lady, you're a pretty clean-cut, fellow, clean-cut sort, a veteran if I'm right well, we can't all be veterans, look at, me, look at, Stewie, I was believe it or, not, I was just, like, Stewie once upon a time, can you, believe it, can you believe it, can you, but that young fellow hasn't found the girl of his dreams yet, but the girls, upstairs, in the office, they all, all, they like him, don't, get, me, wrong, I'm not inferring that he don't like the, girls, no, he just reminds, me, a lot, a lot of myself when I was first starting out on my first job as a messenger, in the garment, yes, the business, remnants, and now as you, see, as you can see, now I wear the white shirt, you see, what, I mean, the, white, shirt, the *white shirt,* if you wanna wear the white shirt you, gotta, I always say to Stewie, you got, to, and let me say it, to you, you got, to, keep your nose clean and get along, all kinds, I don't care coloreds, Spanish persons, one hand, washes, you know, the other, Stewie knows this, oh yes, where his bread is buttered what, side it is, the hands washing, uh-huh, he's got, his, eye on the white shirt, I tell him like a, son, I tell, Stewie you got your eye on, right, the white, right, ha ha, don't you, and Stewie just, well, smiles, because I know his, plans, his, I was just like Stewie once can, you believe, believe it, can you, now, look at the desk, my personal desk, the pens and pencils, the white, shirt, the white, right, pens, pen-cils, my phone, look, you should know you, should unnastan, soon when I go, upstairs, upstairs, soon, Stewie will, be, Stewie will have, this, this will be, his desk, with the daily orders the white, yes, the white shirt, yes indeedy, the tie, the white, uh-huh, so keep your nose, clean, don't be a wise-guy nobody, not nobody, likes a wise-guy yet, we can't all be, no, or like that spick from the penitentiary, with a chip on, somebody will, oh yes, knock, it, off, we can't all, for instance, you're not Spanish, are you, no offense, we couldn't all, all be, take Stewie who tried to join the Army, we can't all be, or sit around in the penitentiary, living off, you know, the taxpayers, look at Stewie, who, tried, who tried to join, the Army the, Marines, but his asthma his, flat feet his, punctured ear, adenoids, some family, you know, problems out in Queens, astigmatic, an astigmatic condi-tion, the National Guard, we're not, all, so lucky, no, can't all run away from obligations, join, the Army the, you know, jail, no, so you shelve the poster, the paints, like Stewie asks he's, got, his, methods, they're good, remember the white shirt if you got, sort of problems, am I right, am I right, am I or am I not, right, you bet your goshdarn life I'm right, now go, take your lunch take, you got an extra, six, minutes, go ahead and, take my, advice, stay away from that shtarker, thug, that, Felix from up in Harlem, I hate, to, say it but, they're all animals up, jabbering in Porto Rickan in, God knows what, language, like monkeys with the knives and, the guns, so keep your nose clean if you, want to get, to move up on, you know, the, ladder, like Stewie, he was nobody just, like, you a couple years, ago, a nothing you hear me.

Bill was fired a couple of weeks later for manifesting what the personnel director of Art Adventures termed "a negative attitude." He disappeared soon after. Mr. Pearl "went upstairs," to assist the purchasing agent of Art Adventures. Six years later, he died in the men's room. Stewie took his desk when he left, wore the white shirt, and then he, too, "went upstairs," leaving his job to one Carl Sheldon. He is still there, dumb as ever. Felix was last known to be working as an orderly at Flower Fifth Avenue Hospital. He is married with four daughters.

≈ *Up and Running Smooth as Silk*
T. Lawless, Branch Manager: *Loquitor*

It's too warm in here. Close the door. It's too goddamned cold. Open the door. Fix the air conditioner. It's stuffy as hell. Turn up the heat. Leave the air conditioner alone. Have a cigar. Fix the copying machine. Fix the light. Help the salesmen with anything they want. Let's see your legs. Put out that cigarette. Let's have some lunch. Fix the door. Get the orders out toot sweet. Unload that truck. Tell your wife you'll be late. What's this. What's that. Cross your legs. Open the air conditioner. Don't piss all over the floor. Call the main office right now. Have a smoke. Always bring in the new stock first. Put the stationery over there. Put the machines over here. Put the machines over by the stationery. Put the stationery over by the machines. Put the machines and the stationery where I tell you. Get me a Coke. Who told you to order this many lightbulbs. Put a tie on for Christ sake. Labels OUT, always. Leave that pallet there. Leave that pallet by the elevator. Close the door and lock it. Ship the machines now, now, now, right now. Go fuck yourself. Don't do what the salesmen want. Come in this weekend. Where's the skid. What's a flat. Turn out the window. Close the bathroom. Wash the windows. Close the heat. Take off that goddamned tie. Take off your dress. Take off your cigar. Green here, red there, red here, green there, blue there, white there, black there, no there, there, THERE. Ship the fucking air conditioner. Put the heat on the shelf next to the stationery. Open your blouse. What do you mean no room. Repair the door. Where is your eraser. Nice cross. Where is your pencil. Where's my pen. Where are yesterday's orders. Ship all the inventory. Forget the paperwork. Come in early tomorrow. Ignore the heat. It's too sunny. Put up the blinds by the cigar. Close the drapes. Bend over. It's too noisy. It's too quiet. I've got nothing against those people. Get my white shirts out of the Chink laundry. Don't hang around the salesmen. Don't hang around the stockroom. Don't come near my office. Deliver the mail to every single goddamned desk. Pick up all the mail all the time. Who told you to pick up the machines. Shovel the snow off the sidewalk. Stack the doors next to the heat. Move the cigars. Put your bra back on. Don't think you'll drink the cocktails. Keep your nose clean. Open the salesmen. Ignore the secretaries. Don't talk to the UPS man. Don't talk to the mailman. Don't hang out with those goddamned truckers. Don't worry about every little thing in the inventory. Why doesn't my pen work. Send back the heat. What do you mean back ordered. Close your blouse. Close your skirt. Pull up your panties. Let sleeping dogs lie. Fix the office. Fix this. Fix that. Fix the salesmen. Who told you to wear a tie. Scrub the floor. Unclog the sink. Unclog the drain. Unclog the clog. Stock your skirt. Red the cabinet. Open the keys. Buy some pencils and Danish. Make the blue. Make the coffee. You'll drink water. No sugar on the orders now or ever. Put your slip on the shelf right here, no here, no there, no here, put it back on. Shut your mouth. Get my wife on the phone. Get that mockie bastard Mr. Pearl on the phone. Get the phone fixed. Cross the green out, no, the red out, no, the air conditioner. Put the files in your socks. It's too damn comfortable in here. No white shirts, no white shirts, goddamnit, no white shirts in the fucking stockroom. Don't eat lunch in here. Don't eat lunch in there. Don't eat lunch over there. Who said you could eat lunch now. No radios in the stockroom. Don't ever wear that old OD shirt in here again. Who hired that guinea whore. Get Sven Bjornstrom on the phone, the crazy Swede bastard. Touch me there, yes, there, and now here. It's too warm in here, sultry, close, no, it's too hot. Fix the vent or whatever you call it. And also the air conditioner goddamn door machine right fucking now immediately. And tell your troubles to Jesus you little faggot prick.

⌐ Cocktails

Hello, I'm Sven Bjornstrom. Often, various people have called me a crazy Swedish person, and I admit that I am of pale skin and have somewhat yellowed teeth. I am fairly skilled though unfluent in three languages, including, as you may surmise instantly, in English. I'm not in liberty to divulge at the present the identity, or name, of the other, or third language, for many reasons which will soon be made as clear as the limping waters. Well, and you wonder why it may be that I admit to being called a crazy Swedish person? That is quite easy! I look forward, to filling you in as my story unfolds. You will see that my life has not been wholly lacking in contented moments and my fair share of a bevy of hearty laughter, along with the rather occasional attention of some partially attractive, running all the way down the scale, to varied homely if not worse-looking ladies. Not all of which I actually knew very well.

I have always tried to act honorably and even with a pinch of stern honesty toward my fellow humans, some sort of trait that is to be continuously knocked into the head of Swedish babies, no matter who they may be. Day after day and year after year, honorableness and honest. Those are what you call the Swedish tickets! Many of these traits of habits are based right on the many teachings of Jesus Christ, or as we Swedish people jokingly daub him now and then, "the first Lutheran." A person or two will sometimes hint that this is very close to blasphemy, and yet Jesus himself often enjoyed a good laugh and a cold glass of beer, yes. The world is filled up with plenty of people who are not actually good sports. Some opine, half as jest, that they should be killed every once in a while, ha ha.

I have sometimes been thought of as a martinet, a word I have looked up, by subordinates, co-workers, and sundry ladies of my past acquaintance. The word has no counter-something in the

Swedish language, but insofar as I know, the closest expression to it might be translated as "fucking corporal." A rude term, I opine, and yet it is in my open nature to speak with rugged vim. The ill will aimed upon me bursts directly out of the fact, like night from day, that I have setted my sights, ever since the proud day that I stepped off the plane from Sweden's greener pleasant land to this great country of opportunity and money, on success of the sort that will, at long last, allow me to purchase, on credit, the Hickey-Freeman suits, the Bally-Bush shoes, the sportlike coats and tastily faded shirts created by Lauren Polo, not to mention the fine foods and the quaffing of the best French vintages. And, upon nearing the pinnacle, I attained the disputeless symbol of success, the signal of the arrival, whatever that truly means, the white shirt! In this last item, I am as much like a man I happen to know slightly, merely to say hello! and hi! and such greetings when we are strolling the avenues and quiet streets of Jackson Heights, which lies in Queens. This is a man who is a self-made man, a man who started his business career as some sort of a grimy lowlife sweaty type of a kike off the streets. Laboring in warehouses, shipping in shipping rooms, packing and taping in dusty basements surrounded up to the knees in old newspapers and excelsior. However, yes!, by dints of cheerful smiles and judicially selected asskissing of those in charge of labor, he rose up slowly to the position of a stern but fair supervisor, as I've carefully pointed to, and one who wears the white shirt to business each and every day, also starched!, with a knockout of a tie. In short. I have always myself dared to have a dream of being atop the hill of the rat race, where I can relax in a sophisticated manner or mode, donned in ascot and smoking gown and velvet slippers, with a pipe filled with the smoldering aromatic tobacco that women adore, and casually just lean back and kick over and drink tasty cocktails to my heart's content with the best of them! And smile gently while I gently toy with my cultured fiancée, a university graduate and not necessarily, believe you me, a Swedish girl.

In brief. My résumé is as thus. First, I toiled in a bookstore where I had to contend, as weekend evening acting assistant manager, with loutish clerks who were constantly hanging about in the stockroom reading trashy magazines and the *Daily News,* and chatting of dirty jokes. As well, they seemed to enjoy eating baloney sandwiches on hard rolls, although I mention these culinarial obsessions only because they ate these foodstuffs in full view of the customers, while paying little heed to sorting and caring for the store's large stock of bullfight posters, an item that we could not keep upon the shelves and walking out the door, as they say. They mocked and razzed at my sense of orderly behavior and fell into bouts of laughter when I employed a tape measure to make sure about the even, neat quality of the stacks of books stacked upon the tables and quite attractive, too. Each stack was displayed so that browsers could view them with ease, even though they were mostly cheapskates and made few purchases. This devoted attention on my part to swift care was not, I insist, crypto-fascist leanings on my part. I am, you must recall, a Swedish person, as I have suggested. I wore a neatly buttoned cardigan while performing my duties, along with a rather jaunty bow tie, somewhat like a college professor, I believe, and such dress is not the signs and such of tyranny in hiding and mental distress. No! I stoutly protest.

I admit, and have jovially admitted in the recent past in both oral and written chats, that I did, I do attest, at times, indulge in somewhat wild arm-waving, hoarse shouts, Swedish oaths, and ear-splitting, uh, screams, while on duty, along with a vigorous stamping of the floor with my feet and a pounding of the counter with my fist. Nothing of a serious nature, yet I saw the desired cocktail shaker floating away from me on a cloud of detested baloney sandwiches. It was a sour pill to watch the silvery dream break up into many pieces. The store manager, a swarty Italian guinea fellow, suggested to me in a harsh tone that I was alarming the customers and frightening them off, the cheap deadbeats! And also that the riffraff clerks were quitting regularly, since I disturbed their sandwich breaks. But what, I asked myself, does this greasy ball know of my desires for ultimate success? You can be sure that he was drinking the cocktails! "Sir," I smilingly averred to him one evening, "you are drinking the cocktails, is this not the fact? What about my chance at the life of milk and honey?" He stepped back from me in what he made believe, I am quite certain, was puzzled alarm, and I was swiftly told to gather my cardigans and leave the premises. I was not working out as weekend evening acting assistant manager, so this gangster stated.

Soon hard upon this, my wife packed her bags and left me, tired, or so she claimed, of listening to my dreams. "Make a living!" the harlot attested. But never saying "die!" I soon claimed another forte as a translator for an import-export firm, until the windows of my mind began their slow fogging over with pesky lustful thoughts, brought on by gazing on a woman in my department who took to wearing the donning of skirts that were disturbingly tight as well as much too short for a lady. My fellow workers all smoked as well, a habit more dangerous to the innocent bystander than a month in heavy combat, so researchers have proved. And to their hearts' content. I am happy to report that with the savings I have saved by not smoking, I have regaled myself with educational treats like various scientific magazines and flashlight batteries. And not just a few! I did not actually know Portuguese, my area of translational responsibility at the firm, and yet I pressed on. My sturdy versions of letters and contracts composed in this barbarous tongue were not exactly as precise as they might have been, and what with my attentive glare upon the body of the immodest lady and the translations, which the departmental chief termed "quite unbelievable," if I recall aright, I was sent unnobly packing as a result of being canned. I had, I may add, drunk nothing but beer with my paltry lunches, while all about me cocktails were quaffed by people no better than I.

The wretched and highly uncultured thug who ran the shipping room at my next job, wherein I performed as the purchasing agent, bookkeeper, correspondent, more and less, really, as the chief cook and bottle washer, whatever that may mean, for a paperback-book distributor, was grossly arrogant. He remarked that I was "fucking crazy," as I recapture his vile lingo, when I insisted, as the acting temporary assistant mailroom overseer, that a promotional mailing be stamped, on its envelopes, FIRST CLASS, twice on the front of the envelopes, twice on the back, and once on the labels. Once again, he muttered an imprecation directly at my benignly smiling person. Thus, I became somewhat excitedly disturbed, naturally, leaped toward the wooden supports tying two bookcases together, and swung there, rather suavely, so as to cool my head off and regain the calmness that was mine. The boss arrived soon after upon the spot. "I merely want to DRINK THE COCKTAILS!" I vigorously claimed. Quickly, in the face of the boss's blustery quiz, I implied that the shipping-room lout, who had never even owned the sort of white shirt I daily sported, was not carrying out my officious orders. Thus doing his best to obstruct my rising to the top of the company ladder. Just then, a woman who had ignored my presence in the company for some time, popped a LifeSaver into her weakish mouth, and the rabble of the shipping enclave unwrapped large baloney sandwiches in front of me, the silent message screaming its disdain! I saw, once again, my American cocktail-like dreams going up in smokes yet again. I must have fainted amid a tidal wave of chuckles, and soon found myself on the "bricks."

For the past few months, I've been calling various colleagues of yore at three o'clock in the morning with stern words of anonymous hatred. Crazy Swedish person? I'll be showing them crazy Swedish person! I've also stocked my larder and pantry, whatever the cupboards are called here in the land of dreams come true, with ready-to-imbibe Bloody Marys and Manhattans, and other alcoholic treats. They are not at their best at a room's temperature, thus I wait for the electric company to accede to my wishes to turn the power back on. However, I am careful of my appearance, white shirt, bow tie, cardigan, all business. I have discovered this is called electric blue in color, what a book I once browsed through called "the color of madness." The author is well-known to be a homosexual pervert, yet I must try to love him for all his improper moralistic leanings. I may give him a brief telephone call one early morning and we will just see how he likes them apples, as you say here. My goal of sophisticated cocktail-drinking with the smartest of the smart set is not, I assure you, but the goal of a feebleminded dumbbell! My Timex now informs me that my boiled potatoes bubbling tastily on my Sterno stove are ready. Along with a cup of savory instant coffee and a few choice pages from a good book, I'll leisurely dine away, although I would prefer to exchange bon mots with discreet, beautiful women in the paled moonlight, as you may have guessed. It is good to be an alien in America despite the crudities encountered.

≈ *The Wheels Turn*
The salesmen, dear new colleagues and friends, who are out in the field, have no time to be answering requests by clients or would-be clients for samples, information, direction, or guidance; nor do they have time to engage in amorous or sexual correspondence with these people. Unless, of course, they feel that such interchange will lead to a considerable account. Photographs of a compelling or arousing nature may accompany diverse missives, along with, at times, gifts of cash, and such items may be able to change the most focused minds. You, as correspondents, here in the Correspondence Department, are in *no position,* nor will you *ever* be in such a position, to judge whether or not the salesmen in the field will have the time or inclination to reply to such letters "personally," if I may use such a word, freighted, oh freighted as it is with velleity and suggestion. It matters little, that is, what your opinions of such letters may be, since all letters that land—and I use the word advisedly— that land on your respective desks, cluttered though they may well

become with odds and ends of folderol and impedimenta, will, of needs, be those that have already passed through the vetting process on the twenty-third floor, that is, in the Alpha Department of the School Division, Southwestern Branch, a department supervised by our Mr. Bjornstrom, a man known to our other supervisors—and they are many—as "the man with the rubber stamp," or, as he often delights in roughly and somewhat jovially, even hysterically, describing himself, "the Stockholm Corporal." Stockholm is, of course, in Sweden, Mr. Bjornstrom's homeland. These instructions, then, are tendered you in the event that an unvetted letter from a client or would-be client *lands* on one of your desks, which will, of course, never happen. If it should, well, no need to go into the nooks and crannies of that impossible eventuality. At *present*.

To your right, you will notice a series of shelves or pigeonholes stocked with stationery of varied hues, shades, tones, and colors. On closer inspection—do not attempt to inspect at this time, PLEASE!—on closer inspection you will see that the stationery contains the preprinted names and addresses of those salesmen who are yours to assist, obey, jolly along, praise, flatter, and take the blame for in all matters epistolary. There are also, in the drawers beneath the shelves and pigeonholes, paradigms, or model letters, which we call "dummies," that will guide you in drafting replies to the various letters sent "your" particular salesmen, letters requesting samples, information, guidance, loans, photographs, reading lists, and, on those impossibly rare if not impossible occasions that I just mentioned, requests for sexual dalliances of diverse types. These, as I have said, will never reach you, *actually*, but in case they should get by Mr. Bjornstrom's seasoned vetters, they are to be ignored by you, and such occasions brought to my attention, whereupon you will probably be, as they say, "let go." For *no reason* should such a letter be answered in your salesman's name, is that understood? Is that *understood?* It may seem unfair that one or more of you might possibly be "let go" through no fault of your own, through, as it were, your devotion to duty and the job. It *is* unfair, but life is always terribly hard on those with neither money nor power, despite propaganda to the contrary. Am I right? Of course I'm right! If you should, how shall I put it?, *cheat,* that is, fail to call such a misguided letter to my attention, the furnaces are always roaring in the sub-sub-basement! Ha! Ha! Ha! I like my little joke!

You will discover that the stationery on the shelves is nothing, really, other than good American paper and nothing but; nothing to be in awe of, letterheads or no. And you would do well to ignore the rumors suggesting otherwise. Rumors of all sorts are born and circulate in a large and virtually omnipotent corporation such as this one. They emanate, for the most part, from the "creative" divisions of the firm, the Professional Trash-Fiction Division, the Memoir Division, the Hip-Youth Division, the Sure-Fire Division, the Dim-Bulb Division, the Texas School-Adoption-of-Everything Division, the Devout-Christian Rapture-Mania Division, the Unborn-Child-Series Division, as well as those divisions that support what the company likes to think of as its old soldiers—those editors, publicists, accountants, and lunch-eaters who have made their lives into one long testament to their belief that they have done their best to make real for all humankind the kind of book that is both an exciting read and a contribution to the general culture of regular Americans—and others, of course, depending on how the rights are spelled out in the contracts. As their unofficial coat-of-arms proclaims: GOOD BOOKS, BIG BUCKS. You may, at times, even hear a rumor that can be traced to the Shipping and Receiving Department, but the nonentities who toil therein are prone to whining, and may be ignored or, better yet, reviled at any opportunity that presents itself. Management and the Correspondence Department tend to think of these employees as we do waitresses—necessary, perhaps, but wonderful targets for insult. Best for you to ignore all information that is not included in the company newspaper, edited by Mr. Pearl, *The White Shirt.*

The stationery, or paper, then, comes in the following colors—or hues or shades: red, orange, yellow, green, blue, indigo, violet, black, and white. The letters that you send to your salesmen's correspondents will be on white paper. Clear, sharp copies will be made on the varicolored stationery and distributed as follows: red to Mr. Bjornstrom; orange to the Correspondence Department Acting Chief Supervisor—currently Mr. Bjornstrom; yellow to the salesmen, for their files; green to the salesmen who are not "your" salesmen and who work in areas other than those in which your salesmen work—this will be explained to you as soon as Mr. Bjornstrom feels that the time is right; blue, for you to take home and study in preparation for what Mr. Bjornstrom and Mr. Pearl call their "popped" quizzes on office fashion and mailing procedures; indigo, which, since the copied material will be wholly illegible, is to be destroyed, but not before a copy on *mauve* paper is sent to the twenty-third floor and the Rejection-Cliché-Files floor; and violet, which is, of course, a file copy. The black copy is to be passed through the paper shredders at precisely 8:45 A.M. each morning, at, ha ha, "your" convenience. Excuse my cruel chuckle. You must not sexually harass the file clerks to whom you deliver the violet copies, but I should point out to you that our Legal Division-Department-Section has approved a list of sexually charged words, gestures, and invitations that may be employed in your interactions with these young men and women. Should a file clerk accede to requests for certain sexual favors or acts, you must sign a "receipt," so-called, prior to the clerk's granting of said favors or performance of said acts. The "text" describing your activities with the clerk or clerks will be added to the "receipt" by the staff of the Alpha Department when and how it sees fit to add this text. There is nothing in this procedure for you to concern yourself about, I assure you. Only a mere handful of employees—or "partners"—has been arrested and prosecuted on evidence contained in the "receipts," and these prosecutions were well-deserved and were welcomed by the employees themselves! In any event, such aberrant and unrepresentative occurrences should not deter you from—if I may employ an earthy colloquialism—getting your ashes hauled. And you might keep in mind that the file clerks can use a few dollars, if you take my meaning?

You will work from 8:30 A.M. to 5:30 P.M., Monday through Friday, although it should be pointed out that this is a *bare minimum,* and those of you who are, ah, wise, will choose to work more hours, *many* more hours, than this, although no one in Management or Middle Management will ever suggest to you just how many hours a day or week are considered adequate. There is a half-hour lunch break, but here in Correspondence we smile upon the bag of chips, the bagel, the soft-drink or mineral water taken right at the good old cluttered desk. Restroom breaks are not really monitored, not at all, and there is no truth to the rumor that you will doubtlessly hear about the cameras in these rooms. White shirts, starched white shirts, are required to be worn each day, with a tie, of course, for the men, as this is, indeed, a "white shirt company." We're pretty proud of that. This is the unwavering standard for our male employees. The women may wear blouses or dresses of any muted and somber color, but they may not wear slacks or jeans, and skirts must come to mid-knee, no higher. They may not wear ties or earrings nor may they "look like" men in any way. Undergarments that restrict the natural movements and shape of the body are highly recommended if not yet mandatory for both men and women. You will be expected to work on weekends, when you will be supervised by Stewart Park, Mr. Pearl's assistant. You may be terminated at any time for any reason, but you may not *leave* the firm's employ save upon Mr. Bjornstrom's personal recommendation. This may be granted should you conduct yourself to his satisfaction on what he is pleased to call a "cocktail-friendly nocturnal," held at a lounge of his choosing or at his home in the Borough of Queens, down whose leafy boulevards he will expect you to accompany him in the "paled moonlight," as he puts it.

Before you begin your first day tomorrow, I would like to point out to you that Management would be very pleased should you come in an hour or two—or three—early, so that you might busy yourselves with the small departmental chores of air-conditioner repair, sidewalk shoveling, pen-and-pencil filling, and the like. The cafeteria is still open if you wish to have a bite. Good afternoon.

THE SEA, CAUGHT IN ROSES

—— ☾ ——

It was not possible to find gathered together rarer specimens than these young flowers. Of course, as the phrase so often has it, there are flowers, and then there are flowers. Some commentators, as always, have vulgarly intruded remarks concerning "figural language," if one can countenance such opinion without displaying some small degree, at the very least, of levity. At this moment, before my eyes, they were breaking the line of the sea with their slender hedge. "The line of the sea," I admit, may be taking things just a little *too* seriously; but events, one hopes, will bear out its ultimate propriety. It should also be noted, and the earlier the better, that the sand was almost uncomfortably hot because of the meridional blaze of the sun, savagely brilliant in the usual white, cloudless sky. They were like a bower of Pennsylvania roses adorning a cliffside garden. In gardens such as these, small domestic animals tend to cavort, on any pretext. The question of why larger animals neglect to "follow suit," if such an idiom may still be employed, is, at present, moot. Between their blooms is contained the whole tract of ocean, crossed by some streamer. This is an ocean "as you like it," which is the message presented by this crumpled note. The note also contains the formula for making roast leg of lamb mavourneen, sometimes called—the formula, that is—a "recipe." The steamer is slowly gliding along the blue, horizontal line. With the aid of a pair of good, not to say excellent binoculars, one can just make out the name of the ship—the SS *Albertine.* On the other hand, it may well be the humble forest cabin which *we have seen before,* albeit in dreams. The line stretches from one stem to the next. As we know, the rose is beautiful, and is often called the queen of the green world because of its cruel thorns. This sobriquet doesn't seem precisely right or just, if I may, for a moment, interrupt the gardening with a gently puzzled remark, as I have, or so it would seem, just done! An idle butterfly is dawdling in the cup of a flower, one long since passed by the ship's hull. Some of the more sensitive guests are leaving, including a few of the young flowers. There are barely concealed grimaces of disapproval, and some of the older gentlemen, placidly elegant in black tie, appear to be trying to *sink* the steamer before it reaches the buffet. The butterfly can wait before flying off in plenty of time to arrive before the ship. But according to a telegram carried by a sweating courier, "Nobody else can wait." And there, once again, is the old, familiar sound of breaking glass! He can wait until the tiniest chink of blue still separates the prow from the first petals of the flower. Two of the women have nervously rushed into the gazebo, despite posted warnings. And, as one might easily have imagined, the "chink of blue"—actually aquamarine—has grown no smaller. The ship, of course, is steering toward the flower. There are cries and imprecations against

Pennsylvania and what some call "salts," whatever they may be. The blue, horizontal line is quite striking in contrast to the blank glare of the sky.

But only last week, the flowers that were flowers had vied with what certain celebrated authors term "the shining turn of the wave," or "the turn of the shining wave," or perhaps "the thundering wall of water." Figural language often defeats one, especially at the seashore, where one's head simply swirls! The *line* of the sea, however, seems, always, somehow to remedy just about any problem. There were vacationers, of course, who, daunted by the white, blazing sand and the cruelly hot sun, stayed in their well-ventilated gazebos, "happy," the roustabouts said, "as cherrystones," to some small degree. Clams are not usually thought of as domestic animals, particularly the large, blue-ribbon specimens often mistakenly associated with Pennsylvania, its farms, wells, knolls, buzzards, and plentiful copses. There is a wonderful photograph of one such prizewinner, "Old Moot," who comes up to the ankles of his master, or, as it pleasurably turned out, mistress. I may as well state unequivocally that I prefer not to use the word "mistress" in such close relationship to the mention, such as it is, of an animal. More than one crumpled note has been delivered to me—post-haste!—from breezy oceanfront cabanas regarding such unfortunate contiguities. The threats therein are what a grizzled editor of my acquaintance wisely called "recipes for disaster." But this time I escaped, and could gaze at the slowly steaming freighter on the horizon in much the same essentially idiotic manner as the other guests. Not, of course, that I was a guest; let us say that I was, simply, very like someone you may well have seen "before." I was, indeed, once billed as "Queen of Flowers" and "Credenza of Cruel Thorns," but that was long before certain curious proclivities led to disturbing psychological effects and an unswerving attention to minute details of dress. My gardening regimen, for instance, was almost completely subverted, if I may use a fashionable euphemism. A few of the young flowers, as I like, I suppose I've mentioned, to call the unmarried women, were leaving for a better view of Saint-Loup, the hotel's pasta chef. He, rapt before his own sense of personal vanity, paid attention only to the buffet, and not even the steamer's insane whistle could tear his gaze from the "*plat complet*" of *vermicelli alla Sciaccatana*. None of the lovely young flowers waited for him to notice them, and the message they blushingly but assertively conveyed to him occasioned one of the master's rare, gap-toothed smiles. He and three of the young ladies swiftly made for the greenhouse, and subsequently were heard the sounds of flustered laughter, creaking wicker, and *some more* breaking glass. Influenced, perhaps, by the current bestseller, *The Hothouse Bacchanal*, certain of the older women charged the cliffside gazebo, despite posted warnings to be on the alert for myriad broken spirits. More than one "chink" of blue, as wags still snicker, was fondled that day, although the several dispatches from the administration's puppets predictably said otherwise. As the sun began to lower itself into the glittering sea, one heard feminine voices everywhere pleading for "salts, my salts, *please,* my salts, if you love me!" The *blue line* of chauffeurs, servants, toadies, and hastily deputized police officers prevented angry crowds from approaching the scene of what had rather quickly become an exhausting debacle.

Later, one had not thought it possible to find gathered together rarer denizens than the young whores, who, at every moment, between their thighs were peeking for signs of glee. Their tender wedges, like bowers in "Pennsylvania poses," were explored by silk-like garters between which perfumes retained a slow, "packed" emotion. Bossed by one schemer, so slow in sliding along the blue, horizontal mime who had stretched from one hem to the next, an idle guttersnipe bawled in humping a whore whom a pimp's trull had long since sassed. *(He* could wait before flying off; I'm to arrive before him!)* Nothing but the tiniest pink-and-blue rill separated these souls from the fine-fettled whores toward which they were leering.

Ultimately, it is not possible to say with any certainty whether or not lessons have been learned, since it is not possible to determine the moral objectivity of the spectators who gathered about like so many wretched flu sufferers, each vying for a moment of an exhausted physician's time, each brandishing a crusted eyecup, or pitifully displaying badly soiled linen in a puerile bid for attention. It is one thing to deal with the orgiastic and the exhibitionistic in an area which is, let us admit, a dreary seadrome like La Bbec, but such activity, such shocking hedonism in a supposedly refined family setting, is, as a rude prospector, in quite another context, put it, "like a Bowie knife 'mid th' aspic." As to these noted activities, made depressingly public, they needed no Rosetta stone of the sensual in order for them to have been clearly—all *too* clearly!—understood. Granted, the balmy temperatures of these climes may have contributed to the general moral collapse, but the erotic pandemonium of gardyloos, shrieks, halloos, yodels, screams, and full-throated bellowings cannot be blamed on the weather, and must stand forever as a blot on this otherwise handsomely managed season. Some grumblers have suggested that morality and discretion were treated by the *rentiers* as mere trade-ins for the considerable monies provided by what this same disaffected group calls (worshipfully), with no reservations whatsoever, an ochlocracy. A small minority of older, successful tradesmen and professionals sneer at the younger and overtly "conspicuous" crowd as "rabid stearin," but that is, surely, going a little too far. In any event, the stencils went up later that day, each bearing its remonstrative jussive in blazing red: DESIST! Yet the very next morning, the butterweed around the ransacked and noisome gazebo was crushed and broken, the machine for instant cupellation lay smashed at the bottom of the sea, and the shipment of New Testaments was but smoldering ashes. A noted conservative humanitarian of excellent family was found, sans trousers and underpants, bound and gagged in the ladies' room, and time itself seemed to have retired—perhaps for good! Yet the antique chipper still had a fine edge to its blade, and the more obstreperous protesters were being, finally, brutally harassed. That afternoon, all the self-proclaimed prudes left, taking their health implements and "green things" with them, and the youthful contingent of regulars triumphantly flew the peter, thereby recalling those compatriots who, earlier in the summer, had unwillingly and unhappily vanished. All in all, the lesson learned, then, might be phrased, "a surfeit of emendation *sometimes* turns to delighted glee," or, as an old proverb teaches, "else."

A BEEHIVE ARRANGED
ON HUMANE PRINCIPLES

So can you predict the exact date on which the "pearly" rain will fall? Are you a slave to such quirks of clairvoyance? Is there a testament, if you don't think that's too strong a word, for or against behavior of that sort? Would red flowers or white, or pink for that matter, be any the less useless to you? Or their motions, such as they are, in the wind? Speaking of wind, do you remember those long-ago parades, held in gales of lilacs, so it seemed, or were they actually merely lilac butterflies? And do you recall how the children and their mothers aped the yokels who marched in those Midwestern uniforms and plumes? Weren't they always the dead white of sails, or snow, of, in short, winter as you once experienced it? Do you think of the usual creaking boughs and bitter frosts when you hear that "music"? Wasn't it on one of those festive days that you butchered the peacocks? Those you claimed lived behind the house of the girl with the out-of-tune guitar? Didn't you tell me her name was Regina, Regina Lake, or Regina Star? Now that I think of it, weren't you and she the closest of friends when she was still a virgin? And isn't she now the Regina Lake or Star whose sex life is the subject of the monographs on perversion that you collect? She and you flew pigeons off the roof, didn't you? I remember, do I not, you telling me that she asked you the meaning of "gobbet," or was it the derivation of "radish"? You say that was April Starre? Why would you think of April Starre when Regina looked, not like her, but exactly like Ursula? Speaking of whom, why did you insist on calling her really beautiful buttocks ugly? And why did you persuade the other women to give her a box of candles and bananas? *And* why did Sheila Christian blush and crack her gum when you arrived? In the photograph you have of Sheila and Ursula, who is the blonde asleep or in a faint or perhaps even dead beneath the hydrangea? Why do women to whom you show this disconcerting photograph mysteriously call that position a "malady"? Why, for instance, do *you* say, "With a malady like that the only cure is Emperor Ointment"? And in the other photograph, isn't that you doing the Tiger Hump? And why do all of you, you, Regina, April, Ursula, and Sheila, insist that Jesus was at the party? And then why do you agree that, despite all evidence to the contrary, he arrived wearing a sleeveless pink dress? Weren't *you* wearing a sombrero like the sojourning Mexicans? Or were they really blackamoors whose curious taste for the fugue depressed all of you? And the turbans beneath their sombreros frightened you? But didn't they kill the parakeets to assure you of their good intentions? Didn't they appear the next morning in slippers and dressing gowns to tell you and anyone else who would listen of sunshine and cognac and the coconuts of Florida? Before we go on, would you like some chocolate? Or would you prefer to sit under a California umbrella and have a glass of orangeade and gin to chase the blues? Perhaps you'd like a free pass to the Bijou to see *The Janitor's Waltz?* Seriously, as they say, why are you waiting this way, so hopelessly, really, for Ramón? Do you believe, despite all you've learned, that he's different from other drummers? Didn't he make you publicly "perform" on a bed covered with white carnations? Didn't you have to eat cauliflower ice cream for him? Didn't he make you sleep on bare porcelain tiles? Don't you consider that being laced, day after day, into that tiny corset was an indication of his true feelings for you? And while you and the Mexicans acted those lewd roles for the camera, didn't Ramón sit there blithely eating *peas?* You say that he sent you bouquets? But didn't he give Ursula the pearl-and-ruby necklace he'd bought for you? Weren't you bitterly hurt when he took April and Regina to Barbados on what he called a "double honeymoon"? Don't you think that there's a *reason* that he makes you live on Willow Way? Don't you find it strange that a loathsome dwarf constantly spies on you? Didn't your very blood sicken when you first realized that there wasn't a crevice of your body that the little monstrosity hadn't seen? Why do you pretend not to know that he's always there, watching and masturbating? Why do you play those madrigals every night? Why do you threaten to call Connecticut, where you don't know a soul, with the news? Why do you continue to believe that the cinnamon cantharides tablets and the sex toys that you get every month are from Ramón? Don't you ever see the misshapen beast watching you in your bath? Why did you let Ursula hide in the family chapel? Didn't you find it odd that Ramón asked Regina to pose for that "emperor" in nothing but pearls and high heels and carrying a tiny Japanese parasol? Didn't she tell you that she was persuaded with hashish nougat? Were you the beautiful brunette rapt amid the flowering dogwood? Or were you naked in that copse of almonds? Why did Sheila name the sparrow that you gave her "Lesbia"? She was living then in the mauve-brick tenement you own, wasn't she? Why did the milkman deliver free ice cream to you and to her every Saturday? Didn't you say that his name was Bud or Billy Starr? Weren't you, during your early days on Willow Way, playing the oboe with the Sapphic Apricot Romance Orchestra? Didn't the leader affect a steel helmet and pretend an interest in antique gramophones in order to seduce you? Wasn't she the woman who duped you with some absurd story about a lost canto of *Don Juan?* Why on earth did you buy her a football for Christmas? And didn't you and Ursula buy her a blown-up color photograph of a plague of locusts? Do you still think that there was a certain "chemistry" between the two of you? Didn't she give you a thousand dollars to "pose," as she called it, in some expensive lingerie she'd bought for you? And didn't you turn white as a ghost when a nude actor suddenly joined the two of you? Why did you, some few years later, regularly refer to the obscene exhibition that occurred that night as a "rendezvous"? And don't you now term the photograph one of crickets, not locusts, as if it somehow mattered? And why do you maintain that the geraniums had a spicy smell? Why do you so dislike Sundays?

Is it because he claims that Ursula "simply adores" Sundays? Don't you think that he carried off that geranium boutonniere very well, considering? Didn't she write, by the way, a book of poems called *The Red Cricket?* Am I correct in recalling that she got a lot of unwanted, so she said, publicity over an obscene sonnet in it called "The Rendezvous"? He was then still what those stupid fags refer to as an "actor," wasn't he? Anyway, she never seemed to stop droning on and on about his "fucking ghosts," isn't that what she called his friends? Didn't she sell his beloved Gilbert Chemistry Set for a dollar and a half? Isn't it unbelievable, especially after *that* night, that she called *him* a locust? Didn't she play football for a time with that lesbian team, the Canto Cunts? She'd tried to get Sheila up to her apartment to "see" that rusty old gramophone she picked out of the trash, didn't she? But wasn't he still living in the apartment then, trying to make a quick buck on those defective pith helmets? Ah, the romance of sophisticated fiction, eez eet not wondairful? Bud Starr, or was his name Buzz, came on the scene about that time with his apricot-orchard and antique-oboes scams, didn't he? With that brain he should have been a milkman, or a congressman, right? Do you remember that he thought a tenement was a building that had ten apartments? But she'd listen to the idiocies coming out of that sparrow brain and love it all, no? Do you remember the almond-juice scheme he had going, and the whole demented routine he'd worked out to ship plastic dogwood blossoms to the Spanish Sahara? Didn't she once make a, Christ help us, nougat stew so that he could enter some goddamned contest or other? Jesus, I think she was better off when she posed for *Sex Chapel* in nothing but pearls and high heels, holding that yellow paper parasol, don't you? All she ever really wanted were her hot baths and her little wind-up toys and her cinnamon lozenges, right? Personally, I don't think she ever gave a damn about that eighteenth-century farmhouse in Connecticut, do you? And then when he stuck her with that phone bill and liquor bill and the unpaid insurance and ran off with Emily Madrigal? Didn't she have, by the way, the nickname of "the crevice," as in, careful sport, you might not be able to climb out? And then if I'm not mistaken he came on with the me and Lorenzo routine, the old dark secret blood, right? She was being "courted," so to speak, by that dwarf, what's his name, by that time, wasn't she? *And* she'd changed her name to Ruby Willow, right? Who was it who said he'd give a month's pay to be a fly on the wall during *that* honeymoon? Do you remember the wedding presents she got from the groom's friends, you'll pardon the expression, the bouquet of pears, oranges, and boiled shrimp, that porcelain corset, the fifty-gallon drum of broccoli ice cream, and oh, what else, the case of Carnation evaporated milk? And the short-armed drummer with the band, Ramón Mastiachi, wasn't he? Didn't he say he'd played the part of Andrés Jones, the typing champion, in the road company production of *The Janitor's Waltz?* Didn't he keep calling it a "bijou" of a role, the fucking cretin, a "perfect bijou"? Anyway, when they returned, didn't she say that they'd lived for the whole three weeks on Rumanian chocolates and coño, whatever that is, orangeade? And do you remember that huge blue umbrella she brought back? From Florida, she said, *Florida?* She wore absolutely nothing but evening gowns after that, didn't she? While he, I *can't* remember his name, took to wearing those pointed slippers, poulaines do they call them? And do you recall those unbelievable turbans he wore, with the parakeet-feather plumes? Didn't she, probably in desperation, spend her allowance arranging for the première of Regina Lake's "Blackamoor Fugue"? I'm almost certain that's the same piece of pretentious crap that she originally wrote "for autoharp," Christ be merciful, called "Sombreros of Rage," wasn't that it? She was a knockout in those tight dresses though, even the one that somebody called "rube pink," wasn't she? Wasn't it right after the *ringing* silence that greeted her "masterwork fugue" that she claimed that Jesus had appeared to her in a tiger-skin loincloth? And right after that, right! she and Ursula, I should say Ruby, started that magazine, *Emperor Sundae?* Didn't she, or they, publish Dennis MacMalady's ridiculous story, "Ointment," in the first issue? Isn't that the *chef-d'oeuvre* in which he has the world-weary blonde, clutching her hydrangeas to her bosom, "look down on the traffic far below"? He said at a party that that was one of his Christian stories, didn't he, the bastard? In contradistinction to what he called, the *dumb* bastard, the stories of his decadent phase, "Gumbananas"and "Who Can Hold a Candle to Her Buttocks"? Wasn't that the party at which he insulted Ursula, Ruby, *and* Regina and locked himself in the bedroom with April June May? Didn't he say he married her, as I recall, because she was the only woman he'd ever met who knew the meaning of "gobbet" and the derivation of "radish"? And, oh God, what about her sister, Stephanie, wasn't she the one who advocated sex with pigeons? Didn't she write that best-seller, *Virgin Lakes and Pure Stars?* And Dennis, oh yes, I'm remembering all this now, didn't he seduce Regina by reading those treacly passages about guitars around the old campfire and the cry of the wild peacock and the frost on the boughs, the winter silence and snow and all the rest of that shit? Wasn't he *insufferable* riding in that China-wagon with the madras sail? And when he wore that Tyrolean hat with the little orange plume and the button that read YOKEL? Didn't he always say that if he could make the butterflies and the lilacs like him, the mothers and children would take care of themselves? It *almost* seemed a shame when Mastiachi shot him as he led that, what did he call it, "perpetual-motion parade"? Sheila was beautiful at the funeral, wearing those lavender feathers, wasn't she? She, or at least the way she looked, was a tender testament, a beautiful and loving testament to MacMalady's *quirks,* remember that's what the drunken minister said in his eulogy? And wasn't that moron put out when it started to pour rain on his Episcopalian toupee?

Then didn't they all tramp through the rain and mud to get sloshed at Sunday's Tavern? Did they actually think, I wonder, that that joint with its watered booze and shanty-Irish geraniums, would help them to suppress their quirks and neuroses? They drafted "Testament to the Crickets" that evening, didn't they, all about eat, drink, and fuck, for tomorrow we die? Did that feather-brained bunch actually think they needed an "intellectual" foundation for their endless sexual rendezvous? At least Ursula, I should say Ruby, went through the motions for two minutes with that deadbeat actor, Briggs Jones, when they pretended to "rehearse" for *Ghost Parades,* wasn't that the name of the turkey they were in? It closed in ten minutes and then they did *Lilacs On My Lips,* a dollar matinee if you brought your old crippled mother along, wasn't that it? Do you remember that line at the curtain when they strip naked and say, in horrible unison as I recall, "The chemistry of love creates the butterfly of desire in the laboratory of the heart"? At that point Satan should have released the swarms of locusts and all the children of darkness, or am I being too harsh? Does anybody know, I wonder, that despite all their third-rate sophistication and dumb artistic pronunciamentos, they lived with their unbearable mothers and watched *football?* All yokels are the same, whether they're out in the cornfields or playing shortstop naked for the Canto Cunts, am I right? Whether they're clumping up Main Street on the Fourth of July in their garish patriotic plumes or selling junk gramophones on Bleecker Street, am I right again? Speaking of antiques, do you remember the time that Bud Starr and Ramón Mastiachi unloaded those "authentic" German helmets, made in Long Island City or Astoria, on Sol Sails, "the poet of the phallus"? That's when they owned that antique store, if I recall, just after they'd given up the ski shop, Snow Use, cute as a button they were, which they had right after Romance Pants, their lingerie store, folded, no? Didn't they, along with April and Sheila and Regina Lake too, I think, have some idea of spending the winter in, as Sol phrased it, "the paradise of apricot country"? They had some harebrained idea about a series of "surrealist" photographs that had to do with oboes on the boughs? Some sort of arty tableaux with pink-and-gold artificial frost on the buds and a dozen peacocks tethered to stakes while they all played horny milkman and lonely housewife, wasn't that the scheme? Then they were going to have an interlude, that's right, about a guitar genius who gets lost forever in a tenement, right? Another Orpheus routine, help! with Regina cast as the Eurydice figure, a rock singer called "The Ruby Sparrow" whom they gang-rape, artistically, of course, right? Wasn't that about the time that they took to making long-distance calls to anybody about the timeless beauties of the nonexistent Almond Lakes? Didn't they all begin stargazing in earnest and subsequently initiate that crypto-fascist ecology group, the Dogwood Conspiracy? Didn't they even call you once about somebody named Nate Nogatz or Nougat, some nonentity who was involved in a land-development deal concerning a so-called virgin forest? With all those endlessly busy days and saving the magnificent cockroach and art and books and of course *life,* I wonder how they found the time to pose all those fourteen-year-old neighborhood girls in nothing but pearls and high heels with those toy parasols just barely covering their sex? Do you remember when April Snow wrote that little pamphlet, "Pigeons in the Chapel"? Wasn't that when the money really started to roll in and they held weekly orgies in the communal bath using, as I recall, "The Gobbet" as a sex manual? Wouldn't you say that the dwarf, what's his name, had the right idea when he shipped them ten cases of marzipan radishes marked TOYS? They say that April became a cinnamon addict there, or am I wrong? And is there any truth to the story that Ursula went out there to "rescue" Sheila and Mastiachi hypnotized her, Bud Starr put a sign around her neck that said I DO THINGS, and they both put her naked on a train to Connecticut? Don't they say, in fact, that that's how Ursula got the idea for the famous coach scene in *Madrigals and Buttocks?* I wonder why they hid all those candle ends in the crevices? Do you remember when Briggs Jones went out there with blood in his eye and they turned him into a fucking banana in a week? The story goes that they sent him back, he immediately bought a thousand dollars' worth of bubble gum and the next day took it over to the dwarf's duplex, what's his *name?* Didn't they like to whip born-again Christians with willow switches, gently gently? Didn't they come back when they got all that money from the blonde who sold those unbelievable rubies that the senile bishop gave her? Didn't they say that she took the old lecher on a kind of honeymoon that she told the cardinal was a field trip to "spot hydrangeas"? They met them at the airport when they got back, His Eminence dazed but ecstatic, and she said that they'd failed with the hydrangea hunt but *had* found "God's bouquets to salve life's maladies," wasn't that the disgusting phrase she used? Didn't they, I think it was Mastiachi and April, give her a jar of aphrodisiac ointment, the slightest dab of which, etcetera, that was made out of rotten pears? I think it was called The Emperor's Fantasy and they suggested that she use it on the old bastard when the mood was one of "naughty corsets, sheerest silk, and daring thoughts," isn't that how the Coney Island copy read? Didn't it go on to say that the product was guaranteed to make a raging tiger out of a porcelain pussycat? Didn't they say that the blonde put some on the old priest's ice cream and he said that Jesus started telling him off-color jokes? Well, they were all capable of anything, especially Mastiachi, who took to wearing a hat made of carnations, and Regina Lake, in that absolutely *unbelievable* pink sleeveless dress that made her look like a woman who found her cunt by accident, right? And, like all depraved people everywhere, they loved to make the drummers they hired wear black sombreros, wasn't that the case? Do you remember the panic that ensued when April Snow and Ursula discovered that Ramón Ramónes was *not* a blackamoor but just your everyday Negro? They "plunged," I think is the word they used, at least Ursula and April did, into their manic-fugue and crippled-waltz phase, right? They didn't let all that culture stop them from having a few "interesting" evenings with that queer janitor with the turban, did they? Weren't they all wild about roast parakeet for a time, that period when everything was "bijou" this and "bijou" that? They were *really* amazed, weren't they, when the cadaverous dowager told them that the old cardinal liked nothing better than to put on his slippers and her chemise and drink orangeade? Didn't that revelation propel them all, once again, out of town, the women in lacy Directoire gowns and the men sheltering under "Romance of Apricots" umbrellas? They say that everybody lives in Florida now, the living as well as the dead, but who was it who insisted that they were always but figures out of chocolate?

PASTILLES

. . . fruits . . .
—TED BERRIGAN, *The Sonnets, LXV*

≈ *Sheew Gweatness*

Although his buddies adored him, and candles nightly burned in each window and "makepiece" of every rude shack in Corsica against his victorious return, Berrigan's adventures, or many of the more famous among them, may well have been optical illusions. One may consider the celebrated opossum story, for instance, as an example. Optical illusions occur when light strikes the subcutaneous fibroid tissues of the eye—actually, the cornea—in such a way as to make certain things look different from the way they look in actual life. This has to do with inverted images, a concept but barely understood in our subject's day, or, perhaps, "heyday."

In addition to the opossum story, a good example of the optical illusion is the homely one of the cantaloupe drawings in divers supermarket ads. Such drawings tend to prey on our minds and disturb certain ethical values, especially since the supermarkets that so advertise these melons sell a product that is inestimably larger than represented in the crude sketches. This phenomenon is defiantly an optical illusion, then, manifested both in the advertisement and as encouraged in the produce section of the oft-bustling market, probably. Of course, we cannot determine whether the market has, has had, or will ever have extremely small cantaloupes, such as those shown in the ads, or, on the other hand, if the ad draftsman will ever be moved to draw cantaloupes to that which is sneeringly called "normal" size. Or "standard." Size. This is the hallmark of all optical illusions.

An adventure of Berrigan's, undertaken some short time after the hilarious Italian campaign (the legendary "Teleuton fortnight"), had to do with citrus fruit, lemons, to be precise, and seems wholly, perhaps uncannily representative of the optical illusions that so tortured him and his friends and camerados. The adventure may be worth recounting. Brightly burns the hearth!

It has been reported, and there are painstakingly crafted mezzotints accompanying such reports, that Berrigan, or "Tod," as he was sometimes called by his intimate friends, perhaps while in Egypt, quite comfortably situated himself amid several lemons of an enormous size, lemons so large that the famed acclimatizer found that he could quite easily hide behind or amid them. What a carnival it promptly became. Some of the lemons were whole, and some sliced in half, or "twain," as "Tod" said, and as he turned from one to the other, first to one, then to the other, turn and turn about, so to speak, crouched in such a way that only his tricorn hat was visible, he trembled with pleasure as he realized that Wellington might never find him! At that moment, Berrigan loved the very paving "blocks" of the local public park, such a fellow had he become.

And yet, this idyll amid the lemons did not quite happen as remembered and reported, first remembered, then reported, like conversation at a table. Luckily we have mezzotints, which seem to prove that the citrus "imagery" depicted is an optical illusion. Nelson's wanton destruction of French boats of almost every class could well have fallen into the same category as far as "Tod" was concerned.

There is also the bizarre possibility that the lemons of the adventure were of "standard" size, or that size at which they are usually picked and placed in cool, dark "lemon sheds," or "chillers," there to ripen slowly into the characteristic fruit of thin-skinned, yellow, and invigorating sour juiciness. If, however, this were the case, it would indicate that the beloved stroller had somehow shrunk to the size of a small creature, e.g., a mouse! In such instance, it seems safe to say that any sighting of "Tod" in such a state, and by unauthorized personnel, would most likely qualify as another optical illusion. The latter, in the innovator's case, seem to be everywhere. Thus does history, by the legerdemain of apparent candor, hide its secrets.

To get his feet back on the ground, as it were, "Tod" quickly decided to engage the Mamelukes, to whom he read the riot act at the Battle of the Pyramids. Later that night, alone in his tent, and by the small light of a battle lantern, he wrote a detailed critique of the day's engagement, replete with the witty *mots* and deadpan "cracks" for which he was, even then, becoming notorious, in, of course, a good way. In the act of writing, the restless fabricator began to nod, and, in a few moments, was asleep. Was he bored with entelechy? Was, finally, the morphology of the workshop reduced to the ultimate ennui? These things usually gave rise to verbal expressions of astounding felicity. Failure had no venue in his relaxed vocabulary! Perhaps it was the odd scent of prairie smoke that had caused his snooze. Whatever, he woke to plaudits and florabelles. Something, too, had addressed the reality of his beard. Ha! he said. He was the soul of wit in those happy days.

There were other engagements, between which "Tod" played quietly among his lemons, or what may have been only the "images" of his lemons, if such a word may be used among the furtive lagniappes of the marathon readings in celebration of the sentient beings then abounding. On the other hand, he had a surpassingly tenuous idea of life when at liberty, so to say, and when his chef created chicken Marengo, Berrigan realized, with what he would scoff to term "a start," that the crawfish were much bigger than he, as were also the *oeufs*(?). But he fell to with a good appetite and finished everything on the platter, despite its or his apparent or real size. This incident was also optically questionable. It, too, must fall under the heading, if you will, of the "phenomenal."

There is little need or desire to speak of the wanton destruction of the fleet by Nelson, the obsessed mariner and scourge of the waters, whose cry, "Put out my other eye, Hardy, for the to'gallants smell o' death!," electrified all of Britain. His spectacular victory brought a ray of hope to citrus-suspicious Europe, which had been in the bleakest of dumps because of the madness and lust of the Jacobins and the publication of Wordsworth's *The Stamp Distributor*. ("A whiff of the grape!" is probably what Nelson hallooed to his gunnery captain, Hardy, or, variantly, "Put out my other eye, Hardy, and give me a taste of the grape!")

By this time, "Tod" had lost all sense of stability, so that when news of Nelson's brave shout was brought to him in his tent and subsequently translated, the reference to "grape" sent him into concealment behind two or three large lemons he'd ordered from home. "Home!" he'd often think. The next morning, of course, the sad retreat from Moscow began, a dispiriting exodus that ended with the bitter tragedy of 18 Brumaire. "Had our restless and well-read *bricoleur* only known," said many a grizzled veteran of the Big Army. The sunlight blazed and shattered off their medals in a curious manner, reminiscent of Apollinaire, one of the many poets whose work Berrigan had learned by heart.

≈ *Lemons*

The lemon is not quite the size of the American cantaloupe, yet it is considerably larger than the cantaloupes that exist in supermarket ads. It is rare that one encounters a lemon even half the size of a rather small man. This conundrum only serves further to confuse the fruit-filled dilemmas of Berrigan's life. Many modern people, anxiously on the go, take the juice of half a lemon in hot water every morning, for the sake of a regular (?), not that it matters, apparently. They will die, even as you and I. "Mostly *bricoleurs*," they protested, prostrate before the highly-regarded interviewer's tent. What did they mean to suggest?

Yet there are cancer dangers implicit in lemon use. New laboratory reports come "in" every month, and while the data are raw, rats used in subject-friendly experiments contracted cancers of the liver, kidney, and stomach after the ingestion of nine lemons daily for the space of four months. It should be noted that certain of the rats suffered from visual hallucinatory episodes, i.e., they seemed to see lemons "everywhere." "Tod" thought long and hard about this, propped, as he was, against a favorite bench.

At Austerlitz, tired at last of Josephine's (name changed) spending orgies, "Tod" took the juice of half a lemon in cognac upon arising. He'd often joke with young Pierre, his favorite shoes, about the pleasures of tipsy (illegible); and even he had difficulty defining the elusive term. And yet the cantaloupe was unknown to him, even though Moravia was then the melon capital of Europe. One apocryphal story has it that Berrigan, upon seeing a cantaloupe for the first time, thought it a bust of Max Jacob. There was a good deal of levity *that* evening in selected purlieus.

At about this time, the chronicler would often put himself to sleep by imagining himself to be a woman. What was it they said, at least most of the time? How would it feel—that was it—to have a vagina? How would it feel to slip a lemon in there? Or would it be "up" there? And can one actually slip a lemon into such a space? Would it be correct to do so, or would such an act be demeaning? And if so, to whom? Thus did he muse on the politics of his era, complex, certainly, but succinct!

The sea would claw gently at the shore, slowly moving the beach to, say, Spain. In years to come, vacationers would be hard-pressed to lark about *here!* And yet, "Tod" thought, he and his pals took it all for granted. Science was funny that way, although science had invented the lemon and sent, as well, our eager astronauts to their hard-earned deaths. Science!

The lemon is native to India, to the Punjab, to be precise, and has quite extraordinarily lovely, though not showy, purple-edged white blossoms. The skin of the fruit grows slowly yellow and pliable, except, of course, in actual life, that is, when the fruit is permitted to ripen on the tree. Fruit thus ripened is called *mague verde.*

The juice of the mature lemon is high in Vitamin c, and is thought, by Lutheran ministers, to be an aphrodisiac, hence the plethora of summer picnics. In hot climates, the lemon is called *l'amour jaune*, perhaps a reference to its amorous properties.

All citrus growers agree that the fruit should be cut from the tree while green and at "standard" or "normal" size, then allowed to ripen in "chill sheds" or "chill shanties" in order to attain its maximum heft and astringent flavor. The problem here suggested, of course, is: What is standard or "normal" size? (See "Cantaloupe, representations of.")

As Berrigan would make for one "chiller" or another along the line of march through the desolate steppe, his constant refrain was "Etonnez-moi!" He may well have been exhorting his weary followers. On the other hand, he may have been commenting on one of the various optical illusions that the wasteland was noted for, e.g., the williwaw and the fairy morning.

≈ *Florida*
Florida, to this day, is much like Corsica, even to its genial and plentiful whores. This coincidence was not lost on "Tod," grown by now into a wonderful person, and an even more omnivorous reader. "Another Corsica, man," he'd assure admiring guests, with the superb touch of false humility he'd recently cultivated as an adjunct. Josephine's (q.v.) healthy bosom quickened with a kind of oddly bourgeois pride, and heavily came her breath. It had been worth it, she knew, to give up her legal work in order to become the wife of this extraordinary man, even though a career was becoming extremely important amid the "new plangency," as the era was

being arrogantly called. There were, it should go without saying, optical illusions everywhere.

Years later, bitterly alone and quarreling constantly with rude hosts on St. Helena, "Tod" regretted not having victimized Florida in the "Sonnet Days," so-called when the fabled *bateaux à noyer* were available to him by the thousands.

Florida! he would think ruefully.

Vive Coral Gables! Vive Miami Beach! Vive Biscayne Bay!

He collapsed in tears onto the bezique.

How he had wished to experience, and absorb, golden sands, pavilion music, swamps, fens, bogs, fevers, malaria, gators, and ringworm.

The Trocadero! The Gold Coast! Malibu! Little Havana!

Berrigan did not, of course, give a thought to the fire ants, skeeters, or raccoons. In his mind was the image of the deathless pantoum, one of the more elusive optical illusions. It always seemed about the size of a very large lemon. So "Tod" startled himself needlessly.

Oscaloosa! Osceola! San Fernando! Dixie, Dade, and DeSoto! Broward and Hernando!

Too late, perhaps, Berrigan realized that it was his artistic destiny to realize the futility of optical illusions—in his life as well as in his work!—for the pleasure and instruction of others. There were plenty of them!

The bezique floated away on a zephyr, followed by cards, tiles, and dice. But the sand, he knew, was forever, if not here, then in, say, Spain or Massachusetts.

⌣ California

History suggests that "Tod" was often effervescent at parties, to which he was rather disconcertingly drawn. His notebook was always in evidence, and yet. . . . He would, more often than not, assume the persona of a football player or ironworker, a sign of the subverted signifier.

Defeat seemed almost sweet to him. He remembered Waterloo and the thrill of surrender. And to Wellington, a covert practitioner of the unnatural! As a contemporary quipped, "You should take a look already at the tight pants he wears by the dragoons!" Was defeat but another optical illusion?

Soon, he was in California, where he spent several months dreaming of a great shining railroad that would connect the stunning beauty of the North with the breathtaking beauty of the South. And over the projected scene there projectively hung the scent of projected lemons, long present in this paradise before the advent of wheat, the advent of the avocado, the advent of the radish and the pear and the apricot! Long before the advent of the guava! The scarlet tomato!, the latter a gift from our proud Mexican "amigos," happy to have been born to the honest hoe, the honest shovel, the honest broom. Not for such the corrupting dreams of wealth!

⌣ The Dream Is Over

Yet official business, in the guise of the Code St. Mark's, the School Cabal, and the Troublin' Mind Committee, forced the restless innovator back to New York. From there, he was dispatched to Elba for the ordeal of the Hundred Days for "extraneous *ibitas*," a charge that whipped him into a cold fury of nonchalance.

Waking one morning in a lather of sweat, he noticed, at the door of his bedroom, two of the largest lemons he had ever seen. Although conventional wisdom scoffed and snickered, they were quite big!

"Josephine," he called quietly into the melancholy darkness. The lemons rustled in the corridor. He felt as if he had lost his mind, or as if he was about to be compromised by radical groups he'd somehow offended by a thought he'd entertained. Now Florida seemed to be no more than the optical illusion he had always suspected it to be even when good friends had assured him of its actual size, more or less. Where now the quiet breeze?

"Josephine," he called again, but the lady was not there. No more would she assure "Tod" that he was of average height and average build, of, in fact, a decent size, much larger, in fact, than any *lemon* she had ever seen. And no more would she explain to him that everything in life is but an optical illusion, or something like it, no more remind him that somebody had once said that a hero removes all fruits from their places.

ALLEGORY OF INNOCENCE

They discovered a cache of old books, replications, wooden fences, a spangled gypon, assorted spheroids, and many other items, as yet unidentified. The Director, despite his unnerving obsession with luminous white dresses—and their ever-varying representations in his collection of Christian Fundamentalist pamphlets—was lucid enough to assert that some of the more common fabrics would forever remain mysterious as to their composition. "Dried grit," "Leaves," "Pebbles," "Rifle," "Fishing rod," were but some of the names they tried attaching to some of the things, although it was clear that nothing quite fit. One of the group of assistants—actually, more than one—thought that certain of the larger umbrellas looked like navy-blue melton overcoats, admittedly an eccentric notion. Hub shards were quickly identified, as were metal brassiere caps, and, though grotesque enough, they were not as grotesque as many of the other "discoveries." At about this time, the Director took to covering himself with mounds of his cherished gossamer evening gowns, the color of new snow, and neglecting, for days, his investigation of the woody perennials that were doubtlessly clues to the identification of the least familiar clumps.

One of the young women in the motivational group said that she'd *seen* one or two of the brightly colored biloxis in what she called "the better shops," but her suddenly recovered memories put the kibosh on that assertion. In addition, the lost items of clothing obscured the logic, so to speak, of the biloxis' arrangement. After one of the most beautifully delicate of the random crystals disintegrated, every puta bag in the area was seized by security, even though such bags had never been used for anything other than extramarital sexual powwows, or, as the bitch of an editor put it, "adventures." "Security must consider puta bags vectors of blazing darkness, rather than the simple, filthy things they really are," a lissome assistant remarked, her beautifully shod feet nonchalantly "parked" on the desk.

A few of the younger women, the "troops," as they were jocularly called, suggested that a harmonics inspissator might reveal the true nature of the symmetrical devices, but they were, predictably, patronized, insulted, mocked, ogled, and ruthlessly complimented on their looks and attire by executive officers. A week later, beneath an economy-size Mammoth Nut Bar, the shipping-room mascot found yet another shocking photograph of the boss.

Amid the confusion and grumbling over the newly appointed Creative Person, another problem arose when Nan Hacktree, the author of tales based on her own warm yet mentally deranged family, stubbornly held that Wallace Wally's novel, *Over My Dead Body*, had to be judged as something more, much more, than a book. "And I do not feature the word 'deranged' to describe my relatives,"

Mrs. Hacktree liked to repeat. At this point, odds and ends as diverse as torn panties, obscure freak cartoons, and an aluminum soap dish were discovered in a collapsed family room. With this, the senior writers' clique that championed redemptive dialogue became emboldened enough to denigrate such malign yet seductive imagery as garden walls, gnomons, Nazi moms in sheer nylons, and stardust. Other corrupt figures, e.g., battered work boots, crusted, sour pipes, and 1956 Chevrolets fared badly as well, especially during the waspish and misogynist lunches that were cynically thought of, by the clerical staff, as postmortems.

Within weeks, lipsticks, especially the shades Red Rider, Black Cloche, Glorious Bimbo, and Sunburn, became the preferred tools with which the more avid tyros surreptitiously polluted themselves during the demanding Creative Writing examinations. Mysteriously, the graffiti in the employees' lounge read, in part, LES GRANDS JETS D'EAU SVELTES PARMI LES CHOSES. It may have been written by the staff comedian, whose most celebrated routine had to do with Philadelphia lawyers, silver bugles, and stupid waitresses— of course! The Collectors Association, already on the defensive because of a smutty joke told *in mixed company* by its Curator, pretended not to know anything about its holdings of pornographic bar mitzvah music and its recent purchase of the revolutionary artwork, "Money Talks." It wasn't long before the Meat Czar arrived at the Association offices with steaks, shoes, books, wind-up tin pigs, white ribs, cheese maps, nostalgia bastors, celebrity indices, etc., etc., more things, in fact, than you can shake a stick at.

As the weather worsened, the more serious sex workers—many of them fresh from the famous porches of the Deep South—spoke of their dreams of empty patios, cold twilights, distant voices, California sunshine, good-time Johnnies, and other crass selections too vile to enumerate. A crude wag was arrested and held overnight by the Sensitivity Committee for opining that what the ladies of the evening did "beats working." Many psychologists attributed the young man's cruel remark to his belief that heterosexuals are, when all is said and done, really homosexuals *underneath*.

At about the same time, the Board of Directors, with the assistance of the Bureau of Culture, ascertained that Wallace Wally's sweeping saga of a man who lost his way on the prairies, *Carnal Jitters*, had discouraged twenty-two young writers from sending gifts to casual friends, although the latter were leading simple yet zesty lives! Many of these same writers had learned their manners from the old frauds who pretended an interest in inexpensive yet robust wines, translucent spheroids, pitiful tennis afternoons, *The Journal of Virginia Woolf Journal Studies*109 aerobic mania, and movie stars with really good and, like, humanistic beliefs. The Stupefatto Poll, to everyone's amazement, discovered that the "things" that had made these young people writers in the first place—blue uniforms, lovelorn fantasies, trees hard by the handball courts, girlish laughter from a small, wooded island, etc., etc.,—were metonymic substitutes for the zeppelin, or, in Lacanian terms, the *path* of the zeppelin. "Who knew?," Rory Stupefatto mused.

And yet, the rigid instructors stubbornly refused to designate as Actual Things the Red Ball Express, the ill-fitting cap, the perfumed and ice-cold Persian lamb coat, the Jodie suit, and the good read. Apprised of this, one of the women, a Catholic Romantic, mentioned, blushingly, that a "baloney" seemed to be "in the feverish grip of dreamlike fingers," an exercise in incoherence that had even Father O'Flaherty holding on to his Rosary for dear life. Others were unanimous in their opinion that secondhand cigarette smoke causes sexual harassment—including unwanted compliments!— and automobile exhaust. A certain Babs, who yearned to wear small black hats with dotted veils, sheer off-black stockings, black suede pumps, and flattering accessories, had to deny herself this pleasure since her husband was seeking tenure and that was that for couture. She wished that she might get up the nerve to roll the razor-edged mileage calculator back and forth over her husband's multicolored overview notes which, as he had often told her, had to be judged, as more, much more, than just notes. Where had she heard such bullshit before? Or had she read it somewhere—under an umbrella, perhaps, amid coffee, cigars, and good ruby port? The sun is often hotter than it seems, or so Babs had learned in the awesome stillness of the mountains.

With the advent of the long winter nights, the black crayons and other gritty things in the Crakkerjax Factory began to look "mighty good" to the personnel of Wonderful Colleagues, Inc. Still, winter or not, Mrs. Hacktree swore that wrong-thinking applicants would be admitted to the snugly idyllic cottages "over [her] dead body" and, by implication, her dead mind as well. Given her ideas, certain of the more daring interlocutors thought it useful to save such models of the mundane life as Worcestershire-sauce constructs, salad-dressing displays, and lipstick multiliths, while others wanted to throw hot spinach at the iconic snowman, at the blinds, the victuals, at, really, every motherfucking thing in sight. They were, it was clear, wholly unimpressed by the fact that the "Beechwood Cabin" had once housed Sarah Orne Jewett's mother-in-law, the author of "Fling My Snood to the Winds."

Outside of the closed world of the motivational offices and research laboratories, private parks and the proscription of urination by the wrong sort of citizens were part of Palo Alto's "Figures of White" program. City Council members, agog with the restoration of historic beer barns and other tasteful edifices, were anxious for the perfect jewel of a town to "Say No!" to poor taste. In the midst of its opening meeting on the subject of punishment for the transient, one member made it embarrassingly clear that he believed that the color of decay, disease, shit, piss, vomit, paralysis, and death is a color that one can't help but see each and every day, right on the quiet, but rather sticky streets. The very *idea* was appropriated by the Council, and a local artiste was commissioned to paint, to actual scale, the mural "Pendejos de Oro," which was already painted to actual scale. The original had, unfortunately, been vandalized by homoerotically inclined athletes, whom all the neighbors really related to.

As the true nature of the cache discoveries and subsequent experiments slowly became known, the Symptomatic Referent Equalizer proved to be one of the very few instruments capable of bringing about successful solutions to rebuses and puzzles. Pearl S. Buck's personal copy of *The Good Earth,* for instance, was discovered to contain disguised representations of fur cloches, rice cakes, vinyl-covered chairs, large goldfish, and many other elements of a traditionally inscrutable Oriental nature. Critics note that this was the special *hors de commerce* edition that featured the peppery Madame Solange, a character who would rather straddle her horse, Ching Chow, than sojourn in the Plum Blossom Mountains of the Golden Jade. It was this text that led H.A. Zipp to his idiosyncratic belief that absolute silence, in combination with the other absolute phenomena, would eventually lead to what he gloomily termed "the crossing-over into numbing terror."

Much of this lore was forgotten or diluted or revised when Professor Andouille asserted that she had just begun to recatalogue her collection of Brooklyniana when a leering man, described by the professor as a "Baptist," entered her office, his trousers neatly folded over his forearm. This seemed an unlikely event, although if one believes that all things are interchangeable, in the Boolean sense, then Professor Andouille's somewhat overheated story seems much like any common dark liquid. Far removed from this sex disturbance, on the edge of the compound's croquet lawn, a solitary camper found it terribly unsettling to realize that the tightly corseted young woman in the sepia-tone photograph is not forever reaching for a hydrangea blossom, but for something that is forever, of course, beyond the edge of the picture. This young fellow had been somewhat Faustian at one time, and was thought to have had something disturbingly weird in mind when he asked Mrs. Walking, his high-school mileage instructor, for a garter of her love. And it was not to his benefit that Captain Theodore Rosa-Rose had, at just about the same time, discovered that the Color of Decay was one of the many forbidden novelties available via mail order, along with spicy short stories and small fallen trees, the latter guaranteed to symbolize things. Plain folks, so to speak, had very little use for his Oxford-gray suit, but liked the oddities they pulled out of his well when he was away on one of his investigations.

A newly hired nurse, Jenny, didn't really *like* to stand, half-dressed, at the window, but it was, she claimed, "a feminist act, or like, statement," much like a false moustache. As a response to these rampant attacks on sacred womanhood, religious folk of all stripes claimed that America needed good old reliable fetishes to make a reappearance in society, for instance, girdles, support hosiery, white plastic handbags, big corks, bobby pins, and serious but wholesome and humorous plays, with nice music. At least, the shipment of navy-blue melton overcoats and other worthwhile garments arrived in time for really hip writers to wear to the "Salute to Rupert Murdoch" celebration.

However, the liberal Jewish transvestites who lived in the lake house threw things like Greek salad around with imbecile abandon in their demented worship of filth, disorder, runaway government spending, and dead Christian babies. And the Physics Department, at one time the jewel of Corporate Entercon Corporation, Incorporated, was foundering amid the faddish hermeneutics of Zeppelino contravariant theory, the *last* thing that anyone would have imagined. The senior scientists' attendant explorations of other entities of banal dimensions, e.g., cocktail-sauce bottles, snow photos, scale-model Packards, Wally pennants, etc., seemed almost frivolous after the new Motivational Therapist, a young lady from France, boarded the company bus in what seemed to be a semi-conscious state, or "trance." The subsequent behavior of the passengers, conductor, and driver surprised and angered many citizens, especially those who believed that the glass ceiling had long since been cracked, if not shattered.

In the end, or, as the Frenchwoman's report put it, the "final analysis," madness, rage, and erotic fury presented themselves as the three most obvious states of being to hold sway over the entire group, each speckled, misleadingly, like a starling, as a New Formalist poet phrased it, yet again! "To write poetry that makes no sense is something like playing tennis," as Chet Blanky once put it in conversation. And so, with work in various stages of completion or decay, and with loved ones whining of closure, the company agreed that although there may very well be more stars than anything else, this probability has absolutely no effect on the meaningless, which remains, stubbornly whole and unchanging. Religious beliefs, appallingly tawdry visions, and harsh legislation proscribing, denying, or outlawing this persistent state of affairs, this "reality," if you will, have all proven useless.

SAMPLE WRITING SAMPLE

≈ *A Desk*

To make a narrative concerning a number of aspects of what we might agree to be life—a simple enough program, and one that will, perhaps, make us feel closer to the world that we inhabit, more or less, or would prefer to inhabit were things as they should be. By paying strict, even rapt attention to the false world that will deal with certain aspects of life, embroidered, as they must be embroidered, we *may* gain an understanding of, well, real things as they really are. This is how literature works, if "works" is the word. I do not describe narrative, or this narrative, as false so as to mock or denigrate it, but to differentiate it from the real world that exists, despite all, for all of us, outside the narrative. And that is so even if the narrative appears to represent a number of aspects of that real world in, as might be said, moving and well-written prose. This seeming fidelity to the actual, while the actual roars on, unalloyed and unaffected, is one of the gloomy mysteries of fiction, a mystery that remains unsolved to the present day, one, in fact, that deepens with each reader who attempts to order his or her life by means of what can be called fiction. Some also use this latter to educate themselves. There is no telling what a reader may do when alone with a book.

To the narrative, then, or parts of it, of the whole, of that which may ultimately "become" the whole. To that blessed narrative that may almost write itself. Then "control" would seem to be the word, although it is not the precise word, nor, for that matter, is "word." No matter, of course, for all may be corrected, changed, polished, all made clear in revision, revision, the handmaid of "the writing process," for which nobody is too good. Writers often insist that they revise, again and again, everything that they write, for writing must be heartbreakingly difficult to be authentic, heartbreakingly and exhaustingly demanding. Even this small item will be, and has been revised, or is in the process, even as I "speak," revised to a fare-thee-well, an odd phrase, that, but one that comes to mind, another curious phenomenon of writing, the things that come to mind. That such things, or "phrases," are mostly old and warm and as well-worn as an old shoe is part and parcel of that inevitable process, so dear to life, called, well, called something. Perhaps good writers don't revise everything, but they do revise a good deal, a lot, actually, if they are to be believed. Even the lacerating yet redemptive personal memoir, chockablock with scenes of guilt-ridden incest and battered puppies must be revised, revised and "touched up" and, well, fucked with, so to speak.

One of the many reasons that the demanding heartbreak of revision is so necessary is its role in making the absolute falsity of the representation of reality more precise; that is, to enable the falsity of the narrative, by dint of laborious revision and the odd polished phrase, to gleam with what seems to be—and why not?—truth. Or at least something that may well be mistaken for it, gleam to a goddamned fucking fare-thee-well, for that matter. So to speak, as it were, after all, in sum, and finally. To insist that the perfection of the false is much closer to the imperfection of the something or other is awkward, yes, but natural and casual. The phrase may be corrected, or course, in revision, or it already has been. Writing takes many drafts, usually, to emerge victorious—well, not precisely victorious—unless the writer is Proust, who was satisfied with one draft, and that a rough one. And, too, there are *Moby-Dick* and *Ellen Finds Out*. Look at them! Book reviewers are often cognizant of such phenomena, but rarely give us the benefit of their profound knowledge, given space restrictions, the demands of commerce, and what readers prefer in the way of a good read. They know what makes a good read, else what's a heaven for, and know, too, that good reads make them—and us, always us—feel as if they know the people within the reads and have spent time with them, for instance, Holden Caulfield and others, good pals all. They will not be duped by cheap falsifications of reality, two-dimensional characters lacking not only flesh but blood, and always insist on well-written representations of the real, representations that read as if seeing something or other for the first time. Craft! Well-written craft! That's—or they're—the ticket. Life that throbs is also a big winner in these serious purlieus. And what of characters who, while throbbing, are redeemed, brought to justice, and speak nothing but the crispest dialogue? Take Sarah Orne Jewett. Take Minister Handy. Authors who have made a world that one can reach out and touch, gingerly, to be sure, but touch nonetheless. Living, loving, lolling, losing, and hating. It's not only as good as life, some argue, but better, at least in selected passages. Can the remarks on *Dark Corridors of Wheat*, pointedly made by Patricia Melton Cunningham, be easily forgotten? Huh? Well, this is what one may call, with little fear of contradiction, writing that matters on writing that matters. Consider *The Paris Review*, and other items, if you dare.

So that one evening, sitting at my desk, a comforting pipe glowing near at hand, a hand that seemed to belong to someone else, as did my face, yes, some other face, or, perhaps, the face of the Other, I put the final touches on a letter to a friend, Pat Cunningham, to be precise, a woman who knew the meaning of trust, friendship, log-rolling, and the lunge for the main chance, when I noticed some impedimenta on the desk, impedimenta that I gazed at as if gazing at them for the first time. Slowly, I came to realize that if I could find a language that permitted these items representation, I could, perhaps, reach out and touch them in all their flesh and blood and flawed humanity. But I had to overcome the terror of the blank page, that famous blank page which all writers confront each and every day that they sit down to cover that blank page with love and laughter, brooding despair and so on and so forth. There is nothing as terrible as the blank page, and so I had informed Pat in my letter, a letter that lay, somewhat forgotten, near the blank page that, too, was slowly in danger of becoming somewhat forgotten. On the other hand, the blank canvas, the blank music paper, the blank notebook are all equally terrifying to the painter, the composer, the notebook-keeper, and there looms, too, the blank stage for the actor, the dancer, the monologist, the hilarious comic. Yet who was it who pointed out that "empty" in such instances would be more precise than "blank"? Good friends are rare, and even rarer are those who pop up just when things are going fairly well. You can count on it, or them.

Could a character be evoked who might evoke the items or disjecta on my desk? A simple noun for each, if properly "handled," might do the job. And yet, what job was it that there was to be done? Lest confusion reign I decided on a handful of nouns, or, as the blank page demanded be uttered, the substantive. Should I show rather than tell, or, better yet, better yet infinitely more difficult, display rather than show? If I could succeed in displaying, or even showing the spondulicks on my desk, *in context*, in picture language, i.e., language that is like a picture, or pictures, lots of them, of course, colorful when needed, it goes without saying, perhaps the reader, ever hungry for actual experience, will be able to reach out and touch them in all their flesh and blood and interesting formal qualities, not to mention all the other things. I know, of course, that the awesome powers of revision may abrogate or defer or even occlude, occult, and abort such heady fantasies of literary perfection, yet I feel that I have no choice but to press on. Revision, as noted by Gide, Irving, Bly, Tough, and Lombardo is a harsh mistress, finally. Consider the work, the entire opus of the "vagabond prose master" of the Western reaches, or at least the reaches of Los Altos, the town whose motto wisely states, "Our Cars Are o.k.," that wise yet warm penman, Wallace Stegner, of whom his various assistants have noted, *as one,* that even his first drafts were revisions, as were, doubtlessly, his ideas, of which there were plenty. Yet the hot, quick tears kept falling. This was what no-nonsense people called "writing, man."

But how to handle items, memorabilia, flotsam, and the like? How to approach the unforgiving blank page with ideas about such a *pasticciaccio,* if you'll pardon my French. For instance, is it enough to say "globe," "pen," "letters," or is that not enough? These sound rather haphazard, at best. How about: "Lifting my eyes from the plebeian fastnesses of the worn carpet, I found myself gazing, as if for the first time, at the moon, sailing through the cloudy skies like a bark of yore, like a kind of globe, a globe that had been sketched on the heavens by a ghostly pen, one used not to the demands of art but to the humble task of writing letters." The clock ticks quietly as the fly buzzes against the window globe, the sun warms my letters. All is but a dream.

But what wise man said that the dream is a rebus? And yet, what is the nature of a rebus? Is it flesh, blood, globe, or desk? Or all three? Joseph Cornell knew precisely what a rebus is, but who else knows, or even once knew? Must I return to the beginning, then? To the world of the empty page? Or the blank canvas? "The silent shit on my desk yearns for the dignity of representation." Yearns and pines, its blood throbbing as it has throbbed, yes, for aeons and aeons of clanging time gone mad with despair!

I rise and head for the window, gaze out at the winking lights far below on the valley floor. The night is cool, the wind sighs quietly, I feel as if I have walked into the kitchen to avail myself of a cold beverage. I feel as if I have lit a cigarette, filling myself and the house, filling all the crystal-clear air with death! Death that asks no quarter, that laughs with the wild laughter of unbridled love, that laughs and laughs and laughs as if laughing for the first time.

⪯ A Joke

A Jewish matron on a jet from New York to Miami Beach introduces herself to her charming seat companion as Mrs. Moskowitz. After a drink and some light banter about the intrinsic problems of the aporia as it relates to *cutting velvet,* the charming companion comments on the clarity, brilliance, size, and cut of the enormous diamond ring on Mrs. Moskowitz's finger. This might have been Mrs. Cohen, by the by, but that's neither here nor there. And is that the glint of cupidity in the charming seat companion's eye? Mrs. Moskowitz sighs and reports, in a whisper freighted with the sort of fear that suggests the ineffable rebus of life itself that the ring, despite its beauty and obvious worth, has a curse on it, the— Moskowitz curse! The Moskowitz curse? queries the charming seat companion, who has, incidentally, beautiful legs, of the kind highly prized by any number of leering men, many of whom have subjected this young woman to a male gaze, gazing and gazing at her legs as if seeing legs for the first time. Their hot, quick tears fall fast as they chide themselves for such crudity. The Moskowitz curse? the seat companion queries again, looking up quickly from her copy of *Dark Corridors of Wheat.* What, in heaven's name, is the Moskowitz curse?

Mr. Moskowitz, is the reply.

Or it could be Mr. Cohen, were this another joke. And it had better come out with numbers on it. What are you selling this year, cancer? Everybody's gotta be someplace, yingle, yingle. Max, carry me?

Maurice Bucks, the entertainment *bigwig,* is so rich, confides Mrs. Moskowitz, that he hires people to count the people who count his money. Ha ha. Or, perhaps, Bucks is so rich that he can find himself in a lather. Has everyone taken note of the fact that he is always immaculately dressed, even on the slopes at Moskowitz Pass? There is, too, that certain Kafkaesque something that he has about him, and even, some say, in him, like bacteria. Many are the nights when Maurice has stared at the blank walls and thought that he might be better off were he still that young actor who wanted nothing more than to direct, nothing more than to be surrounded by the sparkling conversation of the stars. Well, he often sighed.

Schultz is always dead in every joke he's ever lost his virile member in. The charming companion considers this and blushes deeply, rummaging for her biography of Sarah Orne Jewett by Wallace Stegner, the "Prairie Edition," of course.

"Not only is this joke anti-Semitic, misogynistic, and contributory to stereotypes about air travel, it is also, in some as-yet-undefined way, not very nice about the regular family kind of feeling right here in Miami Beach."

Speaking of Miami Beach, I am reminded of a joke, or is it more like a story? It is hard to know what with time, plodding time, clanging outside the window as I write—yet write—what? A man, hired by a rich contractor—a friend, by the way, of Maurice's—as a chauffeur, companion, gin-rummy partner, fellow-bettor at divers tracks, both equine and canine, strongarm, and occasional gunman, finds himself appointed, during those periods when the contractor is away on business, and by the contractor's alcoholic wife, as a dogwalker. The boss's wife, Handy Sarah, a lifelong admirer of diamonds and other precious gemstones, is regularly soused by noon. The dogs, two prize boxers named Scotch and Soda, sorely try this rather refined thug's patience, for they demand to be walked at times that are highly inconvenient to his gaming instincts and erotic impulses. Speaking of the latter, he once contracted gonorrhea from a *fille de joie* whose stroll took in some two blocks of Collins Avenue. Encountering the same woman the next year, he remarked, "What are you sellin' this year, cancer?" This man's name was Patsy Buonocore. "Looks like another eyetalian joke, with numbers on it! Some more spaghetti with meatballs, sir?"

One day, upon returning to his employer's mansion on Biscayne Bay, Patsy, sobbing bitterly, reveals that the two dogs have drowned. "It seems that Scotch leaped into the drink to retrieve a little boy's beloved wind chimes, their *yingle-yingle* poignant on the wind, and Soda, seeing that Scotch was encountering some aquatic difficulties, followed. In jig time, both were swept out to sea." Some few months later, both dogs were fished out of a landfill, their brains scattered by .38 caliber slugs.

This is not actually a joke, but an anti-dog story, as mean-spirited as the one about the professors' wives working in the local brothel on their husbands' poker nights. One must admit to problems before one can be helped by those who have already admitted to problems. Look at the recovering alcoholics who can never top off a meal with cherries jubilee, rum baba, or sfogliatelle à la Proust. And yet rarely is there anything less than a wan smile and a chin up! A thousand drinks are never, ever enough, whatever that might mean. "Well, if you won't gimme another fuckin' drink, how about a haircut?"

Max, carry me to the bar? Who does Mrs. Moskowitz have to fuck to get *out* of this job?

Surely, is one of the most beautifullest rings ever found of a desk, is it not so? And no more lip about Miami Beach, all right? "I'm not certain about that *jig time*. What kinda phrase is that, an aporia?"

"Come see me at the Fountain Blue, dolling."

≈ *A Tomato*

Bill came out of the kitchen, an anxious look on his face.

"Say, Charlie, how about a tomato with supper? What do you say?"

I knew that when Bill mentioned supper this early in the evening—it was barely late afternoon—that he had made plans to go downtown to the Jewel Theater to moon over Dolly Rae, the strange, pretty girl who did the cleaning up after the last show. He was trying, I knew, although I wouldn't let on that I knew, to ask her, once again, about her reasons for trying to raise the gleaming white bicycle from the bottom of the swimming pool over at the other motel in town. Dolly Rae Jewett was a determined girl, and her cooking, as the old phrase has it, had won Bill's heart. Well, it *was* terrific cooking, and her *guaglio, matarazzo,* and other robust dishes were something to talk about indeed. Bill would have been much better off concentrating on Dolly Rae and her great food and her sweet, pretty face, and forgetting all about the gleaming white bicycle that lay so mysteriously, so silently and symbolically, at the bottom of the deep end of that damn pool.

I looked over at him, my mind moving unwillingly to a picture of the two drowned dogs that an old neighbor of mine, Mrs. Moskowitz, used to own. I was twelve at the time, and I'll never forget those dogs being trundled home in a baby carriage, the water leaking out of its sides and bottom. It had been, that memory, a major problem for me for many years, but I'd worked my way through it with the help of a very fine and strong lay therapist, who'd made me realize that I had to admit to the problem before I could even begin to deal with it. "One drink is a lot and a thousand drinks are not too many," she'd say, enigmatically, at the end of each informal session. And sometimes, she'd tell me of her mentor, Schultz, now dead these many years, and mourned, or so I came to understand, by scores of his students, many of them aspiring poets.

I admired Bill, but it was in his best interest, or so I felt, never to say so, at least not to him. It was better to mention my admiration for him to other people whom I didn't admire at all, but who, or so I learned, admired Bill. He liked to repair cars and trucks and with the money he saved over and above his living expenses he planned on buying a very large, green canvas patio umbrella for his favorite table near the pool in our motel's courtyard. "Let me tell you about another great umbrella I saw in Monkey Ward's yesterday," he'd chuckle.

"Tomato sounds good, Bill," I muttered quietly, looking out at the chipped enamel table by the pool as if seeing it for the first time. "Fresh basil O.K.?" Bill nodded but it was a distracted nod. He was thinking, I knew, of Dolly Rae and the bicycle that both obsessed and, in some dark, strange way, frightened her. Then he was gone in a swirl of cigarette smoke, and I wondered how many minutes had been taken off my life *this* time.

Six months earlier, when I'd left school to work for a man who made authentic Shaker furniture for people who loved it for its spirit and its subtle hint of the last Shaker colony on Biscayne Bay, I'd met Bill at the Jewel, the only movie house in town. The Jewel showed the kind of offbeat films that you'd never see at the Octiplex out at the Big River Mall, and had a reputation for being cutting edge. It was run by a man called "Chet," who made up in loud brio what he lacked in subtle verve. Bill had been carrying a bag of what turned out to be ripe tomatoes, and we struck up a conversation almost instantly, although I can't recall a word of it. All I do know is that somehow our shared delight in tomatoes led to an arrangement whereby we moved into the Red Wagon Motel together and split all expenses. So far, it had worked out wonderfully well, but I was beginning to worry about his growing anxiety concerning Dolly Rae and the bicycle. But our first few months together were idyllic, and Bill's pleasure in imagining the green umbrella that would highlight the pool area was my pleasure as well.

As soon as he became aware of Dolly Rae, everything began to change, subtly at first, and then, quite overtly. Dolly Rae, it turned out, not only understood more, much more about Bill's umbrella dream than I ever could, but she had innumerable stories about bicycles and the role that they'd played in the settling—she'd called it "the gentling"—of the hard-bitten Wheat Corridor back in her home state. Her favorite bicycle color was tomato red, and when Bill discovered this, he was a goner. He'd do anything to impress Dolly Rae, and began making up stories about crawdaddies and drinking bouts and God knows what. And then, one day, Dolly Rae took him over to her motel and showed him, shimmering and blurred at the bottom of their pool, a white bicycle that seemed to glow in the water. He stood and looked at it in silence, and then, suddenly, at the instigation of her little brother, Carver, she jumped into the pool and swam to the bottom. She had her hands on the bicycle and was hauling it to the surface, but although she broke the water with it, it was impossible for her to get it out of the pool. And Bill knew, he just knew, that his help wasn't wanted. As she relinquished her grip on what Bill had decided to call a "symbol," and let it sink, dreamily, to the bottom, Carver whispered to Bill that she'd never get it out, she'd been trying for days, it wasn't going to be pulled out of that darn water!

Each day, often more than once, before her stint at the Jewel or after it, Dolly Rae would plunge fiercely into the pool and wrestle with the white bicycle. And each day, Bill, sullen with despair, would ask her why she needed to *do* this. She would look at him coolly, the kind of look that said that she wished she was looking at him for the first time, and asked him to explain, again, what a "symbol" is. It was more and more obvious to me, if not to Bill in his agony of wonder, that life simply goes on and on until, one sad day, it stops.

Sometime after that, so Bill told me one night, looking up suddenly from a patio-furniture catalogue, Dolly Rae began calling people on the phone at random, baiting them, misrepresenting herself, telling jokes about Schultz and Moskowitz and, afterward, crying bitterly. Bill told me that he thought the calls humanized her, softened her somehow—his phrase was "gentled her," much to my bitter amusement—but that Dolly Rae maintained that they were just as frustrating as trying to haul that bicycle out of the pool. He began to see less of her, and as he grew quieter, I noticed that he had stopped mentioning the green umbrella. It had become, at least for me, a symbol to set against the symbol that he had created for Dolly Rae.

"Be back soon?" I asked, staring into the space above the pool. He nodded, and said, "Sure, where else would I be?"

I smiled and made the gesture of slicing a tomato, then mimed swimming up, through dark, cold water, with a bicycle cradled in my arms, a bicycle that would not, that could not ever reveal its secrets. He laughed, ruefully, and as the sun moved behind the outer cottages, I said, quietly, "Schultz is dead."

"And tomatoes are cheaper," Bill replied.

NOTES

⁓*A Desk*

1. The actual, whatever it may look like, does not "roar on."
2. Many people feel that all the mysteries of fiction have been solved, and a good thing too!
3. It is probably not a good idea to "fuck with" memoirs in which the victim-pro-tagonist-memoirist has already been "fucked with."
4. Most critics and biographers dispute the fact that Proust was satisfied with one draft, despite the discovery of the "Toulouse" notebooks.
5. Patricia Melton Cunningham's first novel, *Wrenched from Love*, will soon be published by Gusher Books, a subsidiary of Shell Oil Publishers, Ltd.
6. "Spondulicks" most often refer to quarters and dimes, as in "Drop a spon-dulick on the bum."
7. A *pasticciaccio* may be translated as "a fucking mess."
8. Wallace Stegner, although he owned a car, did not actually *like* it.
9. Death asks no quarter—nor spondulick.

⁓*A Joke*

1. It is amazing just how many jokes people know.
2. "Cut velvet!," is, for instance, the punch line of one of those many jokes.
3. The male gaze is at its most pernicious in the academic world, for reasons which will soon be made clear.
4. *Dark Corridors of Wheat* has been out of print for many years, despite a relentless campaign waged by the cereal industry to make it available at a reasonable price.
5. Maurice Bucks is on the record as saying that he "doesn't really care all that much" about money, and after his successful takeover of the Vietnamese government, noted that "it's got very, very little to do with money, and I want people to know

that." It has recently been reported that Mr. Bucks has contracted AIDS, which fact has led hundreds—some say thousands—to argue for the existence of God.

6. The paper used to print the "Prairie Edition" of the Jewett biography is made of acid-free gopher skin.

7. "Handy Sarah" is a mistake of the sort regularly attributed to this author, who, it is said, can "really write" if he "puts his mind to it," books that are "wonderfully readable."

8. People no longer get soused, but, instead, succumb to their addictions, addictions which they cannot triumph over, or "lick," unless they first *admit they have a problem* and then *get help*.

9. Boxers are excellent swimmers, which should have alerted their owner to the suspicious nature of these two hapless dogs' deaths; of course, the soused Sarah had never admitted that she had a problem and therefore never got help.

10. The "haircut" joke was a favorite of saloon comedians, who often and anon told it while soused.

11. "Aporia" is a Greek word that means "who knows?" or, in certain contexts, "what the—?"

⮌ *A Tomato*

1. A gleaming white bicycle at the bottom of a pool is an example of an aporia— but not in real life.

2. Spaghetti *alla matarazzo* is not for everyone.

3. The author had originally thought to place the gleaming white bicycle in the projection booth of the Jewel Theater, pronounced, at least in this story, "thee*ay*ter," as if you didn't know.

4. The baby carriage trundled home to Mrs. Moskowitz was most probably a stroller.

5. "A thousand drinks are not enough [to pay] for a haircut," or so says the Albanian proverb.

6. Basil is never used in spaghetti *alla matarazzo,* save by natives of the Midwest.

7. The Surgeon General has suggested that the Moskowitz curse is, in all probability, secondhand cigarette smoke.

8. The *green umbrella* by the *motel pool* is a motif that some wag had once thought of donating to Raymond Carver.

9. "Carver," in this text, has no relation to the late writer (see above).

10. That the author does not tell us what "tomatoes are cheaper" *than* may be an instance of a free aporia, or, in the parlance of narratology, an ekphrasis.

11. "Put that in your pipe and smoke it," he laughed.

TIMES WITHOUT NUMBER

These were all very slight experiences, of course,
but the remarkable thing was that they happened all over again,
exactly the same. Actually they were always there.
—ROBERT MUSIL

He rose and fumbled about in an escritoire until he found the clipping: "They stood in the dark in the driving rain underneath her umbrella." Can all this have really taken place in America? Obviously, it was abnormal. Maybe not the men, who mostly go out to work, but the women, who are most inclined to talk and who have nothing to do.

He had a good job in advertising and they lived in Kew Gardens in a brick semi-detached house; certainly the reader will recall such shoddy incidents in his own life.

"Welcome to the scene of the extraordinary . . . outrage!"

Not even fake art or the wearisome tricks of movies can assist them. This was in 1948.

The roar of all the traffic came hurtling in through the wide-open window, the liquid moonlight filling the small parking area outside the gates to the beach. What was the scent of the perfume she wore? Why did he not pick her out of her red plush chair and sit her on his knee? He got up and closed the door, then lay down on the bed with her and took off her jacket and brassiere. Of course it wouldn't be sordid. He knew that it was impossible, when once the material circumstances of a function were altered, for its aesthetic expression to survive. Different thighs. What is a supper club?

"Above all, the presence of the loved person prevents reflection, and makes us women wish to be overcome."

"I don't even know where CCNY is!"

She got up, her breasts quivering slightly, and he saw faint stretch marks running into the shadowy symmetry of her pubic hair.

"I don't suppose anybody ever *deliberately* listens to a watch or clock."

"We can go to Maryland and get married," she said.

"How do you play Mah-Jongg?"

A woman of brilliance and audacity, accompanied by a mere boy, came into the place and took seats near them.

"I want to marry you, I can't stand it."

When she slipped her coat off her breasts moved under the crocheted sweater she wore. Perhaps so much assails him that he has to close down ninety percent of himself to phenomena in order not to explode. Her eyes gray, flecked with bronze. She was fair.

We were ashamed of wanting what we wanted, but something had to be done about it all the same.

She was crying and stroking his hair. Was she happy? No answer probably. Against the tabletop her hand, glowing crescent moons over lakes of Prussian blue in evergreen twilights. Of course, life is a conspiracy of defeat, a sophisticated joke, endless, endless. The next moment she felt a violent blow underneath her chin.

Everybody was drinking Cutty Sark. She zipped open his trousers. All night the February wind would come barreling down the wide keyway of Third Avenue, moving right over them all. He felt his heart rattling around in his chest in large jagged pieces. In her fingers a golden chain and on the chain a car key. And so through the agreeable vacation life there twitched one grim vein of tension. What he remembered was her gray cashmere coat swirling around her calves as she turned at the foot of the stairs to smile at him, making the gesture of dialing a phone and pointing at him and then at herself. How could he bear this image? It was just a rotted punctured husk.

One day, in New York, he bought her a silver friendship ring, tiny perfect hearts in bas-relief running around it so that the point of one heart nestled in the cleft of another.

"Let me come and sleep with you."

"What in the end is most apt to fill me with fever is to leaf through train schedules."

"Let me lie in your bed and look at you in your beautiful pajamas."

"I *mean* it," she said.

He said that he would change the eating habits of man!

She smiled and asked for another coffee, taking the key and dropping it into her bag. Who can bring them to each other and allow him to enter her? No argument or persuasion could ever induce him to set up a female establishment after the manner of his companions. They were concerned about him. (They didn't *really* know him.) He was not yet strong enough to ward off their services, and noted that that brought him into a state of dependence on them which might have evil consequences.

"Help me. I'll do anything you say."

"In a little while, love, you will be dead; that is my burden."

She had white and perfect teeth. Her browned body, delicate hair bleached golden on her thighs. I staggered toward the dresser, and there like a beacon stood the lovely yellow tin. It was a joke after all.

"I'll hide in the closet and be no trouble."

"If only I had seen that decree, which had appeared in an inconspicuous place in the five newspapers I read every day, I should not have fallen into the 'trap.'"

He opened the button of her shorts. "All right."

At these words, Roberte does not know if it is from shame she trembles because the sentence is carried out, enormous, impetuous, scalding, between her buttocks, or whether it is from pleasure she is sweating.

"If one has . . . faith . . . all things will . . . come! All . . . *right!*"

"Think of a repertory of insignificant things, the enormous work which goes into studying them and getting a basic knowledge of them. What is the University of Miami? What does Benedictine cost? I want to rehabilitate this period by writing of it with the names of things most noble."

"A hot and breathless night toward the end of August, the patriotic smell of hot dogs and French fries in the still air?"

He adored her. She liked it very much that he didn't look like a blacksmith. Believe me when I say he wanted to kiss her shoes. White lamps, soft lights.

She was childless herself, and she considered herself to be to blame.

He had perhaps wept bitterly that afternoon as she kissed his knees. She had come up to open the house for the season. (All round the edge was written the date of the wedding and in a corner was the artist's signature.) Her husband was a college traveler for a publishing house and was on the road, her son and daughter were staying at their grandparents' for the day. Her flesh was cool.

"I was on holiday with my wife traveling in a small hired car like a violent toy."

Rebecca was fair. Let me have a mist of tears in her eyes, of acrid joy and shame, of despair.

"The three plates are arranged as usual, each in the center of one of the sides of the square table. This is, of course, old news. How softly we had slid off the edge of civilization."

"The author divides *gardens* into an infinity of styles?"

She lay on the bed and opened her thighs and they made love without elaboration. When he got home he was exhausted.

One day there was a photograph in the paper of a deceased seer who resembled a great bag of holy relics—innocent symbol that tortured his blood.

"What is a Stravinsky?"

"I am forced to assume that the latter was at that time not a *real human being* but a fleeting-improvised man, because he otherwise would have been so dazzled by the light phenomena which he must have seen—they occupied almost 1/6th to 1/8th part of the sky—that he would have expressed astonishment in some way."

"Of course he was insane. It is no wonder lesbians like women."

"He even succeeded in transforming specific pieces of music to his *palate*, following the composer step by step."

"One can hear his precise voice recording these picayune disasters as jokes."

They walked to the edge of the black lake stretching out before them, the red and blue neon on the far shore clear in the hot dark.

Having reached the threshold, she turned and, raising her two hands to the dark veil over her face, she blew a distant kiss to those who had evoked her. Lovely Jewish girl from the remote and exotic Bronx. He put her number in his address book, but he wouldn't call her. To those who have not studied the nature of language in any depth, the experience of number association will show immediately what must be grasped here, namely, the combinatory power that orders its ambiguities, and they will recognize in this the very mainspring of the unconscious. He watched her go into the house and saw the door close. Whose hand had touched her secret thighs?

"From the manner in which the libertine welcomes her attackers, it's plainly to be seen how inured she is to this hard use." He was excited and frightened, and got an erection. But he would *not* call her.

"I get the subject to pass the fingers of his right hand through his hair, so as to get a little coating of the natural oil on them, and then press the balls of them on the glass."

Nothing was like anything said it was after all. When he got off the train in Brooklyn an hour later, he saw his friends through the window of the all-night diner, pouring coffee into the great pit of their beer drunks.

Even then he did not move, but waited until the heavy footfalls sounded to the bottom of the stairs. In the bedroom, she turned down the spread and fluffed the pillows, then sat and undressed. It's too impossible to invent conversation for them. He luxuriously lowered himself on the bed and put an arm over his eyes. The moonlight of her teeth, the smell of her flesh, vague sweat and perfume. All summer long we have heard the chant of the husband's newly discovered perfidy.

"What were they to do? She tottered, holding the umbrella crookedly while he went to his knees and clasped her, the rain soaking him through, put his head under her skirt and kissed her belly, licked at her crazily through her underclothes . . . the story of *that*, Madam, is long and interesting, but it would be running my 'history' all upon heaps to give it you here. They worked desperately at it being August, but under the sharkskin and nylons those sunny limbs were hidden. The maimings of love are endlessly funny . . . as are the tiny figures of talking animals being blown to pieces in cartoons."

But a few days later, we regret that we were so confiding, for the rosy-cheeked girl, at our second meeting, addresses us in the language of a lascivious Fury.

"What sort of god borrows a Chrysler and goes to the Latin Quarter? Give *these* children a Silver Phantom—and a chauffeur!"

"I assume that I have the liberty to withdraw, at any time according to my need or desire, from the large sum small sums?"

"Take your clothes off! Please?"

"In the old days a chamber was a bedroom."

"Oh, oh," she said, and closed the door. "You good fuck, Jack," she smiled in her lying whore way.

While she confessed her sins, I waited, extremely anxious to see the outcome of such an unexpected action.

A Cadillac station wagon passed and then stopped about fifteen yards ahead of him and she got out. The woman was gentle, the light glinting off her gold incisor and the tiny cross at her throat. He stopped to float a match down the brimming gutter and somehow they were moving, even hurrying on.

She lay down on the ground and he lay next to her, stroking her breasts until her nipples were erect under her cotton blouse. She was a little high and he messed all over her slip.

Thus the young ladies there are as much ashamed of being cowards and fools as the men.

She was wearing white shorts and sneakers and a blue sweatshirt.

"You *know* I was sixteen a month ago."

He appeared to great advantage behind the white napery and silver platters of the table and displaying his arms with a knife and fork. He went to get a Coke and brought it back to her, but she only sipped at it, then said O God! and bent over to throw up.

"My period," she said.

He gave the fire a hard look and took to handling absently his yellow stumps for teeth.

She had been to the Copa, to the Royal Roost, to Lewisohn Stadium to hear the Gershwin concert. It would be a great pleasure for me to allow him to meet her there, in a yellow chiffon cocktail dress and spike heels, lost in prostitution, a scene of upstairs where there is a second floor from door to door. I'll put her virgin flesh into a black linen suit, a single strand of pearls around her throat. Did she have to go to the Museum of Modern Art? These considerations crossed my mind with a certain rapidity. Did I say that she had honey-colored hair?

There was one boy who had almost made her—he was never quite still, there was always a tapping foot somewhere. Or the impatient opening and closing of a hand. *He* didn't want to know what the pre-med student she was "dating" said when he held her. He thought he would weep.

Their procession, led by the Hungarian, soon disappeared behind the stock exchange. At three o'clock, he kissed her good night on Yellowstone Boulevard in a thin drizzle. He fought against the thought of her so that he would not have to place her subtle finesse in these streets of vulgar hells, benedictions, and incense. The other three lost their senses immediately, running wildly about the streets with their heads in the air, or suddenly starting off at a furious gallop directly away from the car.

They were at the amusement park at Lake Hopatcong with two other couples. The first time he touched her breasts he cried in his shame and delight. The third time it was simply that he followed the other two. When they went out into the courtyard again in the evening, the late June night so soft one can, in retrospect, forgive America for everything . . . aromatic breeze.

The book being opened, the paper of diamonds was first taken out, and there they were! Every one. Yes, it seemed a possible world: the sound of a car radio in the cool nights, collective American memory.

"Literature is language turning into ambiguity. I grant you it will be unbelievable."

These destructive and bittersweet accidents do not happen every day.

NOTE: *This story comprises 177 sentences, 59 of which are taken from 59 separate works by 59 different authors. The remaining 118 sentences are from one of my own earlier stories. Certain sentences have undergone slight changes in punctuation.*

SUBWAY

She said that she'd got on an uptown local at Canal Street, gone to sleep, and, waking, just fifteen minutes later, found herself in Brooklyn at the end of the line on Ninety-fifth Street, a weird miracle, she said. This is the same girl who got thrown out of Six Happiness on Mott Street a couple of nights earlier for knocking everything off the table and shouting "fuck the Communist bastards!" From Canal to Ninety-fifth Street in fifteen minutes while going the wrong way, dream on, sweetheart, and in the meantime straight, no chaser?

She'd been drinking all afternoon with some friends in a bar that used to be on Greenwich Avenue near Christopher Street but that's long gone now. They all went down to Chinatown to eat and she kept drinking, beer, and vodka from a full pint that she had in her bag. She wasn't really a drunk, but that day she was plastered. The story was that her husband, a really lousy painter who lived off her and spent every day in McSorley's soaking up ale, had been relentlessly unfaithful to her with anybody who'd stand still, but you hear a lot of stories. After dinner, on Elizabeth Street, she got separated from her friends, although they might have conveniently lost her, seeing that she'd become an impossible embarrassment. She must have got a cab and took it to the Cedar, the new one, new then, anyway, on what?, Eleventh Street?, and sat at the bar nodding over a whiskey sour and trying not to fall off her stool. At about 2:00 A.M., she left the bar, walked east to Broadway, then down to Eighth Street and into the subway station. The change-booth attendant had to call the police because she was standing on a bench about halfway down the platform, screaming and sobbing about Canal Street disappearing and her friends disappearing and the whole world vanishing. She calmed down right away, and the cops took her to the Sixth Precinct station house and let her sober up there, even bought her coffee, since she was well-dressed and good-looking. She moved about two months later to a loft in Long Island City, then to some suburb outside Chicago. She'd been, incidentally, an editor at *Mademoiselle* when she married the rotten painter. Not that it matters.

She got on the Fourth Avenue Local at Canal Street for the short trip to Twenty-third Street. It was 2:45 A.M. The doors slid shut, the train lurched and banged, the car's lights shivering on and off. She was alone in the car, and had a violently painful red-wine headache. As far as she could tell, there was no one in the cars before and behind hers. The train screamed into Prince Street's deserted station, nobody boarded or got off, and the train barged on through the dark. After a minute or so, it entered Eighth Street, but when she looked out the smudged and greasy windows she saw that the station signs read Canal Street. She got up, frightened; the train had not gone backward. But this was Canal Street. Bewildered, she took a step toward the doors, and just as they were closing, lurched out onto the platform, losing one of her high-heeled pumps. An old Chinese woman, her face half-turned to look down the silent tracks, stood at the end of the platform, two crammed and battered paper shopping bags at her feet. One read: Jade Mountain; the other: Six Happiness. A panic possessed her as the old woman, abandoning her bags, turned and shuffled down the platform toward her, her face taut with a fear that seemed to be just short of terror.

FACTS AND THEIR MANIFESTATIONS

He doesn't recall this, or pretends not to, but when he first met, many years ago now, the woman who would become his wife, she was wearing a cashmere polo coat, pale beige stockings and tan pumps, and a dark-red silk scarf. There was, or he pretended that there was, nothing odd or unusual about this, since he had forgotten, or pretended that he had forgotten, an incident in the past, an incident that would have made the woman's dress notable. Interestingly enough, at the time, the incident, now, perhaps, forgotten, seemed overwhelmingly important, as a matter of fact, unforgettable.

~

On this warm Florida night, his father is telling him, once again, of the dance at which he met his wife and, of course, *his* mother. Elements of this story change, as they will in stories, but the delight, even the passion with which his father evokes this young woman, just sixteen, and her sumptuous black hair in a chignon and wide, white-silk ribbon, and her green eyes, remain always the same. He fell in love instantaneously, painfully, with her face and figure, her womanly stillness and provocative reserve. After they had been "keeping company," as his father put it, for six months, he gave her a silver charm, a tiny shoe, to commemorate their meeting at a dance. His father falls silent, and he knows that the old man is thinking of his wife's death, the dreamlike suddenness with which she was struck down by a cab outside the Plaza, after a day of shopping. He was barely four at the time, and he recalls, or seems to recall, that she had bought him a maroon wool challis scarf, returned to his father, torn and stained, by the police. Surely, his father told him this, for he remembers no scarf. He makes another highball, and about a quarter of an hour later, his father's new wife enters the kitchen, with a bag of groceries. She is not pleased to see that he is still there, and that both he and her husband are drinking. Her waxy, blue-black hair creates a somewhat grotesque frame for her sixty-year-old face, although she is disturbingly attractive to him. Irrationally, he wonders about the fate of the silver-shoe charm, but cannot ask at the moment, and, later, forgets to ask. A month later his father is dead, and the shoe is lost along with the sad and isolate detritus of gone lives.

On chilly, rainy days toward the end of summer, when it was too cold to go down to the lake, they'd usually walk over to her house and talk and play Monopoly on the screened porch. In the late afternoon, she'd serve iced tea, and they'd smoke and leaf through magazines and look out at the Rose of Sharon tree dripping on the lawn. The grass shone brightly green in the odd half-light.

She was a tall girl, at once slender and large, serious in her body, with profoundly black hair and noticeably clear green eyes. Her skin was smoothly tan and there was about her a reserve that was oddly provocative in its stillness. And although they had all known each other for a half-dozen summers, she remained curiously distant. Some of the girls thought that she was a snob, but it was her womanliness that confused them. She usually wore a modest, black one-piece bathing suit to the lake, and, occasionally, a pearl choker. There were certain things that people simply would not say in front of her; everyone wished her approval.

One gloomy, dank afternoon, while he was in the kitchen helping her with the iced tea and emptying ashtrays, he, in a kind of half-crazed trance, put his hand on the strip of warm golden skin between the waistband of her white linen shorts and her seersucker halter, then leaned stupidly to kiss her upper lip. It was cool velvet, slicked with delicious sweat, salty sweet. She gave him a look of absolute calm, one that came from behind the bright clarity of her eyes. Then, in a strange silence, she held out her hand, opened it, and showed him, on her palm, a Monopoly hotel, gleaming a perfect, symmetrical red. He glanced at it and then at her, bewildered and yet exultant, when she closed her hand and turned to the sink. He knew that this was a private message, he knew this. But it was opaque, cryptic, it was impossible. And it was so because of the adoration of her that had so ruthlessly overwhelmed him: because she knew that he would not understand the message, she sent it. He was stupid, there in that small summery kitchen, with love and yearning. He wanted to kiss her knees, her feet, in their fragile golden sandals. The others were calling for them to come back to the game, and he held his hands up in front of him, awkwardly, and, foolish with desire, said something foolish. He would, he knew, never be a man, it would be too much to ask of him.

The summer moved toward its end, and they never spoke of that afternoon, or her impenetrably candid message. It was as if nothing had happened. Nothing had happened.

Twenty-five years later, he saw her, walking quickly, outside the Port Authority terminal. She was wearing a cashmere polo coat, beige stockings, and tan pumps. She didn't see him. He would have preferred it had she been standing in front of the Plaza. Too late, of course. He thought that her name was Nina, perhaps.

∾

There used to be a downtown hotel in a mid-sized city in northeastern Pennsylvania that had been, forty years earlier, the premier establishment of its kind in the region. But with the advent of turnpikes and the demise of railroad travel, it fell out of favor, and, over two decades, became a mainly residential hotel for retirees who were comfortably affluent, but wholly unfashionable, like the hotel itself. Yet the hotel had a bar and lounge that had been designed as a perfect replica of an ocean liner's first-class saloon: it was a jewel of black and silver and white, with art deco murals, chrome-accented bar stools, and lacquered black tables.

The barmen were impeccable in their tuxedo-like uniforms, the drinks were large and perfectly mixed, and there was neither jukebox nor radio. It was the sort of place that, once discovered, was never spoken of.

He found himself there one night, after driving into town just in front of a growing autumn rainstorm, and unable to find the Sheraton that had been recommended to him. When he saw the hotel's name spelled out, in incandescent bulbs, on its marquee, he smiled and pulled into its small parking lot. He registered, and after a shower in his room, walked downstairs to the bar, and sat in pleased amazement at its ambience. He drank a martini, smoked, then ordered another. He was alone, or so he thought, but when he leaned back on his stool to light another cigarette, he saw, in the soft, silvery light that shone through the racks of bottles, a girl at the end of the bar. He looked at her, quickly, and as she lifted her head from the evening paper spread out on the bar, the light caught her short, black hair and the pearl choker that set off her simple black dress. She looked at him and nodded, civilly, without smiling. He turned to his fresh cocktail, his face burning, a thrill of awe and fear in possession of his entire body. It seemed to be the girl, it couldn't possibly have been the girl, a lifetime had passed, it couldn't be the girl. But it was the girl. He finished his martini and ordered a third, then looked again at the end of the bar, but she had left; only her newspaper, empty glass, and some bills were there. He thought that now he might die, since he couldn't understand his life at all anymore. Surely he had imagined this girl, imagined how she looked. He had imagined nothing. There she had been.

∿

The Monopoly hotel that he'd found in his drawer after Labor Day could well have been the one that she'd held out to him on her palm. But how? She'd closed her fingers over it, and then he'd made a fool of himself.

He had not been especially interested in her, and then he was painfully in love with her. He thought himself into her body, into her stillness, into her reserve and modesty. That she often wore a pearl choker to the beach rendered him sleepless.

She had, he realized later, held the hotel out to him twice, it was simply itself, so obvious, so mysterious in its candor. It was but one element, one figure in a rebus, the rest of which was missing, or never created.

He passed her on the street many years later. Her hair was graying, and all that he could recall after the shock of seeing her was that she had worn a dark-red silk scarf. He'd seen her from a distance, crossing against the light in front of the Plaza. A rainy day, gray and chilly, red and yellow leaves plastered to the wet pavement. It had always, of course, been too late.

IT'S TIME TO CALL IT A DAY

Whatever remnants of stylistic eccentricity peculiar and unique to Clifford's fiction had long since been leached out of it by a dogged series of accommodations, emendations, compromises, and authorial, shall I say, understandings. His current editor was a reasonable man, so Clifford believed, and the suggestions that he made substantive and intelligent. And he had stuck by Clifford, despite the disappointment of his last book, patiently waiting for "his" writer to achieve that perfect blend of the conventionally literary and the cannily specious that would announce a *breakthrough*.

Now, reading the proofs of his fourth novel, Clifford saw, not with anything so dramatic as a shock, but saw with a kind of sudden, pleased candor, that not only had he, at last, quite thoroughly assassinated the prose that was once his, with its errors and tics and flourishes, its obsessions and syntactical aberrations; but that the staid, clean, undemanding—he thought of it as functional— prose within which his characters now suffered their warm and imperfect, their wonderfully human, oh so human! travails, was not only not his, but was, quite remarkably, nobody's. It was an excruciatingly polished, forward-march prose, with suitable, occasional filigrees of clever simile and analogy, and splashes of the contemporary demotic; a prose that seemed happily familiar, as if it had been there all the time, waiting to be read, but just once. And, too, his characters, his flawed and fascinating *people,* were deployed as neat packages, their histories and quirks economically posited well before their thrust-and-parry colloquies. They looked, so Clifford thought, as if they had decided on things *by themselves,* sans authorial interference. "They more or less started doing what they wanted to do," he could imagine himself saying to an interviewer.

This latest novel, created to satisfy the desires of an audience, as Clifford's editor had characterized it, "too hip to actually *read* a lot," educated, so to say, and busy, so, so busy, was, he hoped, the very thing to interest those readers among the favored "target group" who had progressed from slop-and-ramshackle best-sellers to the sort of fiction admired by professional reviewers—well-written, with fully developed characters, a nicely turned plot, and *something important to say.* It was, that is to say, designed for a particular kind of success, a "literary" success, and one that was, God knows, long deserved. So Clifford thought in righteous irritation. His first three novels should have been better received than they were—as he often complained to his wife. She thought of him as "neglected," not, as he was, ignored. The books had been painstakingly constructed, modern in their "sensibility," whatever he meant by that, accessible and possessed of accessible, contemporary motifs, dialogue, and sex scenes. They were, to be blunt, absolute failures, and each got a handful of mostly snide, semi-literate reviews, featuring the self-satisfaction of the ignorant. These were, of course, the usual, but Clifford was astonished by their blithe savagery.

How did all this bad luck befall Clifford? He'd begun his dim career as a poet, one of minor, limited gifts. At unexpected moments, there had appeared to him (although "appeared" may be dramatizing such occasions) the notion of the poem that would invite him to venture beyond his given odds and ends of "talent," that would invite him to give up his conception of the poem as a vector of sensitive thought concerning his own highly edited but sensitive life. But since he had a small reputation, a fear of the untried, and, most importantly, a terror of writing a poem that would not *look like* his poems (he had, he believed, a style), these realities conspired to keep him writing a constipated verse that was, at its best, as some friend cruelly said behind his back, "like Sylvia Plath *without* the rag on." What to do?

Clifford wanted, not fame, he knew better than that, but some sort of recognition and respect, some applause, a little money! He wanted to know that his books of poems would be regularly reviewed in the *Times Book Review,* even if such reviews were by the Winchell Tremaines, Brooke Van Dolans, Samantha Gundersons, and the other haughty corporals of the racket. On a number of occasions, Clifford tried to write the poem that was, if you please, just out of his reach, a poem that refused his carefully "crafted" images ("blue gardenias, slices of a summer sky"), but by the second stanza or the twelfth line, he'd be nervously lost; the language that he read, in a nausea of dislocation, was one that he neither recognized nor had control over. He could not, to put it perhaps too simply, tolerate the evidence of his obliterated opinions. And so he "retired" from versifying, as one might quit a boring job, and decided to try his hand at fiction.

His first novel, rigorously and repeatedly reworked, was, nevertheless, somewhat shaggy and juvenile; yet it had phrases and even scenes in which Clifford seemed to overcome his minuscule talents, if I may be permitted a mystical turn. Perhaps it's better to say that he surprised himself in that he permitted his prose to forgo, on occasion, its rigid professionalism, permitted it to break loose, a little, from the everyday world and its everyday people that the narrative drove relentlessly onward: A died, but B lived; C had a terrible accident, but D, her friend, had a baby by E, C's former husband; and F's son came home, addicted to heroin and suffering from AIDS, sullen and despairing, yet seeking love from G, his father, who, although compassionate, was emotionally distant, even from his second wife, the weaver, and her autistic daughter. And I's alcoholism was destroying his sister, J's life, even though she would not recognize this fact. These exhausted problems did not, I hope it goes without saying, present themselves as banalities of "mere" pop fiction, for Clifford, like any *littérateur* you can think of, knew how to disguise the sentimental as the poignant, even the tragic. Life! his novel said. Life! It was, of course, baloney.

Clifford's editor at the time, who would be disappointed by Clifford, worried about the eruptions of, well, *writing* in the manuscript, and worked with Clifford to temper if not excise them. The book needed to be *friendlier,* more *coherent,* retaining its *toughness* and *quirky insights,* but not at the expense of a *driving narrative.* The book was about, was it not, *the way we are now?*

Without a clear respect and compassion for the characters and their messy lives, just what is a novel? What, indeed? Look at Dickens, look at Hardy, look at Trollope, look at Bellow and Updike, look at them! The novel was published, got nine reviews, one of which called it ". . . carefully written and enjoyably quirky . . . somewhat difficult at times . . rich with compassion . . . characters who, by the book's end, we feel we've . . . suffered with." The book disappeared so completely that it never showed up on remainder tables or in catalogues.

There's not much left to say. Clifford's next two books were like dozens of others, literate if vulgar, "better than" kill-and-fuck trash, and of no account. They were much like the miles of thin, clankingly inadequate independent films that one can spend a lifetime watching blend into one another with an inevitability as depressing as it is foreseeable. Clifford, it must be said, did not "sell out," for he had, as the old phrase puts it, "nothing that anybody wanted." He wasn't bad enough or smart enough to be a successful commercial hack, and he had absolutely none of the luck that would have enabled him to emerge from the slough of writhing literary hacks. Had he, when a poet, followed his Muse, as they say, into the brambles of language that were too formidable for him to contemplate, there is little doubt that he would have written bad poems; and it also seems clear that had he insisted on elaborating on the small eruptions of—art, let's say, for want of a less generous word—in his first novel, it would have done nothing to ameliorate the zombie-like qualities of the whole.

It's a guess, one that pleases me, that as Clifford read the proofs of this fourth novel, as he battered his way through its dreary lines

of prose, a prose that seemed manufactured by a language con-
traption with decorative abilities, he was relieved, even pleased.
This is the McCoy! I'll have him say, or something like it, Oh boy!
perhaps. Maybe *this* book would do it. "Scintillating," even "wise."
And with a pronounced "attention to scenes and their riveting
details, not to mention their dialogue, that is almost cinematic."
You never know.

LIFE AND LETTERS

— ☾ —

Some three or four years ago, Edward Krefitz published a story that, as is the case with many stories, contained elements of his past life, elements, of course, disguised, twisted, corrupted, embellished, romanticized, and wholly fanciful. A few people recognized themselves as models for characters in the story, and were, predictably, chagrined or flattered, depending on the quality of the fiction's distortion of their being. They all wished, surely, to be *accurately portrayed*, certainly; but there is accuracy and then there is meanspiritedness. So they muttered.

Edward wasn't interested in their scattered responses to his story when and if he got wind of them. However, the one person whom he had used as a model for a major character in the story, the one person he dearly wanted to read the story and be hurt by it, never acknowledged it, even though it had been published in a literary magazine that Edward knew this person deeply, even somewhat ridiculously admired—at least he had, years before. Edward was disappointed, since his fictional creation—vapid, obtuse, childishly cruel—was easily recognizable, and he so wanted him to *be* recognized by his ex-friend, if "friend" is not too exotic a word to use. Because of this disappointment, which he chafed into a kind of full-blown irritation, he made a mistake; that is, he sent the model a photocopy of the story, insincerely inscribed, and followed this, soon after, with a letter, thereby, quite perfectly, compounding his original error.

The story, entitled, rather obscurely, "The Birds Are Singing," was a bitter, if frail, comedy of manners (bad manners, as Edward liked to think of it), driven by the wheezing engine of the "adulterous tale," one that was neither particularly comic nor particularly sordid. Its hero, if you will, a young husband whose authorial aspirations are at best halfhearted, has a wife, pretty and possessed of a kind of floundering hedonism. She is content to be "his" because of his aspirations and the spidery talents he owns, as well as by the fact that his literary vocation has thrown the couple into contact with other young literary people, jittery, amoral, indifferently talented, if talented at all. These companions are drawn as rapt in a cheap and shabby, vaguely hysterical delusion, and too selfish or stupid to recognize it as such. At the center of this overdone clique of the pathetic, is the major character already mentioned. This man is presented, in the most patronizing as well as nastiest prose that Edward could knock together, as a vapid dilettante; a poet, of sorts, who is hard at work on a novel that will justify the shameful fact that he is the owner of a successful messenger service for which the husband works as a bookkeeper. The boss/novelist is given to the reader as a tedious lout who confuses his sociopolitical right-thinking with artistic talent, and he is stuffed with cretinous dialogue that even Wyndham Lewis might hesitate to put into his most contemptible characters' mouths. The boss seduces the husband's wife in an ugly scene that boils with loathing for the pair. The husband is aware of this, but has no clear proof, and so ignores it, much as if his wife's probable seducer is no more than a living dildo and she a disembodied vagina. He is sure, however, that this amorous clod may one day be able to help him along in his career, or what he thinks of as his career. This was, then, the bones of Edward's story, one that he came to admire more as it aged, so to speak. The notion that the cuckolded husband finds his betrayer pitifully absurd, and his wife a virtual specter, while he emerges as a genuine if eccentric and as-yet unrealized artist pleased him, even though the story had, he knew, a somewhat manufactured air about it.

The model for the boss was, of course, the man, Peter, whom Edward wanted to anger and wound. The cause of his dislike went back almost twenty years, when he and most especially his wife, Patricia, insisted on thinking of him and Peter as partners in a small restaurant in what was then, the early seventies, a just newly fashionable SoHo. Peter was, in actuality, Edward's boss. There had been a falling out between them as the restaurant began to make money, or, as it is said, "real" money. At this point, the friends' differences quickly surfaced and became unmanageable. Edward felt, on the strength, really, of no more than their joint literary, ah, proclivities, let's say, that he was being deprived of his bonus: his loft apartment, his summers on the Island, his good clothes, his this, his that. And Patricia! It's enough to say that she simply blamed Peter for everything, from her spoiled childhood to her sullen years at Hunter and the School of Visual Arts to her haphazard marriage to Edward—Edward, who had been cheated of his rightful *partner's* place as entrepreneur *and* literary force. She hated Peter, even more, perhaps, than she hated Edward some few years later, at the time of their separation and divorce; hated Edward so cleanly and thoroughly for his varied failures, that in her last conversation with him she'd told him, rather sadly, understandingly, and even sweetly, that in their eight years of marriage he had *never once* made her come. He stood quietly before her news, looking, as an old phrase has it, like death chewing on a cracker.

After the dissolution of the friendship and "partnership," Edward began teaching beginning creative-writing courses at coolie wages; writing reviews for *Booklist, Library Journal,* and the like; freelancing as a copy editor and proofreader; and, in general, living the shaky life of the barely published and virtually unknown author. Patricia worked as an editorial assistant for a small scholastic publisher, and they got by, seeing, if not the same friends they had been seeing, the same kinds of friends. It should be mentioned that, at this time, Patricia was somewhat admiring of Edward for insisting, at her urging, of course, on his rights and perquisites, and so she regularly told him, to his delight. She was convinced that Peter, "that bastard," was much inferior in business acumen than her husband; and as the author of a wretched little book of poems, *Table d'Hote*—published by Peter himself as the Chambers Street Press—he had no right to think himself superior to anybody about anything! In sum, she maintained little but an offhand, careless disregard for Peter; who, in turn, vilified her, pointedly or subtly, to people whom he knew that Edward would run into. She was, in his creation, the scattered and selfish Zelda to Edward's hapless Scott.

The rub was that although Edward broke off his friendship or relationship or association with Peter in a swirl of hurt feelings and envy, still, oh yes, *still*, he wondered if he might have been right about Patricia. About her "interference," her "malicious interference," as he had put it, in his work and career. That Edward's work and career were, to be extremely kind, negligible, is neither here nor there: he thought it was work; he thought it a career. Or, to gloss that particular text, it's the rare mediocre writer who knows how mediocre he is. When Patricia left him, soon after it was apparent to her, or so he figured it, that his dissociating himself from Peter would in no way allow his star ever to grow bright enough to have a chance at dimming, left him with her peroration on his sexual limitations, he thought, he *knew* that Peter was right and had been right. He was ashamed of himself, he was what an earlier generation called mortified. Why had he listened to his bitch of a wife? Why had she so despised Peter?

Over the next several years, as Edward established himself as a reliable contributor of short fiction and reviews to a myriad of magazines, he vacillated in his feelings about both Peter and Patricia. He heard many stories of Peter's financial success, and of his mockery of him and his work, of him and his contemptible third-rate literary niche, of Patricia. And concerning her, concerning her . . . although Edward's thoughts of her were tinged with pain and embarrassment, he yet felt, in some unbalanced way, protective of her—even more absurd, he felt loyal to her. And so he began, again, to blame Peter for this and for that and for, well, for everything. It is simple to understand, then, why "The Birds Are Singing" was written, why it was important to Edward that Peter read it, why it was important that he respond to it with, at the very least, irritation. Edward wanted to demonstrate *things* to Peter, salient among which was that he had, indeed, become a writer, by Christ, and that his writer's eye had been sharp enough all those many years ago to see Peter for what he had been: he'd not been fooled, for a moment, by him!— who had been crude and grasping and filled with contempt for him and Patricia, whom he'd hurt and somehow embittered. Edward wanted, simply, to get even with Peter. And so strong was his desire, perhaps his need, to knife Peter, to shock him with a view of himself as a vulgar, cheap, mean poseur, that, as already noted, he sent a copy of the story to him, followed, a week or so later, by a letter.

Dear Peter,

I hope you got the new story I sent a few days ago. This is all out of the blue, I know, but "the old days" have been on my mind lately. I thought that you, more than anyone, would "see" the story clearly, and recognize the furniture, so to speak. It's maybe a little dark, and nobody comes off too well, but I think it's pretty true to the feel of that time, confused as things were. Anyway, drop me a line if the spirit moves you. I often wonder how we came to part so completely, considering how our differences, whatever they were, seem so trivial now. I hear, by the way, that you are doing fine with a specialty catering business, as well as with a new restaurant in Chelsea. I got this from Marge, who also gave me your address. I'm pleased for you, really. Take care, and cheers,

    Fondly,
    Ed

As suggested, the "gift" of the story to Peter was a mistake, one that was richly compounded by the above letter. And as if to polish these mistakes into perfection, Edward, awash in the lies of nostalgia that his acts had awakened, quite unaccountably and foolishly, began to feel bad about everything that had happened: the story, its grotesque caricature of Peter, its dispatch to him, the letter, and, most tellingly, their shattered friendship, which Edward managed to burnish into much more than it had ever been or ever could have been. This broken relationship he now nimbly contrived to place, such were the powers of corrupted memory, on the shoulders of Patricia. She was, yes she was, yes, yes, she was to blame, the snob, the cynical snob, the bitch. And to think that he had felt that *she* had cared about him, had thought to protect his interests, Jesus Christ! There had been no reason, had there, for him and Peter to break their easygoing relationship, their, in a way, partnership? They were in accord on ideas, notions of the comic and the absurd, politics, books, on notions of *what was good.* Hadn't this been the case? He even thought, fleetingly, to be sure, of calling Patricia, if he could track her down, to ask her, to yell at her, to do something! And so he poked at himself, rereading, two or three times, "The Birds Are Singing" with distaste and regret and a growing sense of shame.

A month passed, during which time Edward thought of calling Peter every day, to maybe make a date for lunch or a drink? To talk, to mend fences. He might, he could, he would, yes, apologize for the story itself. One day he received a letter from Peter, and opened it with hope and pleasure. Peter, of course, felt the way he did; he, too, wanted to resume their old camaraderie, tempered, surely, changed, but still *real*. Patricia's malice would be diluted, it would be banished, at last.

Dear Ed,

I was surprised and I guess shocked to get your piece and the follow-up letter after all this time, it's really been a long time! The piece brought back those days in that little dump in SoHo that we called the cash-eater, remember? I hope that the piece and letter are ways of saying that bygones should be bygones. Maybe things will be o.k. between us again, that would be terrific.

I'm doing pretty well. Marge is right that I have a little café in Chelsea on 20th Street near 9th, the Arles. And the catering business, Peter's Specialty Cuisine, maybe Marge told you, is in a loft building on Hudson near Houston on the 4th floor, you can imagine the hassles with the Fire Dept. and the Buildings Dept. and the Board of Health and so on! But everything is fine now, I'm making a living, as they say, married for sixteen years now with a fourteen-year-old daughter. We live in Bronxville.

Most importantly, Ed, really, I mean really, *is how fantastically brave and honest and forgiving you are to have written this piece, which I've read three times now. It must have taken a lot of courage, moral courage, as they say, to use yourself as a model for the husband character, Ned, that poor bastard who is so painfully and cruelly and flagrantly betrayed by his wife and friend. Who, if I read right, are Patricia and me, of course. It amazes me, just floors me, to realize, all these years later, that you knew, all along, probably from the beginning, that Patricia and I were lovers and stayed lovers for a year and a half. We were so crazy*

that we didn't care whether we hurt you or not, although we were care-
ful not to be obvious about meeting each other, and we were certain that
you didn't know. Patricia's bad-mouthing me really should have worked,
although you obviously saw right through it. What makes me feel worse
than the affair is that we ended our friendship for the wrong reason, or
maybe I should say over something that wasn't even real!

Now, with this marvelous piece, you are letting me know that you
knew, you knew all along, and you let it go, maybe for friendship or love,
I don't know. It's just fantastic. You're a wonderful writer, as I always
thought you were. Please write again, stay in touch!

Your old partner,

Peter

Unlikely as it may seem, when Edward read this letter, he decided that Peter had maliciously and carefully contrived to humiliate him with a confession of an imagined adultery. Peter and Patricia, good God! How ridiculous. Edward felt stupid and clumsy to have thought Peter worthy of his concern. He tore up the letter, and then sat down to read "The Birds Are Singing" once again.

PERDIDO

In 1953, or early 1954, Dan Burke was seeing, as they used to say, Claire Walsh, who was pregnant by another man, a lummox known as "Swede" to his lummox friends. Dan had recently been discharged from the Navy, and while he and Claire had been amorous companions during his rare shore leaves, she was far from averse to impromptu sexual adventures with congenial civilians while Dan was at sea. Thus, her dalliance with "Swede," who was, incidentally, a reinsurance clerk on Maiden Lane: this permitted him to tell the occasional citizen who asked about his job that he was "on Wall Street." He enters our story as a catalyst.

Dan didn't know that Claire was pregnant, but since he and she had never engaged in anything more than what was called—and still may be, for all I know—"heavy petting," he assumed that she was a virgin. Who knows why? When she told Dan that she was going to have a baby, he was, sequentially, astonished, hurt, disgusted, and angry. Then he asked her to "go down on" him, which she did. He felt, in some clouded, blurred way, even with "Swede," whom he did not know at all. Then he asked her to marry him and she consented, with much blubbering, snots, and tears. He didn't love her, nor she him, and nothing that they did at the outset of their marriage allowed love to establish itself and stagger free of the grim truth of their situation, as love, despite the long odds, may occasionally do. So their marriage began, not utterly bleak, but surely not aglow. It should be said immediately, I believe, that their marriage did not succeed, and was over some eight or nine years later. Not bad, considering.

Dan began working at a bookstore in the Village, Marboro, to be precise, on Eighth Street, home of the authentic bullfight poster from colorful Méjico! (It gives me pause—what a comfortable phrase—when I recall that the bullfight poster was once virtually epidemic in the apartments of the hip and chosen, and then the latter and the posters suddenly vanished.) One of Dan's co-workers was a man by the name of James Fremont, a poet who had been published in *Zero, Neurotica,* and *Prairie Schooner,* and had a handwritten rejection note from an editor, or somebody, at *Poetry,* suggesting that he "try us again." Which he did and did again, never managing to make further human contact, however contemptuous, with the famous magazine. In the meantime, Claire had begun to read this and that and have opinions on this and that as well. The plot, as you may discern, is not truly thickening, but it might be jelling a little. These people seem as if they're about to "take a step," probably into disaster.

The serendipitous conjunction of the well-read, and, in the best tradition of the Village of those days, slightly shaggy, tweedy, and insufferably superior *published poet,* and the unhappy, directionless Dan and Claire, created the perfect climate for emotional calamities of many sorts and sizes. Dan began to write poetry ("of course!," I hear you say) under the condescending tutelage of James, and Claire began to go to bed with him on those evenings when she was supposed to be seeing old "girlfriends," attending suddenly fashionable poetry readings at any number of bohemian traps, or going to see "films" at the New Yorker or Thalia. Dan would stay home in their one-bedroom apartment on Blake Avenue in East New York—at that time, not yet the sister neighborhood of 1945 Stalingrad—and dream his old dream of playing jazz trumpet, another enthusiasm that had hysterically played itself out at the New York School of Music (Sunset Park branch), over a little less than eight months.

There had been another "student of trumpet" whose lessons were scheduled on Dan's night, a nervous forty-year-old homosexual virgin, who often talked of Charlie Spivak's "golden horn," and of a photograph—which he would soon bring in—of Joan Crawford "eating pussy," as he put it, his eyes crazed and shining and unfocused, as if *he* were the "pussy" to which Miss Crawford addressed her perverse attentions. Dan got bored by the scale book and spooked by his fellow student, who began alternating his tales of Joan Crawford's adventures with questions as to Dan's toilet-paper preferences. And his lips hurt after a half-hour or so of practice: this would not do. He wanted to *play* and show them what he was made of, what was in his heart. Oh well.

But soon, literature, as noted, became his passion, and James guided him into the strange world of Eliot and Pound and Stevens, Dylan Thomas and Robert Lowell and W.H. Auden, the world of art and life! And life! So he and Claire had found a way to be. The trumpet was one thing, but this was quite another. And where James guided Dan, so, too, he guided Claire. She slowly acquired a slight lisp and a choppy laugh that was meant to be cold and worldly, as in: "Dan and James actually *working* at the Marboro *supermarket* (hak hak hak)! It's too *much!*"

Where, you may ask, was the child in this turmoil of art and love and life? As well you might. Growing up as best he could, which, as it turned out, was none too good. He became dyslexic—known in those days as "dumb," hyperactive—known in those days as "dumb," truant and antisocial—"dumb" and "bad." It's of sad moment, perhaps, to note that he would one day murder rhythm guitar and sing spectacularly off-key in a dreadful rock band, the Unbearables, before leaving for someplace Sunny and Sunny, to be with others of his kind. Heavy! But this is incidental to the story, so-called, and I add it because I know, courtesy of my magical authorial powers, what the kid's future will be, or in this case, was. I could, as I don't have to tell you, have made him into a solid citizen rather than a lout. Since his status is peripheral to everything, I offer him as a bonus, an embellishment, a fillip. A tip.

James Fremont let Dan and Claire know that he was soon going to move to San Francisco, where, he said, "real poetry" was still being written in a city long dedicated to the arts, one far removed from the commercial whoredom of New York, hey nonny no! Although the Beats were much in the ascendance there, a group of poets were working seriously at their "craft," and a friend of his had begun a magazine that published authentic poetry. The magazine, *Lux*, called for "a return to the abiding truths of the vision of America set forth in the thought of Emerson, Thoreau, and Whitman." Oh boy. The poets published therein wrote poems that displayed lines like: "Emerging lust that closely binds us all/In contrapuntal swells of love's dark sea." It need not be said, I'm sure, that the morose hacks who contributed to *Lux* were enraptured by fixed forms, and trafficked in infirm quatrains and sonnets and sestinas, all viciously rhymed to a fare-thee-well. Their avocation kept them off the streets, as they say, and the sacred fire burned bright.

So it was off to happy Frisco for James, and he was soon followed by Dan, Claire, and Justin, the latter slowly sinking into frantic misery under the assaults of Claire's daily readings from the Bible, the *Odyssey,* and Shakespeare. "Today, honey, we're going to find out what Odysseus did when he went to Hades. Say 'O-diss-ee-uss.'" Their rusty Nash, a king of lemons, broke down for the fourth and final time of their hejira outside Bakersfield, and they arrived in The City by piss-redolent Greyhound. How they'd laugh in years to come, etc., etc. Right. They rented an apartment on Gough Street, which, like most residential streets of the town, even in those days—before the hordes of émigrés from the Midwest had stormed the place—was weirdly deserted day and night: in brilliant sun, torrential rains, and freezing fog.

Dan got a septic job working in the classifieds section of the *Examiner,* and attempted to dedicate himself to a study of quantitative verse, and, God help us, Latin; and bought himself a second-hand trumpet, with a leaky spit valve, that gurgled on "c." He fitfully practiced his scales from his old NYSM practice book, and, although half-drunk much of the time on the red wine that was wondrously available by the cheap gallon, got to page twelve, after which he set the absurd horn aside and wondered about the ablative. Claire resumed her ramshackle affair with James, and began what she called a "systematic reading" of "the Russians," e.g., some of *The Brothers Karamazov* and 213 pages of *War and Peace;* and Justin worked out his destiny as an emotional gimp.

One night, when Dan, James, and two other poets of the Grail met to read and critique their latest poems, James attacked Dan's foray into the thickets of a Sapphic stanza, by asserting that quantity is not for modern Americans. "You've got to *count,* man! Not *sing!* Marianne Moore!" Dan laughed even harder than Claire, although neither of them knew what their pal was talking about. Sing? And all they knew of Miss Moore was a poem about a fish. Dan's poem began: "In my living room in blue San Francisco." James remarked that "blue" was extraneous, but without it, "you've got no meter, man." So the mentor said, his thigh next to Claire's. He had brought over a copy of *The Colorado Review* which contained his translation of one of Lorca's poems, further to put Dan in his place. Claire's hand caressed the magazine, which lay among the beer bottles and ashtrays on the kitchen table. Despite all, Dan felt like socking her one. James pulled the bill of his cap over his eyes and rolled, badly, I'm constrained to say, a cigarette. Take him all in all, he was a bad hat. Meanwhile, Justin could be heard in his room, smashing toys against the wall. "Must be a critique, Dan," one of the other poets said, and general hilarity reigned. The evening ended when Dan's beer ran out.

Here is a photograph of Dan, Claire, and Justin, taken on a Sunday afternoon in a little park off Dolores Street. The year is 1956. It's hard to pinpoint the desolation that is enclosed in this image, since it is an almost intolerably bright Bay Area day, "some weather," as the natives like to say and say again. Claire is in a brown suit that is out of fashion, and holds a book in her right hand: it looks like *Ulysses,* and may well be. Dan looks drunk, and probably is, and presents to the world a sour smile that appears to have been cemented to his face, and Justin murderously aims a toy pistol at the photographer, Claire's current lover, a jazz pianist by avocation, a marijuana smoker by trade. The little family is right on the edge of wholesale wretchedness, or so the photograph would seem to proclaim. Herb Caen can't save them, nor Dixie Belle gin, nor the gallons of California red that have become Dan's faithful buddies. His leaky trumpet lies, wrapped in a T-shirt, at the bottom of a closet, in classic style: out of sight, etc. The horn can't save them either. There is a tide in the affairs of men that sweeps them out to sea.

It is the Christmas season, and in the inside breast pocket of Dan's worn covert topcoat is a photograph of Justin on the lap of Emporium-Capwell's Santa Claus. They are both scowling. Claire's expression, slightly demented with thoughts of her current amour, reveals "the lineaments of gratified desire," more or, most probably, less. It is quite possible that the photograph, on closer scrutiny, would reveal that the family has already plunged into wretchedness. I am not the man to scrutinize it.

≈ *Claire's Sentimental Education*
Poundian; sonnet sequence; extended metaphor; hypallage; great poem; James's villanelle in the *Hudson Review,* marvelous; negative capability; Justin's color sense; *Howl?*; Westian; Proustian;

Kafkaesque; Williams?; *Ark II Moby I;* the New Criticism; Rothko and Kline; Pollock and Guston; Jack Kerouac?; Dave Brubeck; objective correlative; *Four Quartets;* Dylan Thomas; pantoum, sestina, ballade, canzone, triolet; show don't tell; O'Connor and Cheever; Herb Gold; timbre; Paul Desmond; Warne Marsh; Brecht; Ransom and Blackmuir and Jarrell; the *Wake;* the mind like a dying flame or something; epiphany; daubs; organic form; the Golden Triangle; existentialism; surrealism; Dada; Lowell and Viereck and Eberhart and Wilbur; *Poetry; Le Sacre du Printemps;* Lotte Lenya; structurally calligraphic; the San Remo; Gino and Carlo's; the Place; the Cedar; *The ABC of Reading;* Jacques Brel; Edith Piaf; Dan's smoky tone; Whitmanesque; The City's Mediterranean quality; Kenneth Rexroth; City Lights; bop prosody?; Sonny Rollins?; Herbert Huncke; *Naked Lunch;* horse, H, smack, schmeck, shit; pot, grass, gage, weed, maryjane; the Magic Workshop; "The Venice Poem"; Don Allen; Projective Verse; Black Mountain; Blind Lemon; Robert Johnson; Gerry Mulligan; Sonny Boy Williamson; Snooks Eaglin; Chet Baker, *quidditas;* fuck me, James; fuck me, Bob; fuck me, Si; the *Ninth;* fuck me, Jack; fuck me, Bruce; fuck me, Eddie; *Three Places in New England;* fuck me, Richard; fuck me, Ron; fuck me, Bill; *Transfigured Night;* fuck me, Jon; fuck me, Charlie; fuck me, Sam; Clancy Sigal; fuck me, Joe; fuck me, Michael; fuck me, Dick; Lee Konitz; fuck me, Whitey; fuck me, Harry; fuck me, LeRoy; Laura Riding; fuck me, Al; fuck me, Boris; fuck me, Brad; *The White Goddess;* fuck me, Jerry. Please, Dan! I'm trying to *read.*

That Dan began an affair soon after Claire had begun to capitalize on her sexual chances, let's call them, is predictable enough to make grown men howl and rend their garments. To call it an "affair," however, is to distinguish it with a modicum of glamour and adventure that it did not possess. Then he had another, and then another, all of them the same in their dismal contours. They were mostly drunken, partially satisfactory stabs at abandoned carnality, amateurish, if the word has any sexual meaning, so much so that they seemed as if inflicted on Dan and his what-the-hell partners, most of whom were unhappy wives caught in marriages to men somewhat like Dan, although he would have been insulted to know this. He, it will not surprise you, thought that none of these women were good enough for him, and his gluey, sweaty spasms with them in divers motels did not soften his contempt for them. They were, my God, unaware of the "scene" all around them in the new Florence, and wished, more often than not, for their husbands to make enough money so that they could move to a house in Belmont and spend a few weeks each summer near the Russian River. They were, that is to say, just folks.

Claire found out about one of these affairs, threatened to leave the apartment, leave The City, take Justin away, to do all those things that she should do to be *free,* did Dan not stop seeing the bitch, bimbo, whore, slut, tramp. Suicide was threatened once or twice. This was all a play that humanity has acted in for centuries, of course, but it was no less painful for being so sublimely banal. So Dan broke off the arrangement, as he thought of it, and was faithful for a month or so; then it was back to the adultery follies. Claire, rescued from emotional collapse, briskly punished Dan by taking up with a *marvelous* painter, a friend of a friend of her last lover's wife. He painted the crystalline exhalations of the Bay and sky and so on and so forth, and suggested to Claire that James Fremont was, well, how to put it? *unimportant.* As was Dan, his bad poems and his bad job and his drunken crap about his trumpet, Jesus, that trumpet. After a month with the adoring Claire, the painter told her that he "found it difficult" for him to work and continue to see her; he was "into" a collage tryptych that was, well, "draining." Claire cried and cried and, two nights later, bashed Dan on the head with a Revere Ware pot. "You!" she yelled. "You! You! You!"

I don't know what happened over the next few years, but Dan and Claire must have reached some sort of accommodation, a grim marital dance of necessary exchanges, with no questions asked about late nights out, unexplained absences, missing articles of clothing, whispered telephone conversations, and the like. Occasionally, there must have occurred a vicious and mean-spirited quarrel over a lover who appeared to exist, for one or the other of them, on a plane slightly higher than the merely sexual, or, to put it in Dan's polished words, "I *know* the fuck is more than just a quick fuck to you!" But by and large they just grew older.

Claire made occasional trips back to Brooklyn to see Dot, her "mommy," and her two brothers, both of whom still lived with "mommy," and, it pleases me to think, were still virgins. There they are, coming out of eleven o'clock Mass. "Lookit her," Brian says to Mickey, of a comely young woman, "what a fuckin' dog." "A dog is right," Mickey snarls. So they diluted their rabid lusts. Let's imagine that on one of these trips Claire ran into "Swede," and after a night of joyous dancing and drinking in a little joint in Bayside, the two old pals went to bed together. "Swede" confessed that he was married, but that he thought of Claire all the time. None of this probably happened, for I understand that "Swede" had fallen off a roof about a year after he and Claire had indulged in their initial dalliance. He had been trying to adjust a television antenna so that he wouldn't have to watch the Yankees play in blurry snowstorms. Of course he was a Yankee fan.

In time, the accommodation mentioned became too boring, too burdensome, so Claire took Justin, by now an NCO in the army of sociopaths forever garrisoned in the Republic, and they went to— oh, I don't know. Lawton, perhaps, or St. Louis. No, Seattle! That's where they went, Seattle. Even then, a *great place to live*. It was just great. Or maybe Dan left Claire after another sour argument, complete with tears and rage as decorations to his insistence that neither Claire nor anybody else would keep him from seeing Justin, by Jesus Christ! Of course, Dan would have been pleased never to look upon his berserk son's face again. In any event, they separated. Some thought it touching that Dan took his trumpet with him, along with his NYSM scales book. Others, infected with reality, laughed.

Five or six years after Dan and Claire had divorced, we discover, as they say, Dan in a Greenwich Village bar. He's in town to bury his mother, and has accepted an old neighborhood friend's invitation to have a drink on the last night of the wake. He is dressed in a gray sharkskin suit, white shirt, dark-blue tie whose Windsor knot is too big for his shirt collar, a gray raincoat with raglan sleeves, and a dark-brown porkpie hat. He looks, not to be harsh, the perfect rube. He lives in Vacaville, which may account for the figure he cuts.

He is being contemptuously superior with his old friend, who, to Dan's patronizing amusement, is an insurance underwriter. Dan, you may be interested to know, works as a clerk in the main branch of the Sacramento Public Library, but has told his friend that he runs a small literary agency in San Francisco, "so *much* fresh talent there," he says. Why he lives so far from the oven of creativity is not brought up. Dan sneers at the friend, the bar, the Village, at poor old New York itself, bastion of all that is wrong with everything. Then, suddenly, and, one might say, belligerently, he begins to recite a rigid poem by James Fremont. When he finishes, he looks smugly at his old friend. "I still write the occasional poem," he says. The old friend is happily impressed, and they order another round. "How's Claire, by the way?" the friend asks. "You ever see her?" Dan looks at him, his face rotten with disgust. "Claire?" he says. "Fuck Claire! You know she won't," and tears come to his eyes, "she won't let me see *Justin?*" He takes out a handkerchief and pokes at his eyes. "That boy was my whole life."

I have no idea what happened to Dan or Claire as the years passed, although somebody told me that he'd heard that Claire married an ex-priest who wasn't quite sure he was heterosexual; he also had a limp. This seems much too plausible to be true. Justin, as you know, became a musician, so to speak. But Dan more or less just disappeared into one of many California towns, most of them in the desolate miles of woods between the North Bay and the Oregon border, a land that bursts into flames each fall, to the residents' enduring surprise.

I have, I'm sorry to say, no nice conclusion to this story, which is, I admit, not much of a story after all. But concerning Dan, at least, I can, and will, borrow a few words from Scott Fitzgerald's chronicle of another splintered and self-deluded man as coda: "In any case, he is almost certainly in that section of the country, in one town or another."

LOST IN THE STARS

The way which can be followed is not the true way.
—TAO TE CHING

People are, for the most part, locked into their minds, and their professions of belief in various ideologies or faiths, their opinions and scattered absurdities are but the knowable aspects of the lives they move through as best they can. This may be because of the regularity with which language pretends a simplification, a clear categorization of the particularized darkness that is the mind's. And so religions and credos and their stupefying shibboleths are often spectacularly successful in duping and soothing us, their creaking yet elaborate language systems shamelessly representing themselves as the contraptions of God or his long-dead confidants. This is comforting folly, and we know that the most reprehensibly smug creeping Jesus lives, much of the time, despite his rigid beliefs, in the midnight of his brain, lost therein like the rest of us.

Consider the young, reasonably well-mannered men who killed so many people on September 11th. There they are, as unremarkably, as sadly ordinary as any representative American one can conjure up: anonymous, with their 5.75 haircuts and Timex "Explorer" watches, GAP T-shirts and overpriced running shoes, Hanes briefs and white athletic socks, and their Dockers khakis. They may well be full of Domino's cardboard pizza or Big Macs, turning, despite their love of Allah, into chemical-laced excrement in their bowels. They might as well be American, citizens of Big Faucet, South Dakota, or Willow Lake, New Jersey. Insofar as their linguistic commerce goes, they are surely the salt of the earth: "I like very much to learn fly big jet plane nice, O.K., good buddy?" Of spiritual matters large and small, they have no doubts, they have no qualms, their relationship with their morose and irritable God is one that would make the most dedicated Bible-thumper, yea, with snakes and timbrels, screaming and writhing, white roses and accordions, and thunder and lightning, wild with envy. Their stern yet loving Father has certainly spoken to these men in thus wise: "Kill, my young stalwarts, this is my inscrutable message to you, oh, don't ask why. And know that paradise awaits for all eternity, with its dark-eyed virgins anxious to make your acquaintance."

These young men know that Allah is pleased that thousands of infidels will soon be slaughtered, and since they are unbelievers, there will be no virgins for them. No halvah or falafel or lamb with rice either. Who knows what becomes of infidel dogs? On the other hand, there may be a shock in store for those soldiers of jihad, if, by some unutterable metaphysical quirk, they are made aware, in the smallest fraction of time, before oblivion, that can still be thought of as time, that "Allah" is a congeries of letters, a linguistic notion, if you will, like "flogiston" or "aporia" or "quark," and that their deaths are—not to put too fine a point on it—meaningless. Oh, oh. Peace be upon them.

Regard this salesman, a meat-cutting-machine salesman, standing at an ice-crusted window in a room of a so-so hotel in Ohio or Pennsylvania, perhaps somewhere in the Poconos, the land, for so many years, of ga-ga honeymooners delirious in their heart-shaped bathtubs. He is looking out on the semicircular gravel drive that leads to Mohawk Boulevard and thence to the interstate; where, even now, as he smokes and tries to ignore the fact of his appalling boredom and small, regular failures, his petty defeats and debts, his emptiness and dismay, overpriced cars slam down this suicide alley, their drivers—let me be blunt—wholly uncaring about God in any of his disguises or costumes. They want to get home alive, just once more, peace be upon them. God can look after himself.

The salesman puts out his cigarette, his mind turning over darkly and heavily, and, with *Barney Miller* playing soundlessly and in washes of anemic color on the Korean swivel television in the corner, he takes off his pants and Hanes briefs, removes from his worn bag a pair of black sateen panties with nylon lace trim at the leg openings, pulls them on, and begins to masturbate. He is careful to keep his erect penis confined, the feel of the sateen on his throbbing phallus always does the trick for him. His shadowed mind with its sketchy and occulted thoughts of love and success, of his wife and the women at the branch office in Philadelphia, is concentrated in this solitary act; his secret self finds some succor in the physical world in which he tries his best to live and live each day. And he may thus soothe, for a quarter hour, his persistent malaise, he may find some small fugitive peace.

This act, tawdry as it is, may be thought of as strange and even perverse behavior, but only because, perhaps, I point it out to you, so that you may realize that you know, casually, this salesman. You both buy the paper every morning at the same store, the paper and Tic Tacs and cigarettes. "Morning," you both say. I agree that it's hard to think of this man, with his balding head and scuffed L.L. Bean moccasins, whacking off, far from home, in a pair of cheap black panties. All secrets are dark.

The salesman, for whatever reason, has told himself that his wife has permitted him to use her panties for this cloistered act, whereas he bought them, of course, a few days earlier in a Wal-Mart outside Wilkes-Barre. Oddly, he is thinking of Mickey Rooney in the film *My Name Is Aram,* at the moment of his orgasm, which arrives blissfully but unexpectedly. As he surrenders completely to the weirdly thrilling and bridelike feelings that over-whelm him, gouts of semen spurt through the panties and onto the coarse bedspread.

The salesman lights a cigarette, and after depositing the soaked panties in the bathroom sink and cleaning himself off with toilet paper and a hand towel, he begins to scrub, nervously, at the soiled bedspread with tap water, the towel, and, for reasons beyond his comprehension, one of his worn, unfashionable ties. He is horrified at the possibility of the maid discovering his onanism when she comes in to make up the bed in the morning. The fucking maid, Oh Jesus, the fucking maid, he says to himself, and then suffers a massive coronary infarction and falls dead, bashing his head on the little writing desk that holds his wallet, keys, change, notebook, cigarettes, lighter, all the now useless junk of his life. Later in the week, his wife, faced with the fact of the semen-clotted panties in the sink, prefers to think that her dead husband was cruelly and disturbingly unfaithful to her with a perverted slut of a whore tramp of the Ohio or Pennsylvania evening. Otherwise—what to think? Peace be upon her.

It is quite possible, perhaps even probable, that one of the dedicated martyrs-to-be performed precisely the same hidden act—Allah notwithstanding—that the dead infidel salesman did, save, of course, for the heart attack. Let's place the intense youth in a Great Western motel during, oh, his fifth or sixth week in the land of the Great Satan. He is standing in front of the mirror in his black sateen panties. Black panties! Evil and foul and cursed underwear made for depraved American women who, half-naked, are everywhere before one's eyes. This young warrior had never even seen a picture of these sinful garments before he arrived in Duluth, he could not even imagine them, and here they were, by the hundreds, the thousands, in black, white, and colors, colors. They hang in plain view in Target and Sears, Penney's and Wal-Mart, Macy's and Ward's, there, right there, so that anyone, even this young unsmiling zealot may buy them. Even this gloomy, rigid, sincere man, purified of all desire save the desire for a martyr's death, may buy them. He thinks that he might buy a pair or two so as to have before his eyes a proof of American corruption and evil. His mind goes black, the truth of his apostate lust is therein buried, and, flushed, holding two pairs of these impossible wisps before him, he says to the salesgirl: "I like to buy this pretty things for my wife now please." He takes the plastic bag, turns and leaves, burning, his closeted scenario forming in his mind, dark and silent and obscure, hidden from the decrees of the stern faithful, peace be upon them. The flesh is weak, weak, the mind a sequestered vault, airless and without light.

The young man is standing in front of the mirror in his degenerate garment, dizzy with pleasure, trembling, half-mad with fear of God's wrath; but God, in whatever mournful guise, is, as always, nowhere to be discovered.

PSYCHOPATHOLOGY OF EVERYDAY LIFE

Even in healthy persons, egotistic, jealous and hostile feelings and
impulses, burdened by the pressure of moral education,
often utilize the path of faulty actions to express in some way their
undeniably existing force. . . . The manifold sexual currents
play no insignificant part in these repressed feelings.
—SIGMUND FREUD

I knew some of the minor details of the following narrative—if I
may so distinguish the somewhat rickety account that follows—but
its basic elements were told me, casually and indifferently, by three
or four people, no one of whom knew the whole story. This did not
prevent them from attempting to fill in its sudden blanks, so as to
make the story cohere, so to say, or, at any rate, achieve a sort of balance—despite the fact that there seems little balance to its particu-
lars. And although its meanderings, its often sad climaxes and
anticlimaxes, are often banal, there is a pathos, I think, at the story's
center, that attracted me, so much so that I found myself also
manipulating its events by elaborating its lapses, clarifying its
obscurities. I flatter myself that I have somewhat improved the tale,
which may be another way of saying that I think I have made it
representatively "American," although I'd be hard put to define
what I mean by that. There are scenes in this account that may
strike the reader as fantastic or melodramatic, or, more often,
absurdly convenient to the unfolding needs or desires of the people
involved. These incidents are sometimes, but by no means always,

my inventions; many are details given me by my "witnesses." Which is not to say that they are not *their* inventions. At one point, I considered employing a simple gimmick whereby I could differentiate, for the reader, those elements of the story given me by others from those I invented or adorned. But this, or so I thought, would needlessly clutter the narrative with literary impedimenta.

It may be useful to remark that these events occurred in 1960, and while the specific nuances of feeling manifested by the "characters," let me call them, might well manifest themselves in our postmodern era of knowingness, of amateurish license, it's unlikely. Our time seems too overtly self-congratulatory, righteous and fretful and worriedly concerned not only that "hip" things must be *known*, but that the responses to knowing these "hip" things be the correct ones. So: 1960, March, to be precise.

Let's put the center of events in a publishing house or advertising agency or public-relations company. Some business on the East Side in the Forties or Fifties. We have, working in this business, two young men, Campbell and Nick. Both are just short of thirty, both married about five or six years (although Nick and his wife are newly separated), both waiting, although they of course do not know this, for the sixties to take up and complete the bloody job begun in 1936 in Spain. They were living, that is, in the odd social somnambulism that was later thought, perhaps predictably, to be a cultural "ferment."

Nick worked for Campbell in a small but important department of the firm, but after a time, since they were both given to and comfortable with collaboration, they began to function as equals, and so they thought of themselves. They were wholly different—in family, background, education, upbringing, class, and in their tastes in music and clothes, in their speech, in everything that is established by family and background and class, etc., etc., or by opposition—of the right sort—to them. Campbell was a "child of privilege," a faded phrase, of course, much like the genteel but spent "man of slender means," which latter he also nicely was. That is to say that Campbell's family at this point had little of the wealth it had once enjoyed, and that their name was its gallant but inadequate substitute. Things had become even harder when his mother and father divorced, soon after Campbell's twelfth birthday, for his apparently scatterbrain mother had no money of her own, and his father's generous settlement on her had been squandered on clothes and jewelry and many ga-ga trips to God knows where; and his alimony payments were far less than what his mother needed to live as she wished—or, as she thought of it, deserved—to live. Campbell's expenses had been "taken care of," he'd gone from Andover to Princeton, after which his father's finances became unaccountably arcane and subterranean, almost, so his attorney argued, nonexistent. Soon after Princeton, Campbell had married a young Englishwoman, Faith, who was, supposedly, an heiress to a huge ale-and-stout fortune, that of a company old and profitable enough to have had presented to its founding Welsh family the trappings, raiment, and decorations of the elite. This fortune turned out to be a fable, but at the time of the story I relate, Campbell didn't know this; nor, for that matter, did Faith. How hopeful and wistful they must have been in their fresh young marriage, thinking but not daring to think of the wonderfully corrupting fortune that awaited them. It occurs to me that these fantasy monies might have influenced, in some tangential, "mysterious" way, Campbell's—and perhaps Faith's—behavior in the events that were soon to develop; but there's no way of knowing, of course.

Perhaps the best way to present Nick is to comment on his wonderment, an amused wonderment, at Campbell's elegant shabbiness, which Nick originally took as a sign of what one might call sartorial dumbness. Campbell's jackets, for instance, were out of style, as Nick thought of style, threadbare, battered, rumpled, and none too clean; and his beautiful oxford shirts, ten years old at least, although perfectly laundered, were faded and frayed at the cuffs. His English shoes, repaired and repaired again, and polished innumerable times to a glovelike hand, were as strange to Nick as was his hair, always shaggy and seemingly combed in great haste; and his ties were carelessly knotted and slightly askew. Nick, of course, had no notion or experience of these persistent prep-school affectations, in place so long that they no longer seemed affectations but laws, cultural truths, the regulations of an Episcopalian God. Nick, nobody's fool, as they say, quickly came to realize that Campbell had chosen this "look," which made him, to Nick, an eccentric, or perhaps an exotic.

There's little point in giving much of Nick's background; we may assume that it was the opposite of Campbell's, i.e.; what Campbell was, Nick was not. And yet, as I've said, they worked well together, they began to like each other, and their daily discoveries of each other's quirks and oddities and cultural opinions served to strengthen their growing camaraderie. The marginalized niche in the department wherein they worked became truly theirs, their work flourished, their work was, in fact, extraordinarily good.

Rather quickly, their daily labors became pleasures to which they looked forward.

It became apparent to Nick, in the first month or two of their acquaintance—apparent and almost unbelievable—that Campbell had never been in an Automat, and had to be instructed in these restaurants' ways. He'd never eaten 15¢ hamburgers at Grant's: bloody rare miniatures topped with rings of delectably half-fried onions, nor drunk their extraordinary birch beer on tap. He'd never eaten a hot dog with mustard and onions in tomato sauce from a Sabrett cart. The 2 FOR 35¢ blended whiskey specials at Blarney Stone and White Rose saloons were a revelation to him—as indeed were the proletarian brands of booze like Kinsey Silver Label, Three Feathers, Four Roses, Fleischman's, Wilson "That's All," and Paul Jones—and he had no notion that these saloons' spreads of sliced cheese, baloney, spiced ham, cherry peppers, pickles, raw onions, coleslaw, pickled beets, crackers, bread, and mustard were free—they were *free*—to anyone who had a beer or two at the bar. What a world this was! Campbell, that is to say, evidently had no knowledge whatsoever of Manhattan west of Fifth Avenue and south of Fortieth Street. Or so Nick said as he charged Campbell with this extraordinary ignorance. He was an innocent, deposited each morning at Grand Central, to which he returned each evening to be taken back to Connecticut, or some other barely imaginable place. This is surely something of an exaggeration, and yet it is true that Nick took a consistently surprised, even charmed Campbell to the shoddy remainder bookstores and back-date magazine emporiums in and around Times Square, to Toffenetti's and Marco Polo's ("Ham 'n' Eggs Are My Game"), to the Forty-second Street Tad's

Flame Steak ($1.69!!), and to God knows how many lost, dark bars in the Forties off Broadway or Seventh Avenue, where they sat with their Rheingold drafts and talked fitfully with the battered whores and bust-out horse-players waiting for The New Day A-Comin' Tomorrow. For Campbell, these mundane comings and goings that he and Nick shared at lunch hour or after five, became romantic adventures, and Nick a knowing guide possessed of the most profoundly arcane knowledge of the city, the *actual* city.

It was no doubt true that Campbell knew little of this New York, unremarkable and workaday New York. Campbell's city was the nighttime metropolis of taxis from Grand Central or Penn Station for choreographed evenings with girls from Wellesley or Smith or Mount Holyoke, of silly rendezvous at the Plaza and the Pierre and the Biltmore for Old Fashioneds, or tables at the Blue Angel or the Le Ruban Bleu, of petrifying string quartets at Carnegie Recital Hall; and then taxis back to Grand Central or Penn Station. The specifics of such evenings may have differed from these, but the general spirit of such entertainments was unvarying. There was no other New York for Campbell, certainly not an actual New York; the boroughs, for instance, with their millions, did not quite exist. It might not be too ridiculous to guess that Campbell's city was a kind of theatrical or cinematic "event."

Campbell, then, apparently looked upon Nick as someone who would soon reveal to him the knowledge of all the wondrously, beautifully commonplace, *essential* things he had missed in his vapid life. That Nick knew how to transfer from, say, the Lex to the Fourth Avenue Local at Fourteenth Street was the commonest sort of knowledge, but to Campbell it made Nick a hero of the street.

This was, it goes without saying, daft, but no more so than the awe of those who wonder at the sophistication of the man who understands and appreciates wine or polo or bridge or antiques or baroque music. All trifling expertise, as Nick might have said had he thought or cared to say it, is as one. Campbell was even more impressed because Nick had no curiosity concerning Campbell's world. If such a world was one made manifest, so Nick seemed to make clear, by Campbell's dopey clothes and annoying accent and the chilly stories he told of "swotting" for exams and smuggling beer into dormitories, Nick was content to remain ignorant of and distant from it. He never said this to Campbell, but his polite yet fixed smile of attention was more candid than any remark might have been: a drink at the Plaza, ice cream at Rumpelmayer's, blinis and caviar at the Russian Tea Room with its *ghastly* pink napkins, none of these things were of any interest or concern to Nick. They were for other people, those who were intent on *being* something. Nick, in his stiff Crawford suits, Flagg Brothers shoes, Tie City polyester repp stripes, under his gleaming Brylcreem hair, was somehow aristocratically self-contained. This, true or not, enthralled, awed, delighted, and charmed Campbell. So their unlikely friendship developed, neither of them knowing one important thing about the other. This turned out to be a serious matter, indeed; although deeper knowledge may not have changed a single impending act or decision of theirs.

One day, after lunch, Campbell told Nick that he'd been telling Faith about him, and their lunchtime and after-work "adventures," as he had taken to calling their peregrinations, self-consciously yet delightedly. Well, they *were* adventures, at least for him, and he had made that clear to Faith. In any event, she'd very much *love* to have him as a guest up in Connecticut, and as for Campbell, it went without saying that he would be so pleased, and so on. In sum, Nick was invited for a weekend at any time, at his leisure: it was up to him to set a date. At this point, things, for Nick, become a little awkward; not only was the invitation sudden and unexpected, but Nick felt, obscurely, that he was being steered into something. Yet he and Campbell got along, did they not?, they worked well together, they were compatible: and Faith was probably terrific. So what was wrong? Nick's immediate response, had he articulated it, would have been a polite "no." For somehow behind or beneath the odd bonhomie that easily existed between the two men, was something that nagged at Nick, that made him feel uneasily like—what? A sap, maybe? He had thought, uncertainly, for some time, that Campbell's innocence and enthusiasm were manufactured, and that his astonished reactions to the mundane this and that to which Nick introduced him were spurious, that he was "putting on an act." He felt that Campbell was maybe playing him—or playing with him—for some hidden reason of his own. And now, suddenly, Faith was supposedly in a state of eager curiosity about him. "Maybe," he said. "I'll let you know—thanks."

About a week or so later, Nick had decided, despite his subtle discomfort, to accept the invitation, his objections—although they weren't really that—laid aside. That morning, by peculiar coincidence, Campbell thrust at Nick a handful of color photographs of himself and Faith on an almost empty beach. He had about him a faintly proud, uxorious air, as if he had said, "How do you like my beautiful wife?" Nick, nodding and smiling, as people will, looked through the photographs of the couple, both in swimsuits, both smiling disarming smiles. There were photos of the two of them together, embracing, mugging, wading in the surf; and shots of Campbell and Faith, each alone. She was very lovely, precisely the sort of young wife who would live, or so Nick thought, in some old New England house, no doubt one that her family had bought the young couple as a wedding gift. She was tall and slender, with a nicely formed, lithe body, long straight hair, glossy rich in the rich sun of the rich beach on which they were relaxing or "cavorting," was the odd word that came to Nick unbidden. But in one photograph, which made Nick, in quick reaction, pull his head sharply back and raise his eyes to Campbell's, then look down again, Faith stood, unsmiling, looking directly at the camera with what seemed an almost painful sexual intensity. Her hands were cupped beneath her breasts, which were half-out of her bra, in an offering. She was, Nick thought, Nick knew, offering *him* her breasts, and herself. This glaringly erotic image had been specifically made for him, of course it had. It had been posed by her and by Campbell for him! As he looked up again, Campbell, blushing to his hairline, was reaching for the pack of photographs, embarrassed, nervously laughing, reaching and saying something, saying, "Oh, *hell*, Nick, I didn't mean for that one to be—it's, you know, it's, I'm sorry. It's personal." And he took the photographs back.

All right, so Nick thought, perhaps, it's "personal," but it was in the pack, part of the group, not removed for their own pleasures or uses. He was meant to see it. Campbell's wife was audaciously offering *him* her body, he was meant to see her breasts, her sensual frown, he was meant to want her. He saw again the soft shadows that were the areolas of her nipples, she might as well have bared herself, for God's sake. Nick knew, for certain, that Campbell wanted him to fuck his wife. And what would *he* do? Watch? Nick saw her slender fingers cradling her breasts. This is what Campbell wanted, but did Nick? He decided to wait and see if a weekend visit would come up again.

It did come up again, within a day or two, accompanied by a squeeze of his arm and a kind of maudlin testimonial to Faith's expectations of his visit: Campbell was "afraid" he'd been "giving her an earful" about Nick. "Anyway," he said, "I think we could have a hell of a lot of fun." The photograph was not mentioned. Tomorrow, Nick thought, he's more than likely to bring in a picture of his wife *naked*. He didn't really believe this, nor did he by now believe that Campbell wanted him as a partner in a sexual adventure; he had come to accept Campbell's assertion that the beach picture was indeed meant to be private and to stay private. He was, or so he told himself, getting a little weird. So he decided to tell Campbell that he'd try to get up to visit on the next weekend or the one after that. On that very day, as if scripted, Campbell brought in another photograph of Faith, this one taken, he was clear on this, *especially* for Nick. There she stood, sweet and obscene, pouting, in flower-print panties and white high heels, at the side of a king-size bed, an iced drink in one hand and the other curved lightly into her crotch. Behind her was a Boston Museum of Fine Arts poster of an Odilon Redon flower painting that echoed her insubstantial underwear. "*Faith* wanted me to give you this," Campbell said. "Even though I wasn't sure, you know . . . about it." He colored slightly. "You, right?, understand?"

Nick was nonplussed, to say the very least, by this, nonplussed and silenced, but aroused and tempted as well. Still, the new image of Faith, rather than pushing Nick into inviting himself to their house, pushed him back into procrastination. He was, as remarked, tempted, but repelled as well—it was all too eager and sweaty. And to complicate and blur matters, there was no way for him to know whether Faith had any notion of Campbell's use of the photograph—of either of them. One might cynically say that Nick, at this point, could not or would not believe that this glorious woman knew that her husband was pimping her face and body, since he was half in love with this discreetly exhibitionistic phantom. It doesn't really need to be said, but the very things that aroused and inflamed Nick were those that made him apprehensive and uneasy. He was no sexual innocent, and had his fair share, as it is said, of amorous adventures. But there was something just slightly off with this particular situation, something that lay just out of sight. And yet—there was Faith, or at least her image, waiting. Am I crazy about this woman I've never seen? Yes. Is she being offered to me like a whore? Yes. Why? I don't know. Does she know or is she ignorant of her role? Who cares? So he simmered and stalled, half-witted with desire.

Campbell somewhat melodramatically pretended exasperation at Nick's delay, but he was, in truth, deeply annoyed. Nick imagined him wondering "what *else* can I do?" But within a day or two, Nick proposed a tentative date, subject to change, oh yes, for his visit. From that very moment, Campbell said nothing more about Faith, nor did he bring in any more photographs. It is, by the way, to be noted that Nick had simply kept what he thought of as the "flower girl" photograph, and it joined the beach picture—which Campbell had silently left under Nick's blotter pad—in his desk drawer. Neither of them mentioned this. Nick would, now and again, and against his better judgment, slyly look at the images that he had by now laid imaginative claim to, but Campbell pretended not to notice this. At any rate, he made no comments. As an indication of Nick's shaky state of mind at this time, it's pertinent to remark that he would not permit himself to take the photographs home, for that, he tortuously believed, would suggest the perverse. On the other hand, it had occurred to him to ask his estranged wife to accompany him on his suburban visit; or to tell her that he was in love again; or to send her copies of the photographs with an enclosed message of vile triumph. After these chimeras passed, he was half-certain that Campbell had turned him into an idiot.

Campbell, to repeat, did not mention Faith or the weekend or how lovely the cool evenings were on the lawn that looked down across dense woods to the river. He stopped "selling" the visit, and was careful not to say anything that might unsettle Nick. He had his plans, although they were more like hopes, as we'll see. He did not know, however, the extent to which Nick was by now enthralled—besotted—by the images that he had memorized. As far as Campbell knew, the photos were erotically promising to Nick, suggestive of Faith's "enlightenment," as he might have said. But Nick, following the sad, trite script that is known by heart to half the world, felt a vast, contemptuous resentment of Campbell, who not only knew the breathless delight of sleeping with this Aphrodite, he had certainly and lasciviously subjected her—this adoring and trusting woman!—to his, to *Nick's* gaze. This blithe contradiction held that Faith had bravely offered her body to the unknown yet noble Nick because she knew that she would immediately love him; but also that she was the unwilling subject of a lewd experiment that forced her modest self to be ogled and sullied by a stranger, the depraved *Nick*. He almost, but not quite, thought of Faith as the victim of "a terrible fate." You see how addled he'd become. That Campbell had been changed into a rival for his own wife's affections, her imagined sexual enthusiasms, was a notion that Nick never allowed fully to assert itself. It was—he *knew* this—absurd even to think of this woman whom he "knew" by means of two stiffly posed photographs, taken and revealed for reasons that were still obscure, and perhaps specious. Yet he could feel her breasts in his hands.

About a week or so before Nick's promised visit, Campbell's manner subtly changed. Perhaps that's putting it too decisively; it's enough to say that Nick caught him, on a half-dozen occasions, staring at the wall, an expression of wretchedness, a kind of bereft gloom, on his face. Nick stifled his anger: how dare he mope around with the beautiful and gentle Faith awaiting him on the beach, at their bedside, half-naked and shamed in the role of sexual victim that had been dishonorably urged upon her? But the coming weekend visit would remedy all, and if love had to be painfully extruded from the vulgarity that Campbell had created, that's what would, what must be done. It's quite probable that Nick, certainly, and Campbell as well, were on the edge of an imbecile eroticism. As for Faith, no one knows, or knew, with any certainty, just what she was doing—if anything—in this shabby drama. She waited, did she not?

One afternoon, glum Campbell told Nick that he and Faith had quarreled "hurtfully" a week earlier, over something that was petty and inconsequential, but which served to awaken the hidden angers and, well, disappointments in their marriage. He'd left the house, bought a pint of vodka, and driven to a little pebble beach on the river. He sat on the hood of the car, drinking and smoking, hating Faith and his marriage, his "fucking charity house," as he put it, envying Nick's separation and freedom. The rest of his story was rushed, fragmented, elliptical, and told with his face partly averted. A young man had driven up in an old coupe and parked next to Campbell's car. He looked like a college student—maybe high school. They'd talked about women and shared the vodka, and Campbell told him of the quarrel with Faith, to which the young man said that he'd just broken up with *his* girl, who was nothing but a fucking whore bitch. He opened Campbell's fly and his own, and they kissed and fondled each other, and then the young man knelt in front of Campbell and sucked him off, although Campbell said, in a whisper, "he mouthed me," while masturbating himself to climax. Then he said good-bye and smiled in the darkness— Campbell could see his teeth—and drove off. When he got in, Faith was asleep, just as well, God! What was wrong with him? He'd never tell Faith, never, he didn't think, some things just can't be told. He looked at Nick with a fake rueful grin that said "but I can tell you, can't I?" Nick shook his head in what could have been disapproval or chagrin or both.

Well. There it surely was. Campbell was letting him know, with a glancing candor, why he wanted Nick to visit. His convenient, halting tale—true or not—was a confession of his desire for Nick, who thought, with scorn, that Campbell didn't have the nerve to make a straightforward pass at him, but had to use his wife as a lure. All right, you son of a bitch! He'd *go* up to their house, he wanted Faith, didn't he?, he was beginning to dream about her. So he thought then; but later in the day, it became clear to him that Campbell would get what he had schemed to get from the beginning if he visited. That would never do! Rather than fend off Campbell, or worse, listen to him speak of his desire and devotion, for an entire weekend, he would give up Faith. So crazed was he that he actually *thought* this—that he would "give up"—*give up!*—a woman who existed only in Campbell's occasional remarks and two small images. He wasn't so demented, though, as to think that she would be crushed by his sacrifice.

On that Friday, he said that he'd have to cancel the weekend, something about his goddamned wife and her shyster lawyer and a division of things that they'd bought and been given for their apartment, they had to meet and talk and do this and that and this and that; on and on he blathered hysterically, while Campbell listened in silence.

Now that this crisis, if it may be called that, had been temporarily resolved, or shelved, a hint of normality was restored to their relationship. It was not as it had been, and they most often ate lunch separately, while their after-five strolls and drinks became rare. All references to a weekend in Connecticut disappeared from their conversation, and Faith may as well have never lived. In the careful politeness of mutual embarrassment, they silently conspired to pretend that no invitation had ever been made to "the Campbells'," or, if one had, that it could not have been "seriously entertained," as they say. For that matter, there were no photographs of Faith in existence, certainly not in Nick's desk drawer. Perhaps there was no Faith, no wife at all. Their friendship, of course, was over, and though they still worked well together, they had few conversations that were not professional or centered on public events. So the late spring and summer passed.

In late September, Nick told Campbell, in his capacity as Nick's superior, that he'd received a job offer from a firm in Chicago, and that he'd accepted. His divorce was almost settled, the final decree a week or so away, and, well, he was giving his two weeks' notice. There may truly have been a job in Chicago, but it's not important. It's possible that Campbell began to say, "*What* job?!," but that, too, is unimportant. His face, despite a castor-oil smile so false as to be grotesque, went bone-white, so that he looked, for a few seconds, like a corpse, or, more hideously, like a theatrical version of a corpse. When there was but a week left until Nick's departure, they managed to have a celebratory farewell lunch at a little bar that served sandwiches and hamburgers to the midday office drunks. It was, not surprisingly, a disaster, unleavened by office gossip or old jokes. Just as they were leaving, Campbell, riding on three martinis and a few beers, demanded that Nick return the "very very personal" photographs of his wife. He seemed angrily humiliated, as if Nick had inveigled him into showing him the photographs, as if he had been blackmailed. In the office, Nick gave him the pictures and Campbell roughly folded them in two and stuck them into the pages of a paperback on his desk. "This is a stupid rotten novel!" he said, belligerent and put upon.

On Nick's last day, he packed up his few things and said that he'd be leaving a little early, what the hell. Campbell got up from his desk as if drunk—perhaps he was drunk—his face pulled into a sneer, and half-lurched, half-lunged at Nick to hold him by the forearms, the shoebox with its odds and ends held in Nick's hands awkwardly between them. He didn't look at Nick but stiffly bent forward and tried to kiss his mouth, missing but wetting his chin. His eyes were wide and slightly out of focus. Nick stepped away from him and said something like "Come *on*, Campbell!," and walked out of the office and to the elevators. Campbell was a few steps behind him and when he reached Nick he motioned to the stairwell. "Please," he said. "Just a . . . please?" Nick, absurdly, looked at his watch, then followed Campbell into the stairwell, where he had slouched against a wall, looking at his shoes. Then, as if he had rehearsed, which he may well have done, Campbell begged Nick not to leave just yet, to come and stay with him—and with Faith—and with this articulation of his wife's name he looked into Nick's face and grinned. He knew, he said, he knew that Nick liked, well, was *attracted* to Faith, the photos, he said, those pictures of her. Then he stopped, simply defeated. "I love you," he said. "I love you." He began to wail very quietly, his hands folded high on his chest in a classic yet ridiculous pose of misery and loss. Nick's face was flushed with anger and pity and, who can tell, perhaps with desire. "I love you, I love *you!*" Campbell said, blubbering now, and he put his arms clumsily around Nick's waist just as the door opened and a janitor, carrying a bucket and mop, stepped onto the landing. Momentarily taken aback by the sight of these two flustered young men, he stood uncertainly, then, as they pulled apart, realized what he was seeing, and smiled a knowing smile, a smile that said he understood and that it was all right with him.

GORGIAS

≈ *Invisible Door*

I once had a friend, a dear friend, who, I believed, or was led to believe, had betrayed me, profoundly and completely. Even now, years later, I can't bring myself to make known the circumstances, the facts, as I then perceived them to be, of this betrayal. That these circumstances, these facts, were, I discovered, malicious inventions created by another man for his own mysterious reasons, did not remedy or ameliorate the estrangement and bad feeling they—no matter how preposterous—created between me and my friend; his putative betrayal, that is, might as well have been actual. The notion that time heals or erases such aberrations and their dolorous effects has not, in my experience, been the case; on the contrary, time makes concrete and salient all initial agonies, missteps, mis-understandings, and bitterness. It takes a spectacularly willful, almost herculean courage to destroy, even to soften these ugly pet-rifactions, after which, and at best, there is nothing left of feeling but rubble. It is better to interiorize the waste and regret than to attempt its amelioration. But I don't want to get ahead of myself.

The third party I've mentioned, the malign, the famous meddler who stalks through so many shabby stories, had been a partner of mine and my friend in a small, ultimately unsuccessful specialty-printing business we had begun together—although the failure of the business was not, I'm fairly sure, a factor in the creation of his elaborate system of lies, painstakingly developed to convince me of my friend's perfidy. It's enough to say that he did his work well, and had, I suppose, the pleasure of seeing my friend and me sundered, quite wrenchingly disjointed in mutual anger and bewilderment. Friendships that collapse in this way attain to a kind of mean per-fection, a hateful balance of irreconcilable integers, each of which is, or most certainly becomes, a treasured wound. I was hurt, sur-prised, and puzzled by the enormity of my friend's acts; he was astonished by my abrupt decision to end our friendship. My action and his reaction were gestures sadly predicated on a corrupt syllo-gism, the major premise of which might have been phrased: "If a man I have no reason to trust tells me that a friend has betrayed me, I'll sever all ties with the friend."

The facts, as I have called them, or what I then thought to be the facts, and the subtle variations of this betrayal, were made avail-able to me over a period of perhaps a month and a half by my inde-fatigable guide to—to what? Cleanliness, let's say, an ethical, even moral cleanliness. "Look at this evidence," he might as well have said, "look at these dispiriting, tawdry documents. *Soon all will be revealed!* And afterward, you'll rid yourself of this false friend, and be clean!" He said, of course, nothing like this, but I'm afraid that I said something very like it to myself. With each piece of *evidence,* of *proof,* that my altruistic "assistant" brought me, I became more deliciously righteous, more insulted, more put upon and victimized. It's now obvious that my need, my desire, perhaps, to be an object of perverse and malicious acts was the base reason for my hunger for more and more *documentation* of my friend's cruel schemes. There was, if truth be told (I use the phrase in full awareness of its pitiful irony), plenty of damning material, early on, for me to accuse and then judge my friend, but I began to enjoy the accumulation of his misdeeds, the sweet pang of the badly used, the moral eroticism of a vast self-pity.

I at last decided that I had enough information (I have no recollection of how I came to this conclusion), and I'd already poked and rubbed at my ego's scratch until it was red and swollen. It so turned out that at about the same time that I'd decided to confront my friend, my false, treacherous, vile friend!, he and his wife had just separated. That is, his wife had left him for a man whom she, and, to a lesser extent, her husband, had known in college, I believe. These events occurred some forty years ago, so my memory is not wholly to be trusted. This man had re-entered their lives so as to "learn how to live," or so I understand him to have phrased it. Learn how to live! There's nothing to say to that. He had apparently known of the couple's marriage, its stability, love, mutual kindness, its happy child—its composure, I suppose, will cover it nicely. And so he sidled into their lives, as old peripheral acquaintances will do, as an unhappy, even miserable supplicant. Yes, he wanted them to teach him "how to live." Nice work, as the old song says, if you can get it. I know that all of this sounds absurd, much too good to be true, as they say, too maudlin, too Hollywood, if it is not affected to say so. I heard this story, with its tellers' predictable variations, over the years, not that any of it mattered to me. It hadn't mattered to me when it first happened, when the loving couple decided to help the sad old pal. That my friend was soon cuckolded by this wheedling incubus and then deserted by his true-blue wife, who would later make his visitation rights anent the child a grinding humiliation, so I understand, was fine by me, fine. Just when he came to me for succor, I suppose I might call it, I was all ready with my dossier. I seem to recall, in fact, that I was somewhat annoyed that his wife was unfaithful to him with only this one man. On the other hand, *he* was a perfectly shameful choice. So that was fine.

It was painful to me for a long time to think of my friend's specific reaction to my charges, and so I slowly forgot what it was like. It's simply gone from my mind, lying in fragments among all the other repressed and doubly repressed and wholly distorted junk of my life. The schism affected me, I've come to admit, in the most thorough way, setting me on a course which has demanded (if that's not too strong a word) that I have neither wife nor children, that I be a neglectful son, a distant, sullen, cold man with no friends worthy of the name, without even the ephemeral human connections that pass for friendships here in the San Francisco Bay Area, where I've lived alone for some twenty years. It's the ideally blank place for me, with its grinning populace and its idiot sense of privilege, its lush flowers, dead grass, and year-round air pollution—the worst of which is happily called "save the air days"—and its "communities" with no sidewalks or visible populations. And then there are the millions and millions of cars, blessed cars that allow us all to avoid each other completely as we go and return, go and return, over and over. It is my country, indeed.

I don't recall precisely when I discovered that the proofs of my friend's betrayal were, in essence, distortions, manufactures, subtle as well as crude lies. This is not to say that my "informant" was a genius of deception. Sadly enough, although sadly is hardly the word—perhaps monstrously is more to the point—the shoddiness of the materials were virtually apparent to me all the time I was collecting them. So that I was not surprised to be brought face to face with the irrefutable *fact* of their falsity. It's the cheapest psychology to say that it is obvious that I wanted to hurt my friend and to smash our friendship, but that I did so with such devious ruthlessness astounds me even now. I find it, perhaps oddly, somewhat admirable.

I have not, as I think I've implied, attempted to "patch things up" with my friend. What would be the point? And what would I say? "I was wrong, and I was always wrong, and I knew that I was wrong. However!" And then there is the fact that I was exasperated, furious, even, with my friend, when I had incontrovertible proof that all my allegations against him were false. He seemed to me, then, as he still does, I'm afraid, so weak, so pitiful, so *inconsequential*, unable to have committed the sins I'd accused him of. Good Christ! He'd had no courage at all, he'd done *nothing*, not one thing that I'd—I don't know how to say this—that I'd wanted him to have done, perhaps. How could I ask him to forgive me, when I couldn't forgive his intolerable innocence, his insufferable friendship? He was much, oh much less than the perfidious monster I'd longed for him to be. It was too much to ask of me that I invite him into my life, such as it is, again; or that I ask to enter his. It is too much, for that matter, to ask anything of me.

Recently, I have come to see that I had been waiting, all those many years ago, waiting for I really don't know how long, for an invisible door I'd yearned to discover, to open, so that I could walk through it and away from life, for good and all.

⬯ *The Diary*

A man I once knew somewhat casually married a woman because she reminded him of another woman he had earlier wanted to, had, in fact, planned to marry, but did not, for reasons that, as he once remarked, "are best forgotten." He loved the woman he ultimately married, but after a few years, this was no longer the case. Forgive me for the triteness of this situation, which is as "common," as my mother used to say, "as dirt," although she was usually speaking of people of whom she disapproved, and they were, believe me, many. For the sake of candor, I should mention that my mother disapproved of the man I once knew and his wife, and I don't doubt that she would have disapproved of the woman he did not marry, as well. I may have been influenced in my own opinions of these people because of this. Or perhaps not. It is very hard for a man to think straight about his mother, which may be why so much psychoanalysis never quite works. With honesty and candor and as much accuracy as he can command from his neurotic mind, the analysand reveals all; but that *all* is, of needs, attenuated, twisted, and fictionalized. If and when the analyst finally peels away the sincere and intricately fabricated layers to get to what he and his patient agree is the truth, they've usually found, as Oscar Levant famously said of Hollywood, "the real tinsel underneath." But this is frivolous digression.

My friend and I met one night, ten years or so into his marriage, over drinks in a bar we had regularly patronized at a time when both of us worked for the same publisher, in its unglamorous school department, a claustrophobic section of the house devoted to satisfying the medieval textbook-adoption requirements of, for the most part, the State of Texas. It was there that I learned that Texas more or less fed the entire company, and that we had a vice president whose job was, essentially, to fish and play golf with the members of the textbook-adoptions board. I find it pleasant to recall these things when I read of publishers and editors speaking of their devotion to good letters.

The bar was off Madison Avenue in the Forties, a neighborhood that has always unaccountably made me feel successful, a harmless delusion. We sat in the back room and ordered martinis, then he abruptly told me that his marriage seemed to be, that it really, more or less, might be, probably, well, *was,* in serious trouble. I didn't care one way or another, for I had come to realize that my mother's notion of this man and his insubstantial snob of a wife had become mine, I really don't know how, and even though my mother had been dead for almost four years. I've neglected to mention that my mother once met this couple in a restaurant. They were not at their best, so my mother let me know. It turned out, not surprisingly, that his marriage was "in serious trouble," because of his adulterous mooning over a young woman in the office of the company he now worked for as something called a "marketing-systems analyst," a term dismal enough to bewitch an academic. It also came out that he had been *driven* to this absurd behavior (this was his version of the story; I never heard his wife's, nor did I want to) because of —what a surprise!—his wife. She, paralyzed with ennui in her job as a legal secretary in a tort mill, after having been equally paralyzed during her brief tenure as what I had been told she called a "gold-plated housewife" (with the implication that she was much too gifted to scrub the toilet), had become a devoted follower of a "psychic enabling" discipline, a combination of Zen, Hinduism, evangelical something or other, and nature in all its glorious something or other. As we began our fourth martinis, I found out, from my sad friend, that the discipline involved some brilliant claptrap that had to do with "energy vortices," access to which would open devotees the path to self-knowledge or self-realization or self-acceptance, or maybe it was self-love or self-actualization—whatever, it insisted on rapt attention to one's inimitable *Being*. It was, no doubt, another polished grift, happily based on the surety that the most petty, vapid, selfish, envious, and useless people can be convinced that they live lives of real importance and consequence, are thinkers of subtly finespun thoughts, and, most importantly, *deserve* to be happy.

I was by now, as you might imagine, stupefied by this soap opera of love gone awry, of love locked out in all the cold and rain, as Max Kester's 1933 lyric remarked, in an aberrant flaring of talent never revealed by Max again, who, clearly, never realized himself. I may have even sung the opening line to my friend, a gin-smeary grin on my face, but probably not; he was one of the troops who pretended never to have *heard* a popular song, his musical tastes running to what has come to be known as, God help us, "easy jazz." Or maybe it's "easy-listening jazz." I wanted to tell him that he was boring me to fucking death, but in the irritation of my impatience, I told him that he should start keeping a diary, in which he could make up lies about his *wife's* behavior, making it all up, making up anything, writing down anything, an-y thing!, that came into his head. Then, after he had thirty or forty pages he could, I suggested, leave the diary where his wife could find it. She'd read it, I told him, because of her suspicions concerning his dalliance with the office siren. Right? Sure! Then, after she'd read his crackpot fantasies, lies, ramblings, maybe, just maybe, in amazed disgust, she'd let him "live life," as he probably liked to say, with, of course, suitable hambone emphasis. I did not, as I remember, have to spell out that by "living life," I meant carefree carrying-on with the assistant assistant. My point, as I recall, was that his wife might think him too weird to annoy with the domestic. In effect, he'd lie his way to freedom. He seemed to like this idea, but my memory of the evening is, understandably, hazy. All I clearly remember after my grotesque suggestion is his maudlin description of Ms. Cubicle's legs as "like a fawn's." Oh Jesus.

About six months later, he unexpectedly called me up to thank me for my advice of that sodden evening, which advice, he wanted me to know, he had taken. I had all but completely forgotten about this boneheaded "plan," and when he refreshed my memory of it (my hesitant conversation, designed to make him tell me what I'd forgotten, was mistaken by him, as I'd hoped, for unassuming, good-guy modesty), I laughed a quiet, friendly laugh, and waited for him to get off the phone. But he thanked me again, and added that his marriage was better than ever, stronger and more assured, loving, fulfilling, wonderfully this and thrillingly that, and that he, his blossoming wife, and the wonderfully giving young woman from the office were together every weekend, sometimes even more often. For "marvelous interludes" (he said this). These "interludes" were "psychic springboards" to self-realization, which led to humble introspection and knowledge, even if imperfect, of self. I wanted to reach through the phone to strangle him, but I laughed warmly, and eased out of the conversation, but not before he said that he'd call me again, and I said *wonderful!* The impossible bastard!

I've lost touch with this adventurous soul, thank God, but I can surmise (one of my mother's favorite words) that my friend's wife did indeed find the diary where he'd left it—probably on the kitchen sink!—read it to discover intelligence about her young rival, and then recognized herself as surely as if she'd written the pages, found herself in her husband's improbable, even neurotic descriptions, as incontrovertibly as if he had prepared a factual report for a detective agency. She saw, or so I imagine, in this unreal woman, this phantom, her real self. And she was moved and even flattered by his acute attention to detail, his acumen, his understanding, his analysis of her many failings. Most tellingly, she wept at his magnanimity in forgiving her for the sins she had never committed. She found, that is, in the pages of that bogus notebook, an instance of her husband's amazing capacity for empathy, sympathy, and compassion; and noted, delightedly, his growth toward a profound self-awareness and self-knowledge. And so they'd fallen in, well, love, more or less, all over again. Common as dirt.

≈ *Bud Powell*

This is a story that was told to me by a man I once worked with as part of a location-and-preparation team at an advertising agency. I repeat it, changing nothing in the way of details, and leaving out what seems to me to be the extraneous, the hyperbolic, and the contradictory. I suppose I might say I've made the story my own. It should be kept in mind that these events took place in the late fifties, which suggests, perhaps, that nothing much changes in the goings on between men and women.

A young man and the young wife of a friend of his found themselves—a nice, neutral phrase, I think—drunkenly dancing in the middle of a crowded, noisy, drunken party on Riverside Drive. This man's wife and this woman's husband were also at the party, somewhere in the sweaty clamor of the apartment. The dancers danced, let's assume, into a dark bedroom, where they instantly gave in to their lusts. Emerging twenty minutes later, they became part of the human furniture of the party again, with no one, as they say, the wiser.

Save that the woman, for obscure reasons of her own, decided to tell her husband of her adventure with his friend. Why she did this is anybody's guess; perhaps it is to be classed with the bitter mystery Yeats ascribes to love. Her husband, in a concupiscent, irrational rage, struck her, raped her, and then left the house, weeping and cursing. Three days later, in a studio apartment in Chelsea, wherein lived a restaurant hostess and her high-school teacher boyfriend—the latter an old friend of the husband's—he drank a quart of vodka and cut his wrists with a penknife, a table knife, and a beer-can opener, which, I just now recall, used to be called a "church key." Those were the days. He came to in

Bellevue's psychiatric ward; more precisely, on a gurney in a corridor of the ward, his lacerations nicely dressed, and with a savage hangover. He felt like a complete fool, and why not? There can be little more humiliating than a failed suicide. When he was finally interviewed by a staff psychiatrist, who spoke, as if chosen to play the stereotype, little English, and asked *how do you feel?*, he said that he felt fine. The psychiatrist noted that he was out of touch with reality, and perhaps manic-depressive (the term used in those innocent, benighted days). A few days later, and to the same question, put to him by another psychiatrist, who was kind enough to offer him a cigarette, he answered, in an excess of candor, *terrible*, and it was noted that he was clinically depressed, and suicidal. Well, he probably was.

They prepared "the papers," or whatever it is they do, to have him sent to Pilgrim State, got in touch with his wife (again, I assume), and put him into a locked ward, where he realized, after a day, that his silent ward mate, in the next bed, was Bud Powell. Bud Powell! Is it possible, he may have thought, that this is *the* Bud Powell? The great Bud Powell? He looked like Bud, although he was emaciated, and his eyes were clouded over and filled with bitter sadness.

The next day, after they'd been given their medication, he asked him, he almost shouted in his nervousness, his question: "Are you Bud Powell? The jazz, the piano, jazz piano?" And Bud said: "I used to be, but I don't think I am anymore. They don't have a piano, you dig?" That's all he said, and the next day he was transferred or released.

The husband, a week or so later, was committed, after a hearing at which his wife testified, if that's the correct word, and then signed him over to Pilgrim State. He spent a period of almost eleven months there, and was then released, no longer a danger to himself or others, as the phrase goes. He returned to his wife, who pretended that nothing had happened between the eve of the party and the present, and that he was a new acquaintance of limited intelligence. She had a lover now, not, of course, the friend who'd been with her in the dark bedroom, but one of her husband's ex-co-workers, a rather pale, somehow flimsy-looking man, with a curious and feverishly enraged interest in the Hungarian uprising and its subsequent suppression by Soviet armor: this is apparently all that anybody had ever really noticed about him. He would soon take over his father's extremely successful and lucrative bathroom-furnishings business, but at the time, he was working as a reinsurance clerk at the Fidelity and Casualty Insurance Company on Maiden Lane. Fidelity and casualty! That's very neat.

This arrangement was all right with the husband, or at least he had nothing to say about it. He wondered, actually, so I understand, what in God's name he had *ever* seen in this taut, smirking woman, who had become falsely obsessed, falsely, mind you, with classic Mexican cuisine while he'd been away at "the farm," as he always smilingly said. He was sure that he was stable, and patiently awaited each weekend, when his wife and the reinsurance clerk would go away on what she called "a jaunt" for two, sometimes three days, and leave him alone. He was, if not happy, no more miserable than many. I understand that all three of these people are dead now, and so, of course, is Bud.

IN LOVELAND

I have attempted to tell this story many times over the past years, the past decades, for that matter. I've not been able to bring it off, for I've never been able to invent—inhabit, perhaps—the proper narrational attitude. I begin to invent plausible situations that soon falsify everything, or unlikely situations that, just as soon, parody everything. I have even, at times, tried to tell the undecorated truth, which attempts virtually clang with mendacity, a callow sort of mendacity that wishes to be recognized as such, and so forgiven. I might call it the mendacity of youth, although I'm not at all certain how youth is currently defined.

At that time, my wife and I were living behind a barber shop, in a small studio apartment that was reached by means of a long, narrow corridor that seemed to belong to the barber shop, I don't quite know how. The apartment, too, seemed more like an adjunct to the shop than it did an entity unto itself, and, perhaps because of this, I hated it. My wife was a very small woman, I might say a tiny woman, but her body was arrestingly erotic. It should have looked, given her size, like a child's body, but it did not: she was a kind of aphrodisiacal miniature, a striking doll. Whenever she, alone, approached the corridor entranceway from the street, the scum congregated on the sidewalk, in a crass parody of the manly chorus boys in the musical comedies of the era, would ogle her, fondle themselves, make sucking and kissing noises, and proclaim what they'd like to do to her. She invariably insisted that they never offended her and I chose to believe her. I really didn't care one way or another: those fools had no sense of her actuality, and I suspect that her calm, dispassionate gaze forced them to see themselves for the curious filth it suggested they were.

Our bed dominated the apartment, and was what, I later discovered, is called queen-sized, a term that almost shines with poignancy. This bed had a presence beyond its fact, probably because of something so mundane as its size relative to the total floor space of the room. It served my purposes, such as they were then, to think of the bed as having some special quality, as more than it was, as a symbol, in fact. As a symbol for *what*, I had no idea. But I wanted to write, more precisely, I wanted to be thought of as a writer, and I had started many stories having to do with the power that the bed exerted over various darkly tragic sagas, whose whining narrators were more unhappy and misunderstood, more irrevocably doomed than is, even melodramatically, possible. The desire to add some more stupid clutter to the clutter of the vacuous world is virtually unquenchable. Our marriage was, at this point, in the early stages of irreversible decay. My wife and I often talked for hours about our problems, our refined problems, sure that we were facing them honestly—a favorite word—sure that although they were unique, they were certainly solvable. We wasted a great deal of time in these thoughtful, respectful, futile colloquies. "Irreversible decay" is a phrase that I permit to stand as a reminder of its use in the first sentence of one of my early stories, "The Bower of Bliss." The sentence read, "Although Amanda and I did not know it, the mutually ecstatic shudder that put period to our lovemaking on that breathless midsummer night, was the first subtle tremor of the irreversible decay that had infected our perhaps too bright union." "Ecstatic shudder," "subtle tremor," "too bright union"! Even "Amanda" proceeds from the abyss of machine fiction. I couldn't write because I so wanted to impress people with the fact that my writing revealed a knowledge of writing. I was, I think, unaware of this.

Our marriage was, indeed, falling apart, for many reasons, none of which is worth commenting on, that is to say, any reason might do. We had been married for almost five years, and my wife was allowing, or helping, perhaps, her boredom and restlessness to surface when and how it pleased. Had she been anything other than glumly dissatisfied, I might have been disturbed. As it was, her quiet and dazed contempt, her wayward anomie, passed right by me, as the phrase has it. I had no way of combating it, or her, anyway, assuming that I noticed. I had no idea *what* to do—assuming that I noticed. All this took place in the benighted days before husbands were sensitive to their wives' needs, as they are now. In any event, I began dreading the walk down the corridor, the sight of my wife sprawled on the bed—the symbolic bed—reading, it seemed to me, always, *The Complete Short Stories of Mark Twain.* That can't be so, but since the title has, so to speak, declared itself, let it stand. I hated to see her there, her perfect little body, her small feet, her blond hair in a carelessly provocative upsweep, her toreador pants defining her thighs and buttocks and softly bulging pudenda. It was a kind of shabby ordeal.

She was too complete and complacent in her tiny model of a body, reading, or not reading, or just there, doing anything, I don't know. Occasionally, I'd find her naked, or half-naked, after a shower, and this was worse: her womanly parts looked as if they'd been supplied her, as if she'd rented them at a costume shop. It was always hard for me to believe that her breasts were teacup-size, that her dirty-blond wedge of pubic hair was not even the size of a business card. Who was this woman?

We had been married almost five years earlier, after knowing each other for fifteen months. At the time we met, she was the best friend of a woman that I had been planning to marry, but who had been seduced, a week before we were to have been engaged, by *my* best friend, whom she was, eventually, to marry. This is neither here nor there, although I believe that their marriage is quite successful. I realize, as I write this, that I have no way of knowing this: the last I heard from them, via a pretentious Christmas card, was that they were living in one of the smug, self-congratulatory towns of the San Francisco Bay Area.

All I clearly remember of my earlier love is that she often liked to be fully dressed when we fucked—she had what may be characterized as a masculine pornographic imagination. I draw no moral from this penchant, but do think of it, from time to time, with a pang of lewd nostalgia, as perfectly befits the dirty old man I have all but become. Sometimes she even, marvelously, wore a hat. It was, she said, like being fucked by somebody she'd bumped into on the street or the subway. And so it was. I say, "all I clearly remember," but that is, of course, only an expression. I remember many, oh, many things about her, for instance, the oddly asymmetrical v of her pubic hair. She was extremely attractive, and I can't really blame my old friend for his loss of control. I blame her, of course, because a woman is more than just—more than just what? I know nothing about women. I remember things like hats.

Perhaps my wife and I were propelled or pushed or excited into marriage because of her mishap, the accident that she suffered shortly prior to our wedding: she somehow slipped and then fell down a flight of subway stairs, cutting, bruising, and very badly abrading one side of her face. I can't clarify what I mean when I say "excited into marriage," but the accident had the effect of making us agree to move the wedding date up by about a month, as if, somehow, we had to marry while she bore this painful blazon. I later considered writing about this injury and the huge scab that asserted itself as its astonishing manifestation, for it seemed—it still seems—a symbol of our disastrous marriage. It was not, any more than the bed was, but the idea that I might force it into one made me feel like a writer. That I even considered a narrative flowering from the fact of her wound was, finally, enough. I never wrote a word.

Her scab covered the left side of her face from jaw to hairline in a grim parody of deformation. There was about it, at once, a sense of the overwhelmingly repulsive and the breathlessly desirable, much in the same way that the human sex organs are hideously attractive. I can't say that I thought this at the time, but I do seem to recall becoming aroused during the ceremony—so much so that my vows came in troubled quaverings. When we kissed to seal our compact, I thought that I might burst into ragged, tense laughter. She smiled at me, one side of her mouth held immobile by the thick scab: I wanted to fuck us into hysteria, there, in the minister's study, before the wedding guests. Later, at the small reception given for us at her mother's house, we found ourselves together in the kitchen, and I vulgarly put her hand on the hard lump in my trousers and then bent to lick her scabbed face. She rubbed me, flushed and quivering, and then, immediately, she was, at a sound from the doorway, in front of the refrigerator, into which she stared. I could see her legs trembling from her thighs to the doll-sized white heels she had on. I leaned against a table and smiled brilliantly at the doorway, amazed at the ruttishness that possessed me. It was her—and my—bitch friend, who looked at us and raised her eyebrows. As if she knew what we knew! As if she could. We glared insanely at her.

But it is not my intention to tell the story of our wedding and the twisted, dreamlike interlude of our honeymoon and first months together. It may well be that the fact of this period has, in the past, asserted itself so strongly that I've lost, again and again, the impetus to tell the *real* story, if you will. Or perhaps I have been distracted by my wife's injury, by my accumulative reimaginings of its reality, its domination of her fine-drawn face, the way I touched it. My consistent, predictable arousal when clutched by these drifting memories and half-memories, these semi-fantasies, always seemed to point toward the necessity of the "wedding story" or the "honeymoon story." This, or these, stories will never be told, but their seeming demands always precluded my telling any story: this story.

I should, however, put the phenomenon of my wife's injury—and the oddly perverse timing of the accident that caused it—to rest, of a sort, by speaking, candidly, of my feelings, as I now construe them to have been, at the time. This can, admittedly, be a supremely inexact business, but I see no way of ignoring it. It is quite possible that my past failures to complete this story have had to do with my avoidance of the centrality of this compelling wound, this fabulous wound. It has always been an assertive image, one that threatens all the other elements of my tale. But to avoid it has always meant to be driven into the faltering discourse that ends in silence.

My wife's scab was the result, as I've said, of a terrible fall down the stairs of the local subway station, although I never quite believed that the fall was accidental. For a long time, I thought that she had thrown herself down the stairs in a seizure of misery, or even despair, at the prospect of our impending marriage. I took, as may well be imagined, little pleasure in thinking this. Later, I began to believe, groundlessly, that her fall was the unexpected and unintended outcome of a subtle sadomasochistic adventure gone awry. I was possessed of an unshakable sense of the truth of this fancy, of its actuality, and spent many hours, many many hours, trying to picture the partner with whom she had been so thrillingly involved.

This spectacularly disfiguring scab that thickly encrusted the left side of her face from hairline to eyebrow, thence from cheekbone to lower jaw, had the uncanny effect, although I have vacillated and hedged concerning this for years, of making me doubt my wife's identity. Not in any melodramatic or mystical or metaphysical sense, reverberant with implications of mystery and anima, but in the simplest and most pedestrian sense, so to speak: the scab was for me a mask that concealed half of her face, a half whose contours I could no longer bring to mind. This mask was all the more efficacious since the part of her fact not affected wore precisely the innocently wanton expression that was habitual to her, a misleading expression, and one that often duped me into humiliating behavior.

The other aspect of the scab, one that I have already adumbrated, was its sexuality: it possessed an erotic component strong enough to make me virtually stupid with desire. Its surface glistened in the way my wife's nylon stockings glistened, and as, too, did her labia. Over and again I was moved by the perverse desire to use the small and perfect architecture of her broken face as I did her sex. To put it crudely, I wanted, for as long as she wore that crusted domino, to fuck it. I remember that my terrific desire made me weak with wonderful fear, and placed a cold, stone-like nausea just below my breastbone. Yet as my desire increased, my nausea lessened, my intoxicated self-disgust and sexual terror were smoothly transcended by what I thought of as the sacramental purity of my undeviating lust. I even felt, and this was indeed so, complacently proud of myself for finding my damaged bride still desirable, for overlooking this egregious flaw in her beauty, for being so understanding. And all the while that I blithely misled myself, my genitals ached with desire: I could not wait to marry this imperfect Venus so that I could have her with me day and night. What did I tell her, what could I have told her? I can't believe that I told her of my distorted lust, but I know that I did. I waited, however, until her scab had been replaced by new, creamy skin, and until our marriage had been pushed, as marriages are, now here and now there, by whatever we took love to be. My confession was an act of meaningless courage that, perhaps, disgusted her.

After our honeymoon, I got a job, not worth describing, as a clerk in a midtown office, and we moved from our gloomy first apartment to the one behind the barber shop. I began to write at night and on the weekends, and to publish occasionally in little magazines. I soon met, as one might expect, other young writers or would-be writers, those who could be writers had they the time, husbands and wives and lovers of these people, and many others. They began—we began—hesitantly at first and then with increasing confidence, to use our apartment as a gathering place, and hardly a weekend, and then hardly an evening passed that did not discover one or more people at our table or bedded down on the floor, trading small-time literary gossip and tales of academic backbiting for beef stew or spaghetti or bean soup and a few cans of beer. It is emotionally numbing for me to acknowledge, to admit, that I never thought of these perpetual visitors as anything other than legitimate, as the cream of the tottering fifties. We made fun, we actually, good Christ, made fun of other people! How we waited for things to happen, successful things, adventures and journeys and relocations to exotic locales, events that would soon metamorphose us into the glittering figures that we knew we were beneath our unfashionable and superior shabbiness. We were, certainly, but deadbeats, impotent, arrogant, lazy, and headed toward peripherally creative jobs in public relations and advertising and publishing, we were perfect American clichés, too good for mere work. Some, assuredly, would become hip assistant professors, bored and jaded and ticketed for the limbo of a hundred committees and MLA meetings. My wife and I were willing members of this clique, as I have suggested.

A few years passed, the scene, ramshackle and unimportant, barely changed, save for the fact that my wife and I permitted ourselves occasional adulteries, I with women I met in the jobs I felt myself much too talented for, she with one or another of our stream of guests and visitors. I did not then know of her adventures but was aware of the longing glances given her by the shifting cast that streamed through our apartment. With true delight, trite but true delight, I was proud of her ability to enflame these freeloaders. I once, perhaps more than once, jokingly, as I recall, asked someone if he'd like to watch her undress so that her lilliputian perfections might be seen rather than merely imagined: her adolescently rosy breasts, her toy vagina with its reticent screen of silky hair, her perfectly round doll's buttocks. She was always furious and embarrassed by these crudities, yet I believed that she would have been more than pleased to exhibit herself. I often, in that period of our marriage, masturbated, fantasizing myself as a guest, and my wife as a willing partner: I would, so to say, cuckold myself, with pleasure. When our wretched apartment was ours alone for a day or so, I would ask her to fuck me with her face partially covered by a scarf or kerchief. I pretended that she was a whore whom I had hired to play my wife. She seemed to like this game, and I remember how her face would flush, loose with pleasure, her lips swollen and slightly parted as she entered the role.

My writing, if I may use such a word for the sporadic affectation in which I was fitfully engaged, had more or less ceased, save for a review or two, once or twice a year, in some ruthlessly mediocre magazine or the pitiful book-review section of a newspaper's Sunday arts page. Thankfully, I can recall nothing of these reviews, except that I'm pretty certain that I usually would take an author to task for such grave sins against the body politic as cynicism, and lack of belief in the redemptive powers of art and the wisdom of the common man. One of my boilerplate remarks, I think, was to the effect that this blight on good letters was self-indulgent, and that it is never enough for fiction to point out the failings of a terrible world for the pleasure of literary voyeurs. These reviews were as insubstantial as they were insufferable. In the meantime, our marriage collapsed a little more each day.

I assumed, or pretended to assume, in my decrepit role in the marriage, that the reason I became aroused when my wife was openly desired by other men, and why my masturbatory daydreams were only of her—as somebody else, perhaps, but always of her—and why I was swiftly carried into erotic dementia when she played her roles, especially those that required her to be someone else pretending to be her—once she was a young man, once my mother, once her mother—was because for some time my wife had, for me, little to do with the woman I married. She was, day after day, for many months, a sort of descendant of the scab-faced woman, the innocent yet somehow disturbingly soiled girl I had wed, the lusciously disfigured victim who had, recklessly and suddenly, asserted her lascivious self to suck me off in the cab that took us from the drunken chaos of our reception to that first grim, brown apartment. As her shining blond head moved ravenously between my thighs in the panels of light that slid, dreamlike, through the dark cab, I heard the slight whispering sound that her scab made as it scraped against my disheveled shirt. When I ejaculated, I had a momentary vision of my semen oozing thickly from the bright fragile surface of her face.

I may be elaborating this scene. I don't truly recall a "whispering sound," and suspect that the word "shirt" has called this fevered description up, for after I came, my wife spat a mouthful of semen into the shirttails that she'd pulled from my trousers for that purpose. At that very point, while we were in the cab, and certainly before we had begun our married life, my wife seemed not to be *precisely* the woman I had just married. I was stunned and delighted by her sexual *savoir faire,* her carnal flourish, I suppose such daring can be called. I can still see, with unsettling clarity, her sly childish face as she looked up from my lap, her slick, wet mouth, her eyes cloudy with lewdness, her visage at once hers and somebody else's. I put my hand, tenderly, on her wondrous mask, and she looked directly into my eyes and shook her head, no. As I now understand things, which is not to say that I understand anything, a different woman looked up at me, and it was she who shook her head: no. So that after the affirmation of her surprising act of fellatio, there was a puzzling negation. And in this way our marriage began.

Which takes me, at last, to the night I wish to speak of, but before I place myself, as a young man, in that dark hallway leading to our terrible apartment, I should correct an earlier misstatement. During our marriage, I did *not* involve myself with other women, and I have no reason to believe that my wife had to do with other men. She had many opportunities, that is to say, I gave her many opportunities, but I don't believe that she took advantage of them, if advantage is not too frivolous a word. I used to believe that she had fucked, everywhere and anywhere, all the men that she met, but now it seems to me that those who suggested these spectacular infidelities to me were simply adding their small donation to the general squalor.

I walked out of a bitter-cold night of wind and snow flurries, the exhausted linoleum of the corridor popping and crackling as I trod upon its crazed and faded roses. From behind the door I heard jazz, elbowing its way through the grit and scratches of an old record. I thought it likely that my wife was alone, for she often listened to jazz while preparing supper, and yet there was no reason for me to assume that, for she often played records while guests were in the apartment. Perhaps, since we were so rarely alone, I blinded myself with optimism: I was still guileless enough then to wish for simple things, to wish for miraculous change. Or for that matter, any change at all. I opened the door to see Charlie Poor on our bed, his back against the headboard, a glass of whiskey and water in one hand and a cigarette in the other. My wife stood next to the bed in an old sweater, a pair of boy's shorts that were much too small for her, and dirty white sneakers. She was gesturing with her cigarette. Everything was calm and still, transfixed peacefully within the perfections of Thelonious Monk.

Now that I have begun the narrative that with any luck at all will lead me, rapidly and cleanly, to its conclusion, I apologize for the fact that I must interrupt one last time to say that this is the point at which, in all my previous attempts to tell this story, I've stopped. At this point, approach this scene however, this moment during which I hesitate at the open door, grateful for the soft light and the warmth, I have been unable to continue. There is, perhaps, nothing, really, to tell, and yet that nothing demands release. I have lied in many ways, lied so as to prevent the truth from escaping, even partially, fragmented and deformed, from the duplicitous narrative in which I have hitherto encased it. For instance, Charlie Poor was certainly drinking my whiskey, and my wife, although I would prefer to clothe her in a loose, full skirt, was certainly wearing boy's shorts that were so provocatively tight that her *mons veneris* was perfectly defined. "Blue Monk" was on the phonograph, yes. But Charlie Poor was not stretched out on the bed—it has always been, in the past, his place on the bed that has made the narrative waver and then stagger to a dead end. This time, I hope, the truth may, by itself, be competent to tell the story, to make its incoherence somewhat lucid, perhaps even to make its incoherence somewhat coherent.

Charlie Poor was a man made out of cardboard, surely not what, even then, I would call a friend, but then again he was not much flimsier than anyone else we knew. There was an almost grandiosely specious quality about his casual facade because of the tense and worried personality that it barely concealed. He had been, quite recently, one of my employers, the part-owner of a small specialty-jobs printing shop for which I'd worked as a general office assistant for about six months. Charlie, when he discovered that I was a published writer, so to speak, so to speak, very much wanted to be my friendly boss, my colleague, my buddy. He had some idea, not that it was, or is rare, that I had some special knowledge of and entrée to the literary world, to magazines and editors and agents, to fashion and glamour. It's too good to be true, but Charlie wrote poetry, oh yes. That my wife had taken to writing poetry is, perhaps, even more remarkable, another indication, as if one were needed, to prove that life insists on the wearisome banal. Charlie slowly became peripheral to my life, to our lives, and I'm fairly certain that within a month of my going to work for him at Midtown Artistic Print he had been to at least one weekend party at our apartment.

Charlie fired me after six months or so. Of course, he didn't want to fire me, not my colleague and friend, Charlie. He was devastatingly, ruinously compassionate, almost parodically concerned with the dignity of existence and the wonders of nature, perpetually simmering with anger over injustices done to all sentient beings—he often *used* these phrases verbatim. Charlie did not want to fire me, no, it was his older partner, who, like, wore suits, man, and, like, ties, and who didn't know what was happening, who really fired me. But of course Charlie had to do the dirty work. I am probably imagining that he wore a hurt look as he told me the bad news, how sad he was, how somber. He said that he hoped there would be no hard feelings, no reason for us to stop seeing each other socially. Of course not, dear Charlie! What understanding scum we were.

I don't recall how Charlie insinuated himself into our lives after that, but he certainly did. It may have been the result of my craven response to his crude act, that is, Charlie responded to what he correctly took to be weakness. With the passage of time, however, I have come to realize that I was possessed of the same bogus emotions and shredded ethics as Charlie, and that I could just as easily, had our roles been reversed, have fired Charlie, my face dark with fake anger and embarrassment, crocodile tears standing nobly in my eyes, the stone-cold world too much for my sensitive spirit.

Charlie knew this, I think. I'm pretty sure that Charlie knew this. It was a question of, well, the breaks.

I closed the door and my wife turned toward me, smiling, welcoming me, cordially and politely, into my own house, into the circumstances of my own life. I was greeted, that is, as a friend who had dropped by to say hello to my wife and to *me,* treated as, for example, Charlie Poor. The apartment was dimly lit by night-table lamps on either side of the bed, and by a larger lamp that sat in the center of a small maple-veneer table flanked by two battered armchairs. Everything was, or should have been, instantly visible as I closed the door and blew on my cold hands. My wife turned toward me, smiling. She was smoking a cigarette and drinking whiskey and water, her skintight shorts wedged into her crotch. "Blue Monk." The bed was empty and perfectly made, tight and without a wrinkle. She turned to me, she put her drink down, or picked it up, she mimed a kiss, she gestured familiarly with her cigarette toward me, toward this old friend come to tell her thrilling stories of the fabled world. Tell me! her gesture said, sit down, dear old friend, and tell me!

For a long time this scene persisted in my memory, until I forced myself to face the fact that it was but fabrication. My wife with a cigarette, my wife in the soft light, my wife chatting with somebody, with Charlie Poor, relaxed on the bed, my wife turning toward me, smiling, relieved to see me home, safe from the bitter night, home again, home at last: this was all gauze.

When I opened the door, she was at the kitchen sink, washing salad greens, from which task she looked up to greet me. She smiled over her shoulder, she said something, probably, hi or hello or cold? I might add here that before her accident, my wife disliked salad, had always disliked it, so she told me, but that afterward, she ate it daily, sometimes twice a day, she, as they say, couldn't get enough of it. I'd completely forgotten about this, and it is only the representation of her at the sink, washing greens, that has brought it to mind. So it would seem that my wife's accident, her ecstatically disfigured face, will insist on intruding, despite my best intentions. Apparently there is no way for me to consider our marriage without admitting how powerfully our lives were affected by her damaged reality, her damaged self. As I have said, too often, I fear, I was morbidly attracted by her scab, and found ways to—use it. I would, for instance, watch my wife dressing, and compare the textures and colors of her smashed face to those of her underclothes and stockings, her skirts and blouses and dresses, her shoes. Gazing wanly, she would watch me watching her in the mirror. Her face would there appear even more strangely hurt, since her wound would be, of needs, on the wrong side. Looking at her reflection, I would feel faint, off-balance, urgently lustful. If, on our wedding night, it had seemed insane for me to imagine that my sweet bride had been substituted for by a sexually sophisticated changeling, who had arrived beneath the veil of a timely injury, this changeling, hooking her brassiere or putting in her earrings, had been, in turn, replaced by the woman in the mirror. I would beg this woman to touch me, satisfy me, while I stared at the reflected pornography of my delusion. I would not believe, should she accede to my desires, that I was not being seduced by a stranger, or by one or another stranger, someone I had met anywhere, at, for instance, our wedding. After my exquisitely shameful ejaculation, I would lie or stand, trembling, next to her, silent within her silence. I think that we were afraid to speak and so, perhaps, define the luxury of disgust we both loved. It was what we really loved.

I walked to my wife and put my hands on her waist, then bent and kissed the back of her neck, smelled her damp, clean hair. I touched my tongue to her flesh and she squirmed, turning her head voluptuously one way and then another, as if in sexual pleasure, but her movements were, and so I understood them to be, theatrical and exaggerated. She opened her thighs slightly and pushed her buttocks against my groin in an ironic, bawdy gesture of invitation. In a gesture equally cynical, I roughly cupped her breasts in my hands and ground my crotch against her, laughing until she, too, laughed, and then we bucked and jerked in a grotesque masque of licentious abandon. My smile must have been that of a corpse, the flesh of her young breasts was dead in my hands, our hearts were frozen. I stepped back from her to end the maniacal scene, then turned to face the phonograph so as to have a pretext to release her breasts.

In the armchair at the far side of the small table, close to the meticulously made bed, there, smiling, I sat, looking directly into my eyes. I felt as if some terrible, clammy liquid, cold and thick, was traveling up my spine, thence spreading into my chest and heart, which, surely, stopped beating. I sat, looking at me standing looking at me sitting. All occurred on a timeless plane, or, perhaps, an atemporal plane, one on which time had never existed and had no possibility of existing. The event hung suspended, removed from the diachronic, yet with no synchronic relation to anything else existent. It was as if death had abruptly usurped life's province, everything around my replica and me continued, but we had stopped, we had slid off the edge of the real. The feeling that overwhelmed me, if I may analogize this uncanny rent in the mundane, was much like the one I remember when, at twelve, I first saw a pornographic picture. It was at lunchtime, down the street from the schoolyard, and the picture, a photograph of two women and a man in sexual congress for which I had neither language nor image, made me dizzy, then nauseated, and then, although my skin was filmed over with cold oily sweat, it scorched my heart: I had become ill, sick with sex, the dreamy corruption of its lustful actuality had beckoned to include me. The creased photograph opened to me the insane adult world: beyond dances, popular songs, dates, marriages, beyond friendships and handholding and parents, school and books, movies and relatives. I saw directly into the sexual cauldron, into its neurosis and pain and obsession, its bestiality, its hairy, sweaty stench, its delirium and darkness and joy. I felt as if raised off the concrete, and then I fainted, although I stood firmly on my feet, my eyes open, fixed on the static record of that trio of happy animals which had been pushed into my hands. I looked at their white, flawed bodies, their entranced smiles, their glazed eyes looking into the secret places of selfish pleasure: I could almost hear them grunting and snuffling in their rapturous absence. Adults, *these* were adults. That their joy frightened and sickened me did not prevent me from recognizing their banality: they could have been, they were, anybody. The few articles of clothing that they had not removed testified to their pathetic humanity. They were vulnerable, ordinary, common, I knew all three of them, they were the neighbors.

The figure in the armchair, the I, was dressed in my overcoat, scarf, and tweed cap, and had on an old pair of my horn-rimmed glasses. He sat unmoving, expressionless, his eyes on my face, which, even now, I cannot imagine. His legs were crossed the way I cross my legs, his cigarette held as I hold mine. He was Charlie Poor, and although I must have realized this almost instantly, as I stood in shock at the apparition, I knew that this simulacrum had stolen my very self. It was all, of course, meant to be a joke, a tremendous joke cooked up by Charlie and my wife to amuse me after my long day at work. I fell, oh, with perfect aplomb, into the spirit of the charade, even as I knew that the two of them had spent the afternoon in the carefully made bed. This bizarre mime was the confession of their betrayal, a confession designed to be cruel and insulting and contemptuous.

My wife joined Charlie and me in the laughter we managed to produce: What an astonishing likeness! What a surprise! Look at the angle of the cap it's marvelous! And the cigarette! How mercilessly casual we were. I have no recollection of my feelings at that moment of joviality, but flatter myself that they were murderous. I suspect, though, that did I experience the violence of pain, I also must have had the sense that I had no right to such feeling, that I was, indeed, the guest in the apartment, and that the authentic I sat in my chair, relaxed, after a blissful day in which this legitimate husband had fucked and fucked again, the woman who was my wife but not, somehow, the woman I had fallen in love with and married.

What else could these two lovers have done but confess their lustful acts, a confession emblematized in such a way as to reveal to me my unreality, my meaninglessness as both a husband and a man? It was not quite enough for them to cuckold me, it was necessary to occlude me and by their revelation, to make me into a cipher, to turn my betrayer into me. I have often wondered how far they went that day in their masquerade. Did Charlie Poor wear my overcoat and my cap as he mounted my wife? Did she cry my name into his bespectacled blank face in the same parody of ecstasy with which she equipped the spurious orgasms she fashioned for me, and by which I pretended to be thrilled?

A long time after, I came to think that Charlie Poor had never quite possessed any actuality prior to that day and its sad events. At the moment at which my wife, for it would have had to be my wife who thought of it, created Charlie as me, when he was ordered to assert himself, so to speak, as me, his always tentative and flickering self slipped away, shed whatever tenuous presence it had. In the quiet of that dim, gray afternoon, he must have absented his precarious self in the sexual act: I believe, that is, that he was able to perform this act only as I, so that I had been with my wife that afternoon, as Charlie Poor. I had entered her familiar flesh, as Charlie first became nothing and then became me. This is too dark for me to understand, or even want to understand, but Charlie Poor was not only the agent of my erasure but of his own as well. By becoming me he obliterated himself and became nobody. I wonder, though, if he had been, for a flash, himself completely, that is, did he have the pleasure of knowing that *he* was fucking my wife?

There is little more to be said. My life went on, as did theirs, although after my wife and I separated, I lost touch with both of them. All for the best. I might end, though, by noting that this recording of tangled events has brought to mind an old friend of mine, a suicide dead now for more than thirty years, whose wife, at a particularly difficult time in their marriage, when he was in a mental hospital suffering from the blackest self-destructive depression, began an intense affair with the man who was her husband's partner in the small business they had started together. This man appeared with my friend's wife at parties, bars, restaurants, at, in short, all those places that she and her husband frequented. He even went with her, doggedly, to the sanitarium on Sundays. On all these occasions, his role was that of the faithful support for the worried and uncertain wife, the strong and selfless escort and close family confidant. It was, as may well be guessed, extravagantly obvious to everyone that he was hopelessly, embarrassingly in love with his partner's wife, so much so that he seemed, in her presence, to be little more than yearning incarnate. Unsurprisingly, he attempted, with her halfhearted assistance, to disguise his desire as hearty bonhomie: he was the good pal, so to speak. No one cared, one way or another, and in the curious way of shifting groups of shifting alliances, wives, husbands, lovers, and friends, the man had no identity for anyone beyond that of the business partner of their familiar friend. He was transparent and weightless, insubstantial. He was, additionally, afflicted with two names, that is, he had two different given names and two different surnames, one set of which, for some private, grimly comic reason, had been given him by his partner, had literally been conferred upon him. And it was by this name that he, despite ineffectual protestations, had been introduced, by my friend, socially, and it was by this name that everyone, including my friend's wife, initially knew him. After her husband had been hospitalized, his partner's insistent revelation of his true name had little effect: he remained the persona known to all.

I've wondered, more than once, if my friend's widow, who married her lover soon after her husband's suicide, accepted—I was about to say knew—her lover's real name. Of course, she must have, yet consider how strange it must have been for her to gasp and whisper her beloved's ersatz name during their first fornications, and then to discover that this name, cried out in passion, was one that had been forced upon him by her mad husband. It might then be thought that the early sexual acts between the adulterers were, in effect, acts performed by the wife with a total stranger, sexual gestures of a doubled infidelity. Perhaps my dead friend, in uncanny vengeful prescience, obliterated his partner's self so that his faithless wife would be unfaithful to his successor as well as to him, despite the presence of that successor's flesh.

Reality, or, if you will, that which we constrain ourselves to believe, is, beyond all philosophies, also that which we make of what happened. Unexpected connections do, of course, sometimes make for unexpected forms. For instance, I see that this story is, essentially, about a set of disappearances. I had not intended that to be its burden, although any further attempt to say what I meant to say is out of the question.

THINGS THAT HAVE STOPPED MOVING

Since Ben Stern's death, I've come to admit that Clara always brought out the worst in me. This is not to say that her husband's death caused this admission; nor do I mean to imply that had I never known Clara I would have been, as the nauseating cant has it, a better person who learned to like myself. I suppose I don't quite know what I mean to say. When I think of the years during which the three of us abraded each other, and of Ben's melodramatic deathbed farewell, a ghastly seriocomic scene in which I participated with a kind of distant passive elation, I feel compelled to get at, or into, or, most likely, to slink around the banal triangle of desire, lust, and expediency that we constructed, again and again. Simply put, we met, became intimates, and relentlessly poisoned each other. With our eyes wide open, to paraphrase the old song. I never really much liked this essentially spoiled couple, and "spoiled" is the word. Somebody once remarked that "spoiled" means precisely what it says, and that spoiled people cannot be repaired; they rot. And Ben and Clara were decidedly rotten. I was no less rotten, although "flimsy" might be a better word, and one could argue that

I brought out the worst in Clara. As for Ben, well, he was absolutely necessary for Clara and me to dance our dance. I was sure, almost from the beginning—a portentous phrase, indeed—that Ben was well aware of Clara's "playing around," if you will, with me and with all the other men with whom she regularly had a few laughs, as she liked so robustly, and somehow innocently, to put it. She could act the real American-girl sport, Clara could, a master of the disingenuous: *My goodness!*, I can hear her saying, *just what am I doing in bed with this stranger?* There was, to speak in figures, a kind of heuristic script to which the three of us had limited access, so that each of us could add to, delete from, and revise this script in the preposterous belief that the others would act according to these changes. What actually happened, as they say, was that over the years, each one of us was continually subject to the whims, betrayals, neuroses, and general vileness of the other two. We pretended otherwise, which pretense thoroughly subverted any possibility of our living lives that were even slightly authentic. I confess that my hope, really more of a velleity than a hope, now that these thirty-five years are good and dead, is that Clara is good and dead as well. Perhaps she is. That I don't know, one way or another, is dismally perfect.

My lust for Clara was awakened and made manifest as an adjunct to a lawful, if rare and surprising coupling with my wife, a sexual diversion that occurred on a Sunday afternoon as counterpoint to Ben and Clara's own marital intercourse. We had known the Sterns a few months when they asked us to their apartment for Sunday afternoon drinks and lunch. My wife had met, I believe, Ben and Clara once or twice, and made it clear that she disliked them: she said that they looked like magazine photographs, make what you will of that. But I had long since stopped caring about her likes and dislikes and their motivations. I consented to go, but said something, perhaps, about my wife already having made plans—something to explain what I was certain would be her refusal to accompany me. But she said she'd come, to my surprise.

I was, by that time, wholly aware of Clara's subtly provocative behavior, but as yet had no nagging desire for her, although I was fascinated by the assertiveness of her body, by her—or its—way of walking and standing and sitting, the way, I suppose, that its femininity situated itself in the world. But she was, after all, married to Ben, who seemed to me then funny, intelligent, and, well, smart and candid. I was very taken with him and found myself somewhat reluctantly, but happily, borrowing his style, for want of a better word.

An achingly cold Sunday in January: we chatted, gossiped, ate, rather lightly, but drank a good deal. As the afternoon progressed, and the streets took on the cold gray patina of a deep New York winter day moving toward its early palest-rose wash of twilight, we began, blithely, to inject the sexual into our conversation. We told lascivious stories and jokes in blatantly vulgar language, and every other word seemed loaded with the salaciously suggestive. My wife blushed beautifully enough to unexpectedly excite me; to put it plainly, the four of us were aroused, and giddy with desire. Rather abruptly, Ben and Clara rose and walked from the living room/bedroom into the adjacent kitchen, and almost immediately my wife and I heard the rustle of clothes, Clara's quick gasp, and then the panting and grunting of their copulation. My wife and I were quite helplessly thrown, by the situation, at each other, and, fully dressed and somewhat deliriously, we fucked on the edge of the couch, recklessly driven by the sounds from the kitchen.

Soon there was silence from that room, followed by whispering and quiet laughter. My wife called out, in a silly, girlish voice, for Ben and Clara not to come in, while we cleaned ourselves and adjusted our clothing. And then we four were reunited, so to say, for another drink. We grinned foolish and oddly superior grins, as if nobody on the sad face of the sad earth had ever been so crazily free and adventurous, as if we had just performed acts foreign to grade-school teachers, waitresses, and salesmen, foreign to our parents and rigorously bourgeois queers. As if sex was only ours to deploy and control.

When we had settled down with drinks and cigarettes in a thin aroma of whiskey and flesh, I looked up, by chance, to see Clara looking at me in such a way as to make clear that she had *expected* my look. What was happening? How can I get at this? Just fifteen minutes earlier, on my knees, between my wife's spread thighs, I had known, amorphously and with a kind of dread, that I really wanted to be fucking Clara, I wanted her perched on the edge of the couch, her legs wide apart, her eyes glassy. This sudden crack of lust had come from nowhere, had no gestation, was not the trite fantasy of a passion I'd long nursed for Clara. But her look told me that she knew what I'd thought, that she'd seen into my desire, and, as importantly, that she'd felt the same way in the kitchen with Ben. I was, at that moment, amazingly, stupidly besotted.

Less than a month later, at a party, I danced Clara into a bedroom, and pushed myself into her to come instantly, in helpless fury. Clara laughed and said that she knew it, or that it had to be that way, or something like that; but not in a manner designed to make me feel inadequate, but so as to make me believe—and I believed, oh yes—that this first carnal encounter with her had to be exactly this sort of encounter, and that it was *right*. My instantaneous ejaculation had been made into a venereal triumph! When we emerged into the lights of the party, our clothes were disarranged, but everyone seemed too drunk to notice or care, except, perhaps, for Ben. Or so I now think. I now think, too, that the quiet laughter from that kitchen, the whispering, was a revelation—one that I did not countenance—of the Sterns' knowledge that I was but a step away from a dementia of lust for Clara: that I was to be their perfect fool. I grant you that this suspicion may appear too fine-tuned, too sensitive, too baseless. And still, whether it was planned or not, a game or not, something happened that afternoon that drew Clara and me together into a flawed affair that virtually defined the rest of my life.

I must add a coda to the story of that Sunday. In a cab on the way home, my wife, smelling womanly and ruttish, stroked me, and then, when we kissed, gently pushed her tongue into my mouth with a voluptuousness that had for a long time been absent from our marriage. And when we got into our apartment, she urged me to the floor as she pulled up her skirt and we made love profoundly, in that serious way known only to the married. Lying, exhausted, next to my sweaty and dozing wife, I thought that this sudden sexual magic would, perhaps, protect me from what lay in wait for me with Clara. I should say that I hoped it would protect me. But I knew that this behavior had been but an aberration. My wife could have driven me into a reeling delirium of lewdness and abandon, yet nothing would have been able to halt the corrosive idiocy that was about to seize me.

∼

I met Ben and Clara about six months before my wife and I separated. We kept putting off steps toward a separation, mostly because of inertia or sloth or cowardice. We lived what I might call a reasonable if delicately adjusted life, but we both knew that the inevitable would soon occur. Once in a while we made love, but this was only to prove to ourselves that we were able to arouse each other, that we were, in effect, still attractive, I suppose. My penis, in such instances, was no more than a kind of mechanical toy that doggedly performed its manly task. We rarely quarreled, for we were rarely together. What my wife did during the long hours, sometimes the long days that we spent apart was of no concern to me. Nor, I knew, were my comings and goings of interest to her. None of this, I assure you, has anything to do with Ben and Clara, but it's the rare spouse who doesn't like to talk about dead or dying marriages, and to turn them, heartlessly, into the grimmest of jokes. The jokes are surely more lethal when children are involved, and when the hatred-infused couple pretends to the world and, of course, to themselves, that they'd rather suffer screaming agonies than forgo custody of or visitation rights with their children. They mean this at the time, through the tears and threats and shouted insults, and it takes a year, or perhaps two, before the adored children bore and irritate them, before they begin to conjure excuses for not seeing them over the weekend, or, conversely, to invent stories whereby the children may be got rid of for a day or two so as to accommodate a new lover—always a really *wonderful* person. This sickening desire to be thought of as busily independent marvel, noble and self-sacrificing parent, and righteously angry ex-spouse seems very American. What both parties usually really want is adolescent freedom and plenty of money to indulge its inanities: that's the glittering dream. As for the children, it's been my observation that Americans despise children, despite the ceaseless sentimental propaganda to the contrary.

In any event, I hadn't known Ben and Clara more than a few weeks—perhaps it was but a few days—when Ben decided to enter into a kind of emotional collaboration with me, an odd partnership, formed in alliance against Clara. I didn't truly realize this until some few weeks later, and by then, Clara and I had already been adulterous, and I had no interest in who was doing what to whom for whatever reason. So long as I could see a future of sex with Clara, Ben's motives were of no importance. I think that I had some notion that she'd ultimately become a wife to both of us, but that Ben, and only Ben, would have to suffer the usual domestic antagonisms. I would possess, unbeknownst to him, the spectacular whore.

Ben and I were sitting in their kitchen, and Clara was out. Ben seemed to me intent on making me believe that he was wholly unconcerned with her whereabouts, although he may well have been enraged and humiliated because of his knowledge of her wantonness. He may have considered that apathy and boredom would play better with me, the stranger on whom he had designs. I don't know. He was playing what even I could see—and I couldn't see much—was a weak hand. And yet, now, when I reflect on our wounded lives, I see that I have made the recorder's mistake of *deciding* that this was but an act on Ben's part, because I had, *then,* decided it was an act. But all memories, as even cats and dogs know, are suspect. As if it mattered.

We had got about halfway through a quart of cheap Spanish brandy, when Ben decided to make me, as I've suggested, a partner in his marital combat. I'm pretty sure I went along with this pathology, because, as I recall, I thought that any revelation about Clara would allow me to get closer to her, to become—it is absurd to say so—indispensable to her. I wanted a glimpse, that is, of her wonderful weakness, her amoral shabbiness. I would have been anything, or played at being anything, to stay in—the phrase is wildly comic—the bosom of the family. That Ben and Clara were, in some absolute married way, as one in their warped lives, was a truth that I would not countenance for a long time. Well, for years.

Ben had got quite drunk, and had pressed on me a book of Robert Lowell's poems, but I had no clear sense of what he wanted me to do about it or with it. I put the book on the table, I took a drink, I picked the book up and leafed through it. Christ only knows what sort of raptly attentive face I had put on, but Ben suddenly remarked that *Clara* had given him the book last *Christmas,* because she knew how much he *liked* Lowell. I nodded and gravely riffled the pages, assuming what I hoped would pass as a pose of deferential admiration for Ben's superb taste. And Clara's! Ben's and Clara's! Ben repeated his line about this being a Christmas present from Clara, and at that moment, I looked, as I instantly realized I was meant to look, at Clara's inscription. It read: *Xmas 1960 to Ben.* That the message was but a flat statement of fact was comically clear: this book had been given to Ben by someone on a date specified. Other than that, all was wholly suppressed. I looked up and Ben was smiling sadly at me, oh, we were partners, we were pals incorporated, but I was not yet wholly aware of my position as Clara's future enemy, only as Ben's confidant. I'm ashamed to say that I believe I felt sorry for him, the put-upon recipient of such cold apathy.

Not three weeks later, I fucked Clara, almost accidentally, or so I believed, standing up in that same kitchen, while Ben was out getting beer. She had her period, but I didn't care, nor did she. Later, I sat in miserable stickiness as I drank one of the beers that Ben had brought back. The kitchen smelled of sex and blood, and my pants were flagrantly stained at the fly. I realized, yet without any shame, what a *brutta figura* I must have made. That Ben did his best not to notice made it clear that I had somehow been played for a fool. For a chump, really. Since I was quite obviously crazy, it didn't matter to me.

~

Clara had been promiscuous long before I knew her, and from what I gathered over time, promiscuous long before she married Ben. She was recklessly sexual, with a vast anxious dedication to erotic adventure, although the word surely glamorizes her activities. She pursued these affairs with the sedulous dedication of a collector of anything, with, that is, the dedication of a kind of maniac. That such sexual avocation is solemnly described as "joyless" or "empty" doesn't fit in Clara's case: she was wholly and matter-of-factly pleased with her churning libido, and the prospect of picking up some happily dazed copying-machine salesman in the desolate lobby of a local movie theater and then silently and efficiently blowing him in his parked car delighted her.

Ben knew, before their marriage, all about her penchant for what she may well have thought of as the free life, and was much too hip and blasé to think that he could change her ways. Such a belief was, to Ben, just so much middle-class bullshit Christian baloney. But he did believe something that was much more absurd than faith in love as rescuer of the emotionally damaged, morally skewed spouse of song and story. To put it as simply as possible, he believed that Clara's marriage *to him* would effect a change in her behavior. He would do nothing, or so I carefully reconstructed his thinking; there would be neither admonition nor recrimination, neither scorn nor anger, neither sorrowful displays nor contemptuous remarks. There would be nothing save an unspoken pity for this poor slut. Clara, annexed to Ben's relaxed, nonjudgmental, affectless, and cynical life, would, so he thought, abruptly stop her frantic couplings in hallway and bathroom and rooftop and automobile, in park and doorway and elevator and cellar and toilet stall, her clothes on or off or half-off or undone. Her sex life would seem, when held against Ben's *sangfroid,* utterly and irredeemably square, the provincial doings of a suburban Jezebel in sweaty congress with her balding neighbor. Of course, nothing of the sort happened.

Clara's honeymoon and marriage was but a brief interlude in her marriage to herself, to her own endlessly interesting desires.

I never asked either Ben or Clara how accurate my guess was concerning Ben's expectations and Clara's blithe thwarting of those expectations. Not that they would have admitted anything of the sort—I can see Ben's bemused stare and Clara's smile. There is, however, the strong probability that it was when Ben came to realize that their union would do nothing to change Clara in the least, that he abandoned the marriage and became his wife's dutiful if somewhat bored collaborator, and a voyeur who followed her erotic meanderings with a detached interest.

Ben liked to reveal, in near-comic confidence, snippets of his life with Clara. He did this, or so I believe, in the hope that I would tell Clara what he'd told me, and so irritate her into thinking that he and I had managed some sort of fragile rapport that wholly excluded her. Sometimes I would pass Ben's confidences on to her, sometimes not; sometimes I'd embroider or condense Ben's stories, and sometimes invent things that he'd never even hinted at.

One of the things he told me, at a time when I was sure that he knew of my affair with his wife, was that Clara had always, and without fail, faked her orgasms. He was enormously amused by this, for, or so he said, he was delighted that Clara thought that she was duping him into thinking that he was a perfect lover. But Ben was as duplicitous as he claimed she was, for his gratified and satisfied response to her moans and gasps and soft screams, to her sated smile, was utterly counterfeit. His fake-masculine response to her fake-feminine pleasure filled her with a sense of, in his pleased words, "smug triumph." At bottom, then, he was unconcerned with her sexual pleasure or the lack of it, and it amazed him—I can almost hear his laughter—that Clara, *Clara* for Christ's sake!—held to the notion that he *cared* whether she came or not, and that, unbelievably, she was disturbed lest he discover her deception. But Ben was interested only in his own orgasm: as far as he was concerned, Clara could have stupendous, wracking orgasms, real or pretend, by the score, lie in bed a mannequin, fall, for Christ's sake, *asleep*—all was immaterial to him, so long as *he* came. What Clara did or did not do was Clara's affair. That she worked so hard at her conjugal dramatics somehow—how can I put this—*touched* Ben, so much so that he never even came close to suggesting that he even suspected that she might be faking. "Deluded, pathetic girl," is what he once called her.

He most certainly, though, wanted *me* to tell Clara this story, of course, and he also wanted me to fret over whether Clara was faking with me. But I didn't tell her, because I realized, despite my attempts to deny and then to rationalize it, that I felt the same way as Ben: I didn't care, either. I once lightly asked Clara what sort of lover Ben was, and she said that he was more of a masturbator than a lover. I think I might have gone a little red at this, for that was what Ben had once said about Clara, and I wondered to whom Clara had said this about me. Outside of, doubtlessly, Ben.

≈

The occasions were rare on which I angered and irritated Clara, and when I did, she'd let me know it, as they say, in devious, often astonishingly petty ways, which she never, of course, recognized at all. To describe them is unimportant to the point I want to make, such as it is.

Sometimes Clara would wear an expression of bored smugness, barely but not noticeably concealed by "good manners." It was quite a face. It was at such times that I would obliquely suggest—in different ways, using different words and emphases and approaches—that her expression was very much like that of a clutch of well-off and marvelously dim white Protestants she unaccountably admired. This was an expression developed and trained early on, at about the time, in fact, that these people find that the world has been constructed and arranged for their pleasure, but that it is also filled with others who want to partake of that pleasure—which is certainly not their due!—*without permission.*

Such a comment would mildly annoy Clara, but she would become angry only when I'd suggest that many of her pals' mundane pleasures quite wonderfully killed at least some of the bastards off: to wit, alcohol, cocaine, polo, fast cars, horses, skiing, sex, mountain climbing, etc. I would add that although this was surely just, it wasn't nearly enough to even the score in terms of the grief and misery they caused just by being alive, with their prep schools and sailboats, monopolies and stock-exchange seats, securities and trust funds, private beaches and stables, custom-last shoes and shark lawyers; and, of course, their terror of knowledge, contempt for art, and the polite fucking Jesus that they trot out when needed. Despite the fact that I would run through this routine, with slight variations, at, as one might say, the drop of a top hat, it would always, *always* get to Clara. She'd sit back in her chair, or lean on the bar, or turn toward me in bed, to treat me to that perfectly constructed face: it was all I could do not to call it cruelly to her attention. But to what purpose? Her anger at my venom—often, but not always, real—toward her beloved idiots was weirdly felt, offered up on what was, figuratively speaking, a tasteful Episcopalian altar. Clara was, for Christ's sake, Jewish! And still, and still, her vapid, excruciatingly imitative expression was an homage to and defense of that ghastly cadre that, quite naturally, thought of her—when forced to think of her—as a vulgar bitch who would not, no, not ever do.

The showgirl with whom I lost my virginity when I was sixteen was only two or three years older than I, but she was so overwhelmingly sophisticated, sexually, that I was awed throughout the entirety of the night I spent with her. We did a number of things that I had hitherto known of only as escapades in pornographic stories and pictures—those rare few I had seen. I was so thoroughly made to realize my own naïveté, that years passed before I could even begin to admit to my callowness. Until that time of candid acceptance, I had managed to turn that night into a liaison of sexual equals, although, as I say, it was nothing of the kind. Her influence, if that's the word, was so profound that I afterward often felt dumbstruck and inept before women with whom I was about to go to bed: that is to say that they would sometimes "become" her, or, more accurately, I would revert to the flustered youth of that night. Such situations, which occurred without warning, usually proved disastrous, as one may well imagine.

My father had arranged this adventure for me, and such was his presence in my life at the time that I thought this arrangement wholly reasonable, even judicious. I can't recall how the night was planned, but I'm quite certain that my father did not ask my opinion. He didn't know if I was a virgin or not, but assumed, given the era and his knowledge of his own life and those of his peers, that I was. He was correct. He clearly believed that it was his paternal duty to introduce me to sex in, as he would surely have put it, "the right way." And so he arranged for me to spend the night with a showgirl from the Copacabana, in those days a glittering tawdry nightclub near the Plaza, emblematic of flashy, four A.M. New York, whose clientele was predominantly made up of tough men in silk shirts packing wads of cash, little of which had been honestly come by.

I should make it clear that my father had not asked me my thoughts concerning his plans, not because he held me cheap or thought of me as insignificant, but because, as a Sicilian, he knew that his decision was unerringly correct, beyond cavil, and that this was so because he was, all in all, perfect. Sicilians, as somebody said, cannot be "reformed" or taught anything because they know that they are gods: and it was as a god that my father planned my entrance into manhood. Sicilians are essentially serious people, never moreso than when smiling and chatting pleasantly with strangers, that is, with people who are not part of their lives in any way that matters. The smiles and warm, intimate stories are but devices that serve as charming barriers behind which little can be seen or known. A Sicilian can talk with someone for years and deliver a sum total of information over this time that, considered objectively, comes to a handful of comic anecdotes and a gigantic mass of the most elaborately empty details. And all of these data seemed deeply personal, private, and revelatory. Under the easy conversational brio, the Sicilian has been continuously sizing up his interlocutor, and arranging the stories and putative intimate details that will be perfect *just for him*. I have no way to analyze or explain such odd behavior: it is simply the fact. My father, being this way, wanted me to be this way, expected it, really. And so, the loss of my virginity as a prerequisite to becoming a passable man, could not be the result of some dalliance with a "nice girl," both of us a little drunk after a party. Such frivolity was for The Americans, as my father called those citizens who, whatever else they may have been, were surely not gods. These digressions lead me to another, a kind of exemplar of my father's way of thinking. When he was an old man, some few months before his death, I heard him tell some men with whom he had struck up a kind of friendship in the hospital while recovering from a triple-bypass operation, that he had been a trapeze flyer in his native Italy but had been forced to flee Mussolini because of his Jewish mother, who had been one of the great equestriennes in the Hungarian circus world. He told this story with such an expression of wistful regret that for a moment I thought it might be true, that he had kept some fantastic secret from me and my mother, that he was actually Jewish! But it had to do with his lack of concern about what he told these hospital acquaintances. They were, in his mind, mere Americans, with no idea of what a man's life is and should be. He was, that is, amusing himself by seeing how far he could go with these childish men, eager to swallow childish lies in the same way that they swallowed childish games on television. I now believe that what he wanted, at all costs, was to assist me in avoiding such American childishness, and thus help me into his ideal of manhood in what he knew to be the only proper way.

On the morning of my erotic christening, there was no teasing, no off-color jokes or winks or grins, and there had been none for the preceding week, during which time I had been wholly aware of the arrangement. I can't remember what my mother had been told concerning my night away from home, but my father had con-cocted something having to do with the business. I was, as my mother well knew, expected to ultimately join my father's business as a partner.

That night, after dinner at Monte's Venetian Room in Brooklyn, during which my father talked to me about school, and thrilled me by complimenting me on the dark, sober tie that my mother had insisted I wear, one of his cronies drove me to Manhattan in my father's Fleetwood sedan. He was tall and very dark and disconcertingly still, and we had nothing at all to say to each other. I was intimidated by him, really—his name, not that it matters, was Lou Angelini—by his taciturnity, his air of respect for me as the boss's son, and his rigorously conservative dress. We arrived at the Hotel Pierre, in those days even quieter and more ele-gant, more *raffinée* than it is now. I hardly remember what hap-pened then, but I recall my sense of clumsiness and awkwardness as we walked through the lobby, terribly slowly, because of Lou's slight limp, the effect of what he called a "war wound." But we did, finally, get on an elevator, and then, finally, reached a door in the long, muffled corridor.

Lou knocked quietly, twice, and when the door opened, a pretty girl of nineteen or twenty smiled at us. She had ash blond hair and although her eyes were elaborately made up, her lips were their natural soft pink. Lou looked at her, in her silk robe, up and down, and then left without a word. From that moment on, I was in a detached state of blissful shock, or perhaps happy stupor, as Grace, who later told me that she was half-Italian and half-Polish, showed me, in her words, a few things, more than a few things, that I might like. In the middle of the night we ordered room service and ate ham and eggs and drank cognac-and-ginger-ale highballs. There was nothing romantic or spongy about Grace, and yet she wasn't cold or bored. She was, in fact, what my mother, the circumstances of course being different, would have called "full of fun." When, at maybe four in the morning, she and I danced—that is, she taught me steps to the samba—to the soft radio, it was with a grave sense of play. It was intensely erotic and yet, although we were both naked, not bluntly sexual. Everything seemed magical, and I was obviously insane with pleasure. I had lost all sense of shame with this girl and had, too, of course, fallen in love with her. I even asked her if I might, maybe, call her sometime, a request that was met by a big smile whose import was instantly decipherable: it said, *You are a boy.*

I remember Grace's body pretty well, her long waist, small breasts, the dark auburn of her neat pubic hair. She told me that she thought my father was a real sport, and I knew, instantly, that he had often spent the night with her. She would be, to my father, a nice kid, but a whore, and had her womanly role; not, surely, my mother's role, or the role of the nice unknown girl that my father assumed I would discover and marry, but a valuable role. I always thought to tell Clara that had she been more like the whore that Grace was, rather than the bogus whore that she so contemptuously fabricated, I could have really, well, really loved her. I never said a word, and it has only recently occurred to me that I remained silent because I had no idea of what I truly meant to say, without sounding more like a fool than I had already proven myself to be.

On a very cold winter Saturday, I got two phone calls, not an hour apart, from Clara and an old sometime acquaintance, Robert. Both calls carried the news that Ben was very near death, that he had, indeed, about ten days to live. Robert was serious and somber, his voice an annoying mix of manufactured sadness and the self-important tone that bad news seems to make, for many people, mandatory. I did not, of course, let on to him that this was not bad news to me. Clara was her usual glacially sardonic self, much too ironically detached to be affected by something so banal as death. As always, I found in her distantly gelid tones the erotic quality that had unfailingly undone me. It had been perhaps six years since I'd heard from either Clara or Ben, and my first reaction to this sudden news was no better than apathetic. As the phrase has it, I didn't care whether he lived or died.

Ben, according to Clara, would be very happy to see me, and would I come? There was, Clara told me, plenty of room in the big wooden house that they'd bought on the Hudson, and my presence would make for a sort of reunion, I think she said, an *event*, which word she used without the hint of a dark smile. Robert also insisted—he told me that he was speaking for the, God help us, "family"—on the wondrous quality that my presence at the deathbed would add. I was tempted to say "to the festivities?" but kept my mouth shut. It had been so long, what a long time, it's been years, and years, and so long, and on and on. So we chattered, the three of us. It had, really, not been long enough, it would never be long enough. And yet, I agreed to go, knowing what a disgusting carnival it would be. There would be present the shattered rabble from Ben's past life, along with the fawning students, the grim, scowling artistic platoon from the nearby town, the arts reporter on the local rag, and, surely, the predictably ill-dressed colleagues in the English Department, who were too hip, too distracted by art and ideas to care about clothes, man, but among whom, I was virtually certain, Ben had cut a bohemian, Byronic, urbane figure— the dandy amid the rubes—for almost fifteen years. And, too, there would be Clara, the discreetly bored, aging bitch about whom the panting saps to whom she'd thrown the occasional sexual pourboire of one kind or another, would circle to proffer drinks, sandwiches, lights for her cigarettes, and condolences. They would, each seedy associate professor and second-rate graduate student, smile tenderly and longingly at the strong wife, this astonishing woman who hid her grief with wit and repartee. And each would be happy to believe that this fascinating tramp had taken him, and only him, into bed, car, bathroom, cellar, or backyard. What passion had been theirs! Etcetera. Meanwhile, the smudged and blurry wives and girlfriends lurked on the far side of this erotic Arcadia, being, as always, good sports, anonymous in their calf-length skirts and terrifyingly red lipstick.

Later that day, I regretted my decision to travel up to that grim third-rate college into whose zombie life Ben had settled. But when all is said and done, whenever that may be, I really did want to see Ben die, or, more precisely, watch him slide toward death out of, so to speak, the corner of my eye. None of his destructive asides or poisonous denigrations could save him, and for this I was thankful. I felt no guilt about any of these thoughts, or, better, desires, for I'd always, as I've already mentioned, hated Ben for putting me in the way of Clara, and then for getting in the way of me and Clara. The son of a bitch couldn't win, as far as I was concerned. Of course, the three of us had conspired in this plan of desire and need and demand and destruction, and it was somehow contingent upon our simmering dislike of each other. I was curious, too, to see if Clara still held him—and me—in the venereal contempt that was the perfect expression of her nature. I had cuckolded Ben for years and years, although "cuckolded" is not the right word, as I think I've pointed out. I had, from the beginning, been permitted to discover that there was a good chance that Ben had, early on, found out about our passionate indiscretions. I have no authentic recollection of what I then thought of this, but I can guess that I somehow, in some skewed pathology of gratitude, felt a sense of privilege at being the recipient of this couple's comradely attentions. I do know that I had come to worship what I took to be our wondrous freedom with an intensity that went beyond the imbecile.

The next day I got on the train at Grand Central and went up to watch Ben die, and to look into the cold, blank eyes of his wife. She was composed, remote, and sisterly, settled, uncomfortably, it seemed, into her flesh, as if she were finally alive, but not quite sure of life's demands. On the way home, I thought of how we had laid waste to our sensibilities, with a truly genuine devotion to waste: we grew old amid this waste. We would not stay away from each other until we were sure that it didn't matter any more whether we did or not.

~

At the very moment that my mother died, Clara and I were in bed together in the Hotel Brittany. She and I had met by accident on Vanderbilt Avenue and had gone downtown together in a cab. Clara, in her careless and reckless way, lied to me that she was going to meet an old school friend from Bennington in the Village, and I contributed my own god-awful, transparent lie. We wound up drinking in a bar off Sheridan Square, and I was soon taking liberties, as the creaking phrase has it, with her in a booth. We had, some six months before, decided to break off our affair of three years. We had no concern, of course, with Ben's feelings, even the ersatz ones we handily ascribed to him, but we were somewhat anxious over the possibility that a full-blown adulterous romance might impinge upon our freedom to have romances with others. We had spent some hours thrashing this out, for we were serious indeed about our prospective lusts.

The afternoon had turned into a windy, bitter night, and a thin, powder-dry snow lashed the streets with a stinging drizzle. I bought a bottle of Gordon's and we walked through the harsh weather a few blocks to the Brittany, a faded and somewhat decrepit hotel that still retained a semblance of old glamour in the appointments of its raffish bar and taproom, a locale that featured a weekend cocktail pianist, some gifted hack with a name like Tommy Jazzino or Chip Mellodius. I had always liked the rooms in the Brittany, mostly because of the large closets, a strange thing, I grant you, to care about, since I never once registered at the desk with anything even remotely resembling luggage. The desk clerk nodded and smiled at us as I signed and paid; he probably thought he knew us from the night before, or the week before. God knows, the desperately sex-driven all have the same lost, hopeful look, the same imploring face that seems to whine *please don't disturb me before I come.* Such half-mad people are called lovers, a fact usually denied by lovers. This denial is most often rooted in the dreary fact that most people fall, or once fell, into this category, and no doubt think it unique.

One of the inconsequential things that I remember about our night in that warm room, thinly edged with the smell of cigarette smoke and gin, is the fact that Clara, as she undressed, revealed herself to be wearing an undergarment that looked like a pair of rather fancy culottes: they were a kind of pale raspberry in color, trimmed with black lace. She described them, apologetically, for some reason, as a fucking goddamn slip for idiot girls. I can't say whether they were effectively arousing or not, but they were remarkable and quite unforgettable. I've always wondered whether Clara, of all the women in the world, was the only one to wear this particular item of underclothing; I wonder, too, what Ben thought of her in this extravagant lingerie. I never asked her.

Clara told me that Ben was currently screwing one of his graduate students, a serious, annoyingly smart young woman from Princeton, who was, according to Clara, well ahead of academic schedule in the dowdiness department, almost in the same nonpareil league as assistant professors. The girl thought—what else?—that Ben was really aware, really brilliant, really wonderful, his blinding light hidden under the conventional academic barrel. And so young, so young to be so aware, so brilliant, so wonderful. She thought, according to Clara, that Ben would one day write an academic novel to surpass Randall Jarrell! And, in this novel, she dreamed that she might figure, barely and flatteringly disguised, as a complex and wonderfully difficult graduate student. I'm more or less painting this particular lily, as may be obvious, although Clara *did* actually say that Ben was screwing a graduate student. For all I know she might have looked like Rita Hayworth. Rita Hayworth! It pleases me to be given this glorious woman to use as a term of comparison, for this time has no understanding of her at all. She speaks, her face and body and the timbre of her voice speak to men on their own, as they say, morosely distant from wives and homes, half-drunk in the dim bars of half-empty hotels. She stands in bathroom doorways, in a skirt and brassiere, waiting for a light. She is perfectly and ideally dead, as she should be. What, in this age of speeding trash and moronic facts, would such a beauty even have to *do?*

We drank and smoked and Clara cried, not about Ben, certainly, but about her father's recent death. Then I fucked her and we slept. I woke at about five in the morning, and, touching Clara's naked body next to mine, I was instantaneously nutty with lust. As I again fucked her groaning self with a dedicated selfishness, my mother called to me. I could hear her voice as clearly as if she stood next to the bed, or in the bathroom doorway, and as I came, she called to me again, from somewhere out of the darkness of the closet, a wistful, flat, soft statement of my name. At that moment I knew that my mother had just died. How strange and perverse a moment it was, my mind on some eerie plane, Clara pushing me off and out of her, in raw annoyance that I had jounced her awake. I made, I believe, some apologies to get off the sexual hook, probably delivered with a stricken look of guilt on my face, one that suggested how wretched I felt for my lack of concern for her. She lit a cigarette, as did I, and I got out of bed to stand at the window, smoking and looking down at the freezing streets, thus completing with exhausted flair, I think, the two-bit melodrama. Clara, of course, bought none of this.

I thought, although it wasn't really a thought, that Clara, rather than my mother, should have died, and that I could kill her, right there in the bed. The night clerk would never remember us, and I had registered under my usual fake name, "Bob Wyatt," a moniker so insipid as to be blank. Kill her to even things up for my sad, uncompleted mother, and then commiserate with Ben and Miss Complit. I could imagine their sensitive literary comments, the lines from Hardy or Yeats, and Ben's dim smile as I delivered the *envoi* with a snatch of Dylan Thomas, a poet whom Ben loathed.

I was sick with guilt, intolerable slug that I was, and waiting for despair to fall on me in its black rain. Good old despair!, that most durable and aberrant and selfish of pleasures. But despair eluded me, or I it, and as the room began to admit pale January light, I went down on Clara until she very happily came. She was more or less sweet after that, and let me give her my bacon at breakfast. We sat at the table a long time, drinking coffee and smoking. I didn't want to call the hospital and be told about my mother, I didn't want to be right. I didn't want to have to take care of the terrible details of death, the business angle, as Ben had once called it, prick that he was. But mostly, I didn't want to have to pair my mother's flesh and Clara's, but it was already too late to escape that.

Of course, I write this now, years after these events, as the phrase goes. What I then thought, I don't recall. We ate, by the way, in an Automat on Broadway, just south of Eighth Street. It's long gone, along with all the other Automats, along with all the other every-things, but every time I pass the spot where it stood, I can smell Clara. Her subtle sexual odor is uncannily apparent, an odor that she claimed was generated exclusively for me—a preposterous confession that I, sweet Mother of God, believed for a long time. Now I'm *righteously* permitted, I feel, to think of her as nothing but that sexual odor. As nothing but a cunt.

~

The phenomenon of my mother's death in the Methodist Hospital in Brooklyn at the moment at which I was drunkenly fucking Clara, became, some months after the funeral, the source of what I quite irrationally believed would be a revelation of sorts. Of what, I had no idea, but the temporal conjunction of the two incidents seemed too sinister not to be meaningful. I thought that I might now be able to understand the feverishly obsessive erotics occasioned in me by the thought of Clara, because of the coincidence of death and fornication. I apparently really believed that my flatly banal night in the Brittany held some lesson for my life. And yet, if truth be told—if truth be told!—the adventure was, as always with Clara, intrinsically void. My mother's death lent it no importance; in fact, I was, surely, intent on teasing some meaning from this drunken shambles to avoid the shame of self-confrontation: that is, my mother's death, if rightly manipulated, would redeem my debased adultery by lending it a tragic mystery. What childish perversity!

I know that had I been gifted that night with second sight, so that I could have predicted my mother's sudden fall into death; and had I seen such catastrophe in my mind's eye while kissing Clara's sex through her glowing lingerie, her demise would have occasioned nothing that my lust had not already decided on. To be crudely frank, I would have crawled to Clara under any circumstances, come corruption, hell, come anybody's death. So, then, my desire to make those two incidents yield meaning was nothing more than a way of avoiding the truth about my own lust; I wanted, that is, to make my lust important, in the same way that blinded lovers know that their ordinary couplings are unique and astonishing and bright with amorous truth.

Even now, when I think to luxuriate in self-pity, I conjure up that particular night and try to extract, from its various acts, a moral, no, a lesson, a pensum, that will serve to partially explain my general failure as a man. This failure *must* be somehow dependent upon the circumstances attendant upon my mother's death. Or so I hope; for otherwise my life seems to have no meaning at all, not even that of its being. But I am always sidetracked, because I link that night with the night spent with Grace, and that, without fail, allows my father to enter the bleak world of recollection.

~

I occasionally dream of my father, especially when I find myself vexed by memories of Clara. In these dreams, he does workaday things, nothing strange or even unexpected. He lights an English Oval, he leans against one of his gleaming Cadillacs, he turns to me and says "Lavagetto," he buys me a Hickey Freeman pearl-gray pinstripe suit, he takes me to the fights at the Garden where we sit ringside with big, loud men, he tells me he's sorry about my mother, whom he always loved. When he confesses to the latter, he says something about the good veal and peppers in the Italian grocery on Baltic Street, but I know how to translate this secret dream language. But whatever he is doing or saying, he invariably wears a snap-brim fedora, and much of the time it is a white Borsalino. This hat is, I think, a figure for authority and grace and strength, for arrogance, for manhood. A figure, that is, for everything that I once wanted to possess and exhibit.

When I was sixteen, my father took me, on a hot day in August, to a pier in Erie Basin, where he was doing a complete overhaul on two Norwegian freighters. His foreman, a short, dark man of forty-five or so, whose name—the only name I ever knew him by—was Sorrow, took his cap off when he approached my father, and made a slight bow to me. I was embarrassed by this, and looked away at the huge rusting and peeling hulls of the *Kristiansand* and the

Trondheim riding high in the water. Sorrow said something to my father in Sicilian, and my father answered in English, and gestured toward the ships. As Sorrow walked away, my father put his arm around my shoulders, and said something about the old greaseballs and their goddamn Chinese, and laughed. I should note that by this time in his life my father, who had been born just outside Agrigento and who had passed through Ellis Island at the age of ten, had invented an American birthplace for himself, and had given himself a wonderfully burlesque "American" middle name, Kendrick. My mother often delightedly said that he claimed a birthday on, sometimes, the Fourth of July, and sometimes Flag Day. And yet my mother, for all of her bitterness toward this man from whom she had been separated for twelve years, never spoke of him without a subterranean admiration and affection that I had no way of reconciling with her anger and sense of betrayal. He was to her, I now think, the only real man in the world, and she had often told me stories of their courtship and early marriage that were suffused with details that were at once innocent—almost girlish— and oddly erotic. On that pier, though, whatever he may have been to my mother, he seemed to me a magical stranger in a beautiful hat and a tropical worsted suit of so creamy a tan that it seemed to blush. I knew why Sorrow was so deferential, for my father radiated an authority that created him a figure endowed with authority: he made, that is, a self that was, then, his self. It was not, that is, the creation of someone that he was not, a kind of con-man invention that, for some reason, many people admire, but was infinitely more subtle than that: he had successfully endowed, in some mysterious way, certain traits of manhood with a style that was not naturally or specifically intrinsic to them, but which became so at the moment of his appropriation of them. It was this, I suspect, that so enthralled my mother.

Norwegian ships, back in the forties, were generally agreed to be, by the longshoremen and stevedores, scalers and painters who worked on the Brooklyn and North River piers, the filthiest afloat. This may or may not have been true, but it was accepted as such, until even the Norwegian seamen who sailed on these tubs came to believe it, and, in a perverse way, to flaunt their ships' squalid conditions. They may not have been any cleaner than those sailing under different flags, but their reputation for egregious feculence had been solidly fixed.

My father and I walked about half the length of the pier, and when we were about even with the fo'c'sle of one of the ships, he struck up a conversation with a man called Joe the Ice. He was in a powder-blue gabardine suit, white shirt and navy tie, and wore a little teardrop diamond in his lapel. I had come to learn that Joe had something to do with what my father called "collections," not that it here matters. He seemed to me benign and rather affable, but he had an air of being, so to say, all business. There was a story that my Uncle Ralph told about a deckhand on a Moore McCormack tug who was still paying the weekly vig to Joe on a loan he'd made some eleven years earlier. He rarely complained, so my uncle said: he was whole and working.

I suddenly realized that my father had a wad of cash in his hand, and he said to Joe that five grand was jake with him. Joe took out a handful of cash from a tattered red manila portfolio, and counted out five thousand dollars. My father called Sorrow over, all three spoke briefly in Sicilian, and Sorrow took the ten thousand. I was astonished and bewildered, amazed, really, at having seen ten thousand dollars produced, so to speak, out of the air, in the oily heat of the Red Hook summer afternoon. My father smiled at me, and told me, in as few words, that he'd made a bet with the Ice, even money, that he could walk through the *Trondheim,* from the holds, up through all the decks, onto the main deck and the bridge—walk through the whole ship—without getting a spot or smudge or smear of oil or dirt or rust on his clothes or hat. Then he left me to Sorrow and Joe, and walked up the gangplank. I stood with the men, and, by now, a few scalers who were coming off shift. In a minute, the entire pier knew of the bet, and men waited patiently to see my father appear at the gangway. My father insisted that an electrician who worked for the Navy accompany him to make sure that everything was done right.

My father won the bet, came out spotless, and then took me to Foffés on Montague Street, where he had a scotch or two, and I drank 7Ups, and then we drove to Phil Kronfeld's, a haberdashery near the old Latin Quarter. He bought me a dozen lusciously soft, white broadcloth shirts, and, deferring to my somewhat dim taste, a half-dozen silk ties, the latter spectacularly "Broadway," ties that my mother called "bookmaker" ties. She swore that my father had no sense at all, buying a high-school boy such expensive things, but then told me a story about his spending his last twenty dollars on a hat to impress her before they were engaged. I had heard this story, with subtle and loving variations and embellishments, many times.

When I think of that sweltering Brooklyn, so long dead, and my father in his beautiful clothes, with his strong face and huge hands;

and when I think of the casually arrogant way in which he bet five thousand dollars, on a kind of whim; and when I, still and always amazed, realize that he had that money in his pocket, I sometimes get up and look at myself in the mirror. I look like my father, but I am not, not at all, like my father. What would he have said about my deformed relationship with the Sterns? About Clara standing me up God knows how many times? About the weakness or lack of will or courage that prevented me from abandoning the whore, prevented me from marrying some woman whose flaws were, at the very worst, the flaws of sanity? What?

When I dream of my father in his spotless hat and, waking, wish that I could have somehow appropriated the authority and confidence that I, of course irrationally, think it to have possessed, I am unfailingly left with the truth that it was my father's Borsalino. And only his.

Patsy Manucci, one of my father's drivers and a kind of sidekick who provided my father with a gin-rummy partner and a brand of raucous and mostly unintentional comedy, had a brother, Rocco, of whom, as a boy of fifteen or so, I was in awe. He was a horse of a man, almost, indeed, as thick through the chest and shoulders as a horse, and he spoke in a gravelly voice that was, as the phrase has it, too good to be true. Patsy possessed the same voice, and when the brothers had a discussion or argument about handicapping, the din of their colloquy could be heard through closed doors and even walls. My mother, who liked both brothers, said that their voices were the result of years of shouting the results from the candy store out to the street corner. I did not know what "the results" meant, but I knew that Patsy loved this crack, as he worshiped my mother, and thought it so funny that he repeated it everywhere.

He often said, with the most solemn and respectful of faces, that Rocco was a graduate of Fordham, where he'd studied medicine, a lie so preposterous that nobody ever had the heart to call him on it, or for that matter, even to laugh: people would listen to this wistful, crazy revelation and nod their heads in understanding. *Life!,* their nods regretfully said, *Ah, that's how life is.* Once, my father, in a context I no longer remember, broke this unspoken rule of solemnity, and said that Rocco had graduated from Fordham's "upstate campus," which caused the men with whom he'd been talking to burst into laughter. I laughed too, but had no true idea why.

Rocco was a runner for a policy operation headed by a man named Jackie Glass, who was always dressed beautifully in oxford gray or navy blue suits, white shirts, repp-striped ties, and French-toed shoes that seemed as soft as gloves. He was married to an ex-showgirl, a tall, hard redhead, and they had two spoiled blond children, Marvin and Elaine, who got everything they wanted, or so it appeared to me. His wife's name was Charl, short, I discovered, for Charlene. Jackie was connected, as the phrase had it, with one of the New York families, I don't know which one, which gave Rocco, in my adolescent eyes, the most weighty authority: he worked for a man who worked for serious people who had a great deal to say about the running of many things, including the city.

But this was the lesser part of what enthralled me insofar as Rocco was concerned. Rocco was a gambler, but a gambler who existed in a kind of Paradiso, an Eden, an empyrean of gambling that was wholly unreal to me. One night he won sixty thousand dollars in a crap game up on Pleasant Avenue. Even in this time, when people who can barely sing, dance, act, hit a ball, or throw a punch make millions for barely doing these things, sixty thousand dollars is a lot of money; in 1944, when a seventy-five-dollar a week job was thought to be the key to a big apartment on Easy Street, it was, simply, a fantasy amount. Rocco lost the sixty grand two days later in another crap game on Elizabeth Street.

To win it. To have it. To let it all go. To say to hell with it. That's what fascinated me about Rocco. It's the way I've always wanted to live, the way I've wanted to act with the men and women I've known, with, of course, especially Clara. I've never had the courage, that is to say that I've never had the courage to act on my belief that the world, beyond all its endlessly rehearsed wonders and beauties, is absolute shit, that life is best when ignored, or somehow turned away from, and that nothing should be taken at face value. In sum, that everything is a pathetic bust. But I have always acted otherwise, as if there is, perpetually, the possibility for change, for amelioration, for friendship and love. I have, that is, always and unforgivably, acted as if there is hope. But to say: Fuck life! I've never managed it, or if I have, it was momentary, melodramatic gesture, empty and contemptible. I think, in effect, of losing sixty thousand dollars, and, without fail, make my craven accommodations. I will not, ever, let it all go.

Some few years into my absurd relationship with Clara, a friend of mine who had rented a ramshackle beach house on Fire Island for the month of September, had to return to the city with a little less than two weeks left on his lease. He asked me if I wanted to take the place, gratis, for this period, and I agreed, thinking to ask Clara to make some excuse and spend this time on the island with me. She had been, for some months, disconcertingly faithful to Ben, and I thought that a time alone together, as the strangely lugubrious old song has it, would work to revive our passion, a passion that, I'm afraid, I remembered as a series of dissolving pornographic tableaux. I think that one usually remembers love as a totality of experience and feeling, a complex in which the sun that falls on the kitchen table in the morning is part of the emotion attendant on the beloved; whereas lust is simply the recall of the purely and metonymically salacious. Clara was a duchess of lust, as I have tried to make clear, and images of her in diverse erotic scenes were, overwhelmingly, images of dazed carnality. In any event, I told her of my sudden luck and asked her to come. I implored her to come.

A day or two later, she told me that she'd invented a story for Ben, complete with a sick school friend or a spontaneous reunion, faked phone calls, a fantasy airline reservation, something, everything. I had no way of proving that Clara had done any of this, and I've long been convinced that Ben had joined in this spurious drama, had helped to fashion his own betrayal. Clara was, and probably always had been, one of the machines by the use of which Ben was assisted in his seductions of fragile students and frowzy colleagues and the wives of friends—the butcher and the baker, for all I know. Perhaps even my ex-wife. At the time, all I cared about was Clara involved in lovemaking with me. With me!

We took the ferry from Bay Shore one warm morning, and then clomped along the boardwalk to a disreputable, weathered shack in Ocean Bay Park. Clara had laughed on the ferry as she described Ben's sour expression as she prepared to leave. She had a neat, well-turned story for almost every occasion, and in me the most willing of listeners. Nothing was on my mind but her, I had become desire, ah, how wonderful and dirty she was, her light perfume piquant with the salt air of the Sound. The moment we slammed the door of the musty shack, Clara almost coyly pulled off her T-shirt and stepped out of her shorts. Was I not the most finished of seducers?

Those ten days, however, ended with my morose wallowing in bitter nostalgia. Clara, of course, noticed my tragic expression, and, although people's feelings held little interest for her, she was manifestly disturbed that this germ of misery might make me less reliant a sexual partner than she had bargained for. She had given me two weeks of her time and had spent her energy to be with me; she did not expect gloom and silence. My ill-concealed distemper and preoccupied air turned the last few days of our sojourn into a chilly period of reading and glum card games.

I had been made wretched—blue is, I suppose, the best word—by a delicate, faded memory evoked by ocean and beach, a memory of fifteen years earlier, when I woman I had loved, loved to distraction, spent a summer with me in a rented cottage on the Island's North Shore. There is little point in rehearsing the serene joy of that summer, other than to say that I could not, perhaps did not want to drive from my mind the image of her sitting across from me in the early twilight on the little flagstone patio behind the two-room cottage. She was, in this image, always in white: shorts and T-shirt, skirt and blouse, pinafore, crisply dazzling summer dress, and her tan glows warmly against the candor of her lovely white clothing. She holds a gin and tonic, and as she leans forward to light her cigarette from my proffered match, she looks up and her dark eyes astound me.

I did a really thorough job of destroying this love when we returned to the city in the fall, by means of a cruel apathy, one that I even more cruelly pretended was a distraction caused by painful personal concerns that could not be shared with anyone—especially with her. So that was that. I saw her, many years later, well after my marriage and divorce, while Clara and I were in the early phase of our demented, futile eroticism. It was in sad Tompkins Square, on a gray, humid day just made for mania. We did not acknowledge each other, but the look of understanding that crossed her face, the comprehension of my flimsy reality that registered on her calm, beautiful features, almost stopped my heart. She had, as the phrase so aptly puts it, seen right through me. I thought to speak to her, to ask her—I don't know—to help me, perhaps? I thought I'd vomit, but was spared at least that shame.

∾

Wittgenstein famously closes the *Tractatus* by writing that "what we cannot speak about we must pass over in silence." I'm not certain that I agree with this beautifully subtle, frigid refutation, or, perhaps, critique, of the empty blather with which we are surrounded every day. My rejected and buried Roman Catholicism rouses itself at this proposition, flaunting, quietly to be sure, the garrulous sacrament of penance as counterbalance to Wittgenstein. God knows, the very act of confession, the snug dark of the confessional, the confessor's aloof profile in the gloom—all these virtually guarantee that the penitent will most certainly attempt to speak, in halting improvisations or rehearsed platitudes, about those sins and crimes and dark longings which cannot ever be represented in language. Silence will not do in the confessional, and the unspeakable always finds a voice, garbled and inexact though it may be.

Yet outside of the fierce niceties of the elaborate ritual that makes Roman Catholicism a sly, gay, and mysterious game, never to be understood by functional and palsy-walsy Christianity, I do indeed understand Wittgenstein's blunt postscript. It has been my experience that we cannot speak about anything at all, and yet we rattle on, our ceaseless chatter so much a part of our lives that even the hackneyed concept of "last words" is enshrined as a phenomenon of grave importance, as if it matters what anyone says entering the dark nullity. We refuse, really, just as if we were all ensconced permanently in a universal confessional, to pass over the unspeakable in silence. We start. We continue. We go on and on, through childhood and adolescence, fornication and pain and disease and death. Talking to make sense—how sad the very idea!—of childhood and adolescence, fornication and pain and disease and death.

This story that I have told, or made, such as it is, for instance, with a half-submerged truth here and a robustly confident lie there, with a congeries of facts and near-facts everywhere, this story is an exhibit of speech about something of which I cannot speak. For years, I did pass over it, quite obediently, so to say, in silence. Then, for no reason that I can point to, I decided to ease my mind by speaking, if not the unspeakable, then the difficult to speak. As I half-knew they would, each page, paragraph, clause, sentence, each word pulled relentlessly and stubbornly away from that which I had thought to say. So that my speech, I now see, has made the past even more remote and unfocused than silence would have. But I declare that I have spoken the truth, or something very close to it.

When I say that my narrative is not quite representative of the actuality of the experiences it purports to represent, I play no semiological games. That is to say that were the act of signification a wholly successful transaction with the real, I could still never have effected the proper transaction. I have no language for it, there is no language for it. Just as well that words are empty. How terrifying true representation would be!

This story is dotted with flaws and contradictions and riddled with inconsistencies, some of which even the inattentive reader will discover. Some of these gaffes may well be considered felicities of uncertainty and indeterminacy: such is prose. The tale also, it will have been clear, occasionally flaunts its triumphs, small though they may be. I am afraid that the final word about the gluey, tortuous, somehow glamorously perverse relationship that Ben and Clara and I constructed and sent shuffling into the world hasn't been arrived at; but perhaps the unspeakable has had created some sad analogue of itself, if such is possible. Something has been spoken of, surely, but I can't determine what or where it is.

In any event, I've spent a fair amount of time and attempted a degree of care in the creation and arrangement of these fragments. There are moments or flashes when I believe that I have seen myself, in a quirk of syntax, as I really was, when I can swear that Ben or Clara are wholly if fleetingly present in these simulacra of the past. Moments, flashes, when this admittedly inadequate series of signs seems to body forth a gone time. But I know that this is nonsense, nothing but a ruse with which I have been faithfully complicit so as to make the landscape of my life seem more valuable and interesting than it ever was.

The coffee house of seventeenth-century England was a place of fellowship where ideas could be freely exchanged. The coffee house of 1950s America was a place of refuge and tremendous literary energy. Today, coffee house culture abounds at corner shops and online.

Coffee House Press continues these rich traditions. We envision all our authors and all our readers—be they in their living room chairs, at the beach, or in their beds—joining us around an ever-expandable table, drinking coffee and telling tales. And in the process of exchanging the stories of our many peoples and cultures, we see the American mosaic being reinvented, and reinvigorated.

We invite you to the tales told in the pages of Coffee House Press books.

FUNDER ACKNOWLEDGMENTS

Coffee House Press is an independent nonprofit literary publisher. Our books are made possible through the generous support of grants and gifts from many foundations, corporate giving programs, individuals, and through state and federal support. This project received major funding from the National Endowment for the Arts, a federal agency. Coffee House Press has also received support from the Minnesota State Arts Board, through an appropriation by the Minnesota State Legislature and by the National Endowment for the Arts; and from the Elmer and Eleanor Andersen Foundation; the Buuck Family Foundation; the Bush Foundation; the Grotto Foundation; the Lerner Family Foundation; the McKnight Foundation; the Outagamie Foundation; the John and Beverly Rollwagen Foundation; the law firm of Schwegman, Lundberg, Woessner & Kluth, P.A.; Target, Marshall Field's, and Mervyn's with support from the Target Foundation; James R. Thorpe Foundation; West Group; the Woessner Freeman Foundation; and many individual donors.

This activity is made possible in part by a grant from the Minnesota State Arts Board, through an appropriation by the Minnesota State Legislature and a grant from the National Endowment for the Arts. MINNESOTA STATE ARTS BOARD NATIONAL ENDOWMENT FOR THE ARTS

To you and our many readers across the country, we send our thanks for your continuing support.

*Good books are brewing
at coffeehousepress.org*